ME AND

Drew Gummerson is the author of one previous novel, *The Lodger* (2002). He works for the Leicestershire Police.

BY THE SAME AUTHOR

The Lodger

ME AND
MICKIE JAMES

Drew Gummerson

JONATHAN CAPE
LONDON

Published by Jonathan Cape

2 4 6 8 10 9 7 5 3 1

Copyright © Drew Gummerson 2008

Drew Gummerson has asserted his right under the Copyright, Designs
and Patents Act 1988 to be identified as the author of this work

First published in Great Britain in 2008 by
Jonathan Cape
Random House, 20 Vauxhall Bridge Road,
London SW1V 2SA
www.rbooks.co.uk

Addresses for companies within The Random House Group Limited can be found at:
www.randomhouse.co.uk/offices.htm

The Random House Group Limited Reg. No. 954009

A CIP catalogue record for this book is available from the British Library

ISBN 9780224082440

The Random House Group Limited supports The Forest Stewardship
Council (FSC), the leading international forest certification organisation.
All our titles that are printed on Greenpeace-approved FSC-certified paper carry
the FSC logo. Our paper procurement policy can be found at
www.rbooks.co.uk/environment

The Random House Group Limited makes every effort to ensure that the
papers used in its books are made from trees that have been legally
sourced from well-managed and credibly certified forests.

Mixed Sources
Product group from well-managed
forests and other controlled sources
www.fsc.org Cert no. TT-COC-2139
© 1996 Forest Stewardship Council

Typeset in Adobe Garamond by Palimpsest Book Production Limited
Grangemouth, Stirlingshire
Printed and bound in Great Britain by
CPI Mackays, Chatham, Kent ME5 8TD

for Mum and Dad

HUNCHBACK CHRISTMAS

Me and Mickie James were moving down to London together. We were both twenty-four. We were going to be pop stars, Mickie James on keyboards and me on lead vocals. Mickie James had a hunchback but that didn't matter. Even I knew it. He was the talented one.

We talked about how famous we were going to be on the train on the way down. 'The world is fed up with manufactured pop,' I said. I put on my Ronan Keating voice. 'I'm a talentless Irish twat,' I said. Mickie James laughed at this. He likes it when I'm funny. It takes his mind off his own problems.

During the journey people going to the toilet kept tripping over our Korg keyboard. 'It's not my fault it's long, is it?' I said to this skinny bloke. Then this big bloke tripped over it. I apologised to him. You can't be too careful these days; there are a lot of nutters about.

When we got off the train at Euston, Mickie James asked me to take his photo. He wanted a souvenir of our arrival. I took the picture on an angle, slicing off his hunchback. It was the sort of thing I'd done before. I'd been at Leeds Art College for two years. I hoped I'd got it right. To be honest, these disposable Kodak cameras are crap.

This guy we knew from a pub in Birmingham had told

us to contact his mate who worked at St Pancras Station. He said that he would sort us out for somewhere to stay.

We eventually traced the guy to the station manager's office. He was wearing trousers that were too small and you could see the outline of his knob. Or it might have been a key chain.

'What do you want?' he said.

'We heard you had a room going,' I said.

He shook his head. 'This is a bloody station not a hotel.' The other guys in the office laughed at this.

'You want to get some glasses, mate,' said one of the guys. He added, 'What's in Quasimodo's case? Is it a banjo?'

'Come on,' I said to Mickie James. 'Let's go.'

Between us we had over three hundred pounds. I'd been working in HMV at weekends and Mickie James had been doing stuff for the council. He'd worked in this office but eventually they'd sacked him because he wouldn't take his coat off. He had this coat that he always wore. It had padded shoulders and he thought it made his hunchback less noticeable. It did in a way, but then people were always going on at him for wearing a sheepskin jacket while sitting at his workstation.

We were halfway across the St Pancras concourse when the bloke from the station manager's office caught up with us. He was a bit out of breath.

'Sorry about that, lads,' he said. 'Didn't want the other guys to know about the room. Come on, this way.'

The guy, Dave, led us through this door that said 'Janitor' on it and then through a room stacked with cleaning stuff. At the back of this room was another door.

'I warn you,' said Dave, 'there's a hell of a lot of stairs.'

'That's all right,' I said. 'We can do stairs.'

I counted them as we went up. I thought this was one of

those facts that we could use in competitions. You know, when we were on MTV in the future they could flash it up on the screen. 'How many stairs did Down by Law have to climb to get to their room when they first arrived in London?' Down by Law was the name of our group. It was Mickie James's idea. *Down by Law* was the title of his favourite film. It was directed by Jim Jarmusch and it starred the singer Tom Waits. That could be another question. 'Which singer starred in the film *Down by Law*?'

After the 256th step Dave came to a stop. The stairs didn't have any carpet here and wallpaper was peeling off the walls. There were two doors. We were all pretty out of breath and I could smell Mickie James in his jacket.

'This is it,' said Dave, and he pushed open one of the doors. 'The sink works, and also those two sockets. There's a fan heater knocking around somewhere, that'll keep the place toasty. I'm not asking much for it. Twenty quid a week. It's not official, you understand. I'm doing this on the never-never. I'll give you both a smock. If you could put them on when you come in or out then people will just assume you're a cleaner. If anyone does stop you then send them to me. I'll sort it out.'

But we weren't listening. On one side of the room was this big window. From it we could see what we assumed was the whole of London. It was all there, roads and parks and trees and cars and shops and it was ours for the taking.

'So you want it?' said Dave.

'Sure,' I said. I felt this big ball building up and building up in my stomach and it felt great. 'We'll definitely take it.' Then I looked at Mickie James. 'This is just the start,' I said. 'By Christmas, I promise you, we are going to be massive. Down By Law will be the group on everybody's lips.'

'Christmas is only five weeks away,' said Mickie James. He was kind of nodding his head and counting on his fingers at the same time. 'Maybe six if you include this week as well. It *is* only Tuesday.'

'Um,' said Dave. 'The twenty if you don't mind. The 12:17 will be leaving soon and yours truly here is on the barriers.'

The room next to our new home was like this big loft. Actually it *was* a big loft. There were ladders and old rolls of wire on huge spindles and all these iron girders in there. God knows how anyone had got them up there. They had probably been there for years.

It was the perfect place for us to practise in. It was a forgotten urban backdrop to our sophisticated electronic groove. That was what Mickie James said anyway. Although he said he didn't like the word groove. Pared-down electronic lo-fi hi-fi beat was better he said. That sounded too long for me. And what was lo-fi hi-fi?

Our best song was 'Manos Sucias'. We got the title from this play by Jean-Paul Sartre, *Les Mains sales*. Mickie James translated the title into English, *Dirty Hands*, and then he translated it into Spanish. It had to be in Spanish because the tune we were working on had this whole flamenco section in it.

The song is about a crippled Spanish boy. He lives in a tiny hut with his mother and she is dying of cancer. His only companion is a donkey called Manolo. Manolo was a hard word to find a rhyme for.

Jean-Paul Sartre was an existentialist and he wrote stuff about what is the point of life and all that. That is what our song's about, what is the point of it all when you are different to everyone else. I think it's about Mickie James

4

himself. 'Manos Sucias' is going to be our first number one.

Our room has one bed in it, one sink and a box that we use as a table. We found this old tin bath at the back of the loft and we use that to bath in.

I love it when Mickie James has a bath because that is the only time I get to see him naked. When we sleep together he always wears at least a T-shirt even if he has taken off his underpants for sex.

I'd like to take a picture of him when he's in the bath. He looks so vulnerable there. His hunchback is on the left side. The spine curves dramatically to the left and then forms a loop under his skin. Sometimes when Mickie James is asleep I run my hand over this lump. I say 'I love you I love you I love you' over and over again. I wish that he would learn to love it as much as me but I don't think that he will.

A couple of years ago I read a book about those astronauts who went to the moon. They were the first people to see the Earth from space. They were amazed, full of wonder. Nowadays everyone has seen those images and we don't think anything of them.

That's one of the reasons I want us to be famous. I figure that if Mickie James sees his hunchback everywhere, on every magazine cover and billboard, then he will get used to it. He won't care any more. Of course, it would be nice to have loads of money too. That's something I've always thought about.

Another friend of ours from that pub in Birmingham had given us the name of this guy who he knew from a friend of a friend.

'He has this concert hall,' he said. 'He's got a real nose for up-and-coming talent.'

Apparently everyone who was anyone had played there before they were famous: Razorlight, the Killers, the Scissor Sisters and so on. Even Bucks Fizz had played there, but that was a different story.

Having such a good contact was one of the main reasons we had moved down to London in the first place.

'You do the talking,' said Mickie James. 'I don't know that I can speak.'

'Come on,' I said. 'This way.'

As instructed we took a left and then a right out of the tube and we found ourselves in front of this three-storey pink building. It had a large pink fibreglass breast above the door and the word 'Knockers' in pink neon lighting above this.

'Do you think this is the right place?' said Mickie James.

'Knock and we shall find out,' I said. I was trying to make a joke of it. The place was supposed to be called 'The Venue'. Going on the evidence before us it looked like it might have changed hands.

Mickie James rapped once on the door and it was opened almost immediately by a blonde woman in a tight black negligée.

'Have you come about the bra fittings?' she said.

'We're Down by Law,' I said.

'This is a concert hall, isn't it?' said Mickie James, and even to me he didn't sound confident.

The woman pulled a face. 'We're a hooters bar,' she said. 'You know, breasts, tits, womanly things?'

I got the picture. 'Don't they normally come in twos?' I said, nodding upwards to where the one breast hung above the door.

The woman glanced up. 'Oh shit,' she said, 'don't tell me

it's gone again. You haven't seen a large bosom down the street, have you?'

We both shook our heads.

The woman looked over her shoulder. 'Ronald!' she shouted. 'Ronald!' and then she slammed the door in our faces.

As we made our way back to the tube station I saw these two sixteen-year-old lads loitering outside a newsagent's. I beckoned them over.

'You know that bar around the corner with all the women?' I said, and they both nodded. 'Go and knock on the door and tell them you've come about the bra fittings. They'll let you do some measuring, if you know what I mean.'

Both the lads laughed at this and then set off almost at a run.

'I don't see why everyone should have a crap day,' I said.

Mickie James laughed as this. As I said, he likes it when I'm funny and if Mickie James is happy then so am I.

Those next few weeks on what we called 'our unstoppable climb to success' were spent trooping around bars, music venues, concert places. It wasn't nearly as easy to find gigs as we thought and on top of this London was a very expensive place to live.

We got into an argument one night with this guy who wanted nine pounds for a couple of bags of chips and a pair of hot dogs.

'You haven't even put sauce on mine,' said Mickie James.

'There's no discount for the physically disabled,' said the man, and I would have gone for him only I was hungry and I didn't want my chips to go everywhere. Besides, you have to rise above such things. That's one of the things being in

Down by Law had taught me. We weren't just a pop group, we were a way of life.

Mickie James said the problem was that we had the right look but before people would book us they would want to hear us. We came up with the idea of making a demo tape. Only we didn't have any recording equipment.

We went from music shop to music shop only to find everything was out of our price range. Then I had this last-ditch idea.

The woman in Ryman's had us over a barrel and she knew it. The Sanyo Dictaphone was just what we needed she said and at £49.95 in the pre-Christmas never-to-be-beaten sale it was well within our price range.

Back at the rehearsal studio we tried the Dictaphone in various locations. It sounded crap wherever we put it. Not crap because we were great but more of a sound-quality issue.

Mickie James said that as manager this kind of thing was my responsibility and I said that if he hadn't got sacked from the council then we would have had more money to buy better equipment. He pulled his sheepskin around him and stormed out. I shouldn't have said that.

I sat down on one of the spools of cable wire for about half an hour and then I came up with an idea. I remembered this documentary I'd seen about the whole *Pop Idol* phenomenon. The bit I was thinking of was when Will Young came to record his first song, 'Evergreen'. In my head I could see him in the recording studio singing into a microphone. What surprised me was how big the microphone was; it had this really big head like an Afro. That must help, I thought, with sound distortion and stuff. It was the kind of thing we needed.

I took off my left shoe and my sock. I wrapped the sock around the Dictaphone and sang a few notes into it. I played it back. It wasn't recording-studio quality but it was better. There was no doubt about that.

I found Mickie James out on the roof. He was crouched down at the edge, gazing out towards the British Library.

'I've done it,' I said. 'Listen.'

I pushed the button on the Dictaphone. Mickie James stood up and clapped his hands. Then he looked down at my feet and asked why I was wearing only one sock. He told me to be careful that I didn't stand in any shit. This was the part of the roof we used as a toilet.

Armed with the tape we went round a few venues. The guy at the Blue Note was more than interested.

'I haven't got time now,' he said, 'but if you leave me a tape then I promise I'll listen to it and get back to you. I'm always looking for new talent.'

I took the tape out of the Dictaphone and slid it across the bar.

'What's this?' said the manager. He picked up the tape.

Now that I was looking at it with his eyes I could see his point. It was only about an inch long.

'You're having a laugh, aren't you, lads?'

'We'll be back,' I said.

Outside it had started to rain. We had ten pounds left and Dave would want his money the following Tuesday.

'We're going to have to get jobs,' I said to Mickie James. 'Just to tide us over until the money comes flooding in.'

It was Mickie James who saw the sign. It was outside this shop called Bloomsbury Cheeses. The sign said 'Help Needed'. That sounded us to a T.

As we went in, a bell rang above our heads and a fat man with a large moustache came out from behind a curtain.

'We've come about the job,' I said.

'You'll do,' he said to me. He looked at Mickie James. 'Not him though. He'll frighten the customers.'

'I wouldn't work here if you paid me,' said Mickie James.

'Calm down,' I said to Mickie James. I turned to the man. 'It's illegal to discriminate.'

'Cheese is a cut-throat business,' said the man. 'I can't afford not to.'

'Are we going?' said Mickie James. 'All this cheese everywhere is making me feel sick.'

The man put his hands on his hips and stared at me. 'Do you want the bloody job or not? I'm rushed off my feet. Between you, me and that rack of Albanian blues, Christmas is a prime cheese-buying period.'

I nodded my head and I told Mickie James I would see him later. He said was I going to take the job then after the way the man had spoken to him and I said I was. I knew this would make Mickie James angry but I had no choice, one of us had to do something. Sometimes I felt that that hunch was on my back as well.

My new boss's name was Constantine but he said that I should call him Con. He said that he'd been in England since 1976 and that he'd hated it from the day he arrived. I said why didn't he go home then and he said he hated home more, and besides, who then would look after all this cheese? He told me to go down to the cellar and bring up three Edams. I did know what an Edam was, didn't I?

'Made backwards,' I said.

The job was easy enough, going down to the cellar, cutting up cheeses and then displaying them on these big plates.

Con said that he stayed open late as he liked to catch the commuters.

'That's one thing I've learnt about the English,' he said. 'You are impulse cheese buyers.'

It was nine o'clock and on orders from Con I was about to close the door when someone stepped through it. He was tall but that wasn't what was most noticeable about him. What did stick out was that he was wearing a large pink fedora.

'Can I help you?' I said because he was staring at me. Then I added, 'Gorgonzola's on special today. Buy a hundred grams, get a hundred free.'

'Don't I know you from somewhere?' said the man.

I get that quite a lot. 'I'm in a band. You might have seen me around.'

It was as I was wrapping a whole kilo of Gorgonzola that the man introduced himself. He told me that his name was Ivan Norris-Ayres and that he had been a singer in a band once too.

'Keep it under your hat,' he said as he leant conspiratorially over the counter, 'but we supported the people who supported Japan on their 1990 comeback tour.'

'Wow,' I said. I was impressed. It is not often you get to meet someone who has actually made it.

'Our band was called Pravdu. The name came from a misspelling of the Russian word for truth.'

I asked why a misspelling, as this kind of music folklore fascinated me, and Ivan Norris-Ayres replied that it was because he felt the misspelling said something about the nature of truth.

'You could have called yourselves Tuth then,' I said.

'We thought of that, but there's already a band called Tuth.

They're three dentists and a chiropractor from Balham. They do Kansas covers while wearing gumshields. They're quite successful. They tell all their patients about their gigs.'

'Advertising is the key,' I said.

'Look,' said Ivan Norris-Ayres. 'I see the shop is about to close. Could I interest you in a little beverage of the alcoholic kind?'

I thought about Mickie James waiting at home, but then I thought that Ivan Norris-Ayres was just the kind of connection me and Mickie James needed to be making. And besides, serving cheese all day had turned out to be thirsty work.

There was this swanky gastro pub right next to Bloomsbury Cheeses and we nipped in there. Ivan Norris-Ayres asked me what I would like to drink and I said a beer, a large one, and took a seat near the window. I watched as the pink fedora made its way towards the bar. I had this feeling that something good was about to happen and on top of this I was getting a free beer, which was always a bonus.

Ivan Norris-Ayres came back holding the drinks, at the same time as Wizzard's 'I Wish It Could Be Christmas Everyday' came on the jukebox, and because of this the conversation quickly turned to all-time favourite songs and then music in general.

This continued for nearly an hour, us talking about the music business and Ivan Norris-Ayres buying drinks and then it came out. Ivan Norris-Ayres said although he was no longer in a band he now did promotions and other stuff. He said that it just so happened that he was putting on a Christmas Eve concert and although the bill was full he might be able to squeeze us in.

'It's at the Astoria,' he said.

'Charing Cross Road!'

Ivan Norris-Ayres shook his head. 'No, the Southend Astoria.'

Still, that was huge. I'd never been to Southend but I'd heard of it.

'You say you're in a duo. Where's the other one?'

'He's at home, practising. Hang on, I've got this tape.' Luckily I had the tape me and Mickie James had made tucked away in the pocket of my jeans. I pulled it out and slid it across the table, 'Have a listen.'

Ivan Norris-Ayres picked up the tape and looked at it carefully.

'It's a Dictaphone tape,' I said. 'Long story.'

Ivan Norris-Ayres smiled. 'You've got character. Let's say I take this away, see if I like it. We can meet up Friday. Häagen-Dazs shop on Leicester Square. Six on the nose.'

'I'll be there,' I said.

'Or be square,' said Ivan Norris-Ayres. He tipped his pink fedora and he was off, out through the doors of the pub and into the night.

So this was it, our first big break. As I walked back to St Pancras I had this idea for a song in my head. It would be the new finale to our set. The title would be 'Hunchback Christmas'. I could already hear the chorus: Nobody wants a hunchback for Christmas, Just ask that old guy from Notre-Dame, Nobody will love a hunchback this Christmas, So spare a thought for the lonely this Christmas.

It needed some work, but I was pleased with what I had, especially the last line where I rhymed Christmas with Christmas. Not many people could do that and get away with it. It was a talent I had, a talent both me and Mickie James had.

As I got to the top of the stairs I was surprised to find

Mickie James was in neither the bedroom nor the room we used for practising in. I was just poking my head out of the window to see if he was using the outside toilet facilities, i.e. the roof, when I noticed the note on the table.

'Got a job too, back late. Love you, Mickie James.'

I clapped my hands. Things were really looking up for us. We both had jobs and, better than that, we were going to be famous.

Friday found me sitting in the window of the Häagen-Dazs shop watching the people go past. Only I didn't see people, I saw potential fans. I imagined them on their way to the Virgin Megastore to buy Down by Law's first single. I hoped they had enough money left after buying all their other stuff. London is an expensive place.

Me and Mickie James had had an argument earlier that morning. I had wanted him to come with me to meet Ivan Norris-Ayres but he said he had to go to the theatre; 'the theatre' being the place where he was working.

'You're always there now,' I said. 'I think you like it there more than you like Down by Law.'

Mickie James had pulled a face at this. Then he had stormed off. Then he had stormed back. 'I'm sorry,' he said. 'I'm not good at meeting new people. Not with this thing on my back. Can *you* sort it out?' He had squeezed my hand. 'Honestly, I can't wait for the gig.'

At five minutes past six I finally spied that distinctive pink fedora through the Häagen-Dazs window. It made its way through the crowd and stopped at my table. Ivan Norris-Ayres was under it.

'Well,' I said, 'what did you think?' Of course, I was referring to our tape.

'Wait,' said Ivan Norris-Ayres. 'What are you having?'

I followed Ivan Norris-Ayres's eyes to the menu. 'Banana split,' I said.

'Good choice,' said Ivan Norris-Ayres. 'You do have style.'

When Ivan Norris-Ayres came back I was almost bursting with excitement. He put down the banana split in front of me. Then he slid a CD across the table. It had 'Down by Law' scrawled across it in black marker pen.

'Something of that quality needs to be in the correct medium.'

'What?' I said.

'I loved it,' said Ivan Norris-Ayres.

'I knew it,' I said and I clapped my hands. In doing so I knocked my ice cream off the table and it landed on the head of a small child in a pushchair. He started to cry and then his dad, this big bloke with tattoos, came up and called me a rent boy and Ivan Norris-Ayres a paedophile. The security guard from the door came over. The ice cream that had been on the child's head had now slid off onto the floor and unfortunately the guard didn't see this. He slipped on it and landed on his arse. Several minutes later Ivan Norris-Ayres and I were escorted from the store.

'So,' I said, as we stood outside in the cold, 'you want us to do this gig?'

'Top of the bill is Showaddywaddy and next will be you.'

'I don't fucking believe it!'

'However, there is one thing.' Ivan Norris-Ayres took off his pink fedora and then put it back on again. He coughed into a balled-up hand. 'As I said, I do promotions and other stuff.'

'Yes?'

'You see, I'm in this little fix. We're making this movie.

The actor has buggered off and we need a replacement post-haste. You're a good-looking lad.' Ivan Norris-Ayres did that thing with his hat again and this time looked around him. 'It would require some nudity and a matter of intercourse with a person of the contradictory sex, if you know what I mean?'

I did. I'd heard of this sort of exploitation in the music industry, only I hadn't expected it to happen to me. It was the kind of thing that could come back and haunt you when you were famous. I could see my arse splashed across one page of the *Sun*. Or worse, two pages; one cheek on verso, the other on recto.

'Showaddywaddy could, of course, be moved down a notch if needs must,' said Ivan Norris-Ayres. 'And also, this little film will need a soundtrack. Could I interest someone of your talent in such a thing?'

I didn't say anything but I nodded my head.

'What's the bloody matter with you?' said Con. 'You been fiddling with yourself for the whole of this past hour.'

Ivan Norris-Ayres had given me a Viagra tablet. He'd said to take it two hours before the shoot. I'd taken it three hours before just to make sure.

'I don't want your cheese on the cheese,' said Con.

I looked at my watch. 'It's OK if I go now?'

'You going to make love with that hunchback again? I told you, you'd be better off without him.' Con bent over and pulled his mouth aslant. 'Esmeralda! Esmeralda!'

'I'll be back by six,' I said angrily.

The shoot was in a room above Paddington Station. Ivan Norris-Ayres knew this bloke who knew this other bloke. The story was that this new train driver turns up on his first

16

day and finds that as part of his training programme he has to sleep with all the women who push the trolleys through the train. They'd already got most of it on camera except for this one bit where the train driver surprises the woman who is in charge of making the tea.

In the room they'd done a mock-up of a buffet car. There was one table and a couple of napkins. The guy who was doing the camera was called Maurice. The guy in charge of lighting was Colin. Ivan Norris-Ayres was hovering in the background.

'Loved what you did with the soundtrack,' he said.

'Could you take your clothes off and put this on,' said Maurice. 'This' was a big Afro wig. 'The guy who you're replacing is black.'

Colin said, 'I'm going to have the lighting on low. I don't think anybody will notice. Audrey! AUDREY!'

A door at the side of the room opened and a naked woman with massive breasts in a tiny bra stepped through it. She looked me up and down.

'He's cute but he doesn't look like a Leroy. What's your name, honey?'

'I don't think I can do this,' I said.

'Just think of Showaddywaddy,' said Ivan Norris-Ayres.

I took my clothes off and Colin wheeled in this large silver tea urn. Audrey bent over it and spread her legs.

'Which hole am I putting it in?' I said.

'He's a professional,' said Maurice. 'He's asking all the right questions.'

'Can you get on with it?' said Audrey. 'I've got bingo at seven. Whichever hole you want love only not in my ear. Last week I couldn't hear the numbers for lube.'

Afterwards Maurice passed me two tissues to clean up

with, but I still felt dirty. Ivan Norris-Ayres came over and patted me on the shoulder. 'You did great lad. You blew Showaddywaddy right out of the water. If the other half of the pop duo is anything like as cute as you we could use you both in a film next time.'

'Mickie James has a hunchback,' I said.

Ivan Norris-Ayres pulled his mouth down and moved away a step. 'There is a certain market . . .'

'Can someone help me off this friggin' tea urn?' said Audrey. 'I think I'm stuck.'

While Maurice and Colin helped Audrey off the tea urn Ivan Norris-Ayres and I discussed arrangements for the concert. It was only a week away. Ivan Norris-Ayres said he had a lot to sort out so he would be in Southend beforehand. He told me to get the train – they went three times an hour from Liverpool Street Station – and then a taxi to the club. He said we should get there early to avoid the crowds.

'Are you ready to be famous?' he asked.

'Fuck yes,' I said and then I noticed the time. I was due back at the cheese shop.

Con scowled at me as I stepped through the door. There were quite a few people waiting to buy cheese. Most of them were heavily laden with various Christmas packages.

'I'll deal with these,' said Con. 'We've got a takeaway order to deliver. Some poxy theatre off the Strand. It's all wrapped up and ready to go. Address is on the label.'

The name of the theatre was the Regency. I'd passed it once before with Mickie James when we were both out looking for work. The name had stuck in my mind because I remembered the play they were putting on: *When I Was Famous*. It was supposed to be the story of an eighties boy band, only one of the band members got wind of it and had it closed down. He said he was *still* famous. It didn't get in the papers, although once upon a time everything he did had got in the papers.

When I arrived at the theatre I looked up on the board to see what play was on this time and straight away my heart went in my mouth. No, I said to myself, no, no, no. Then I said, Please no. I meant it. Sometimes you can want something but it has to be in a certain way.

The woman in the box office enquired where I was going and I held up the package and said 'Bloomsbury Cheeses' quietly under my breath. She nodded and I went through to the auditorium. I sat down in a seat at the back.

Onstage a small man with a large loudhailer stood before a number of people in costume. One boy was in green. A woman was in a pinny. And there was an animal that might have been a cow. When the small man wanted to address any of these people he would move close to them and angle the loudhailer upwards.

'I SAID THROW THE BEANS, NOT DROP THEM!'

'YOU'RE A COW. MOO!'

It was obviously a rehearsal for the play. Despite the constant stopping and starting and all the shouting I could still follow the story.

The boy lives with his mother and he wants to be a pop star. Only the mother doesn't like this and is always sending him on errands. One day she sends him to the cow circus to try and enrol their cow as a trapeze artist but on the way the boy meets a pop guru. This pop guru says that he will help the boy by giving him some singing beans if he will give him the cow. The cow starts to cry and says it dearly wants to be a trapeze artist. The boy takes the beans.

What happens next is that the cow appears in all the papers as a pop sensation and the boy gets upset and throws the beans out of the window and a big beanstalk grows up to the roof of the stage. The boy climbs up the beanstalk and then comes the moment that I feared.

The stage is changed and then there is Mickie James. He has some brown leather trousers on but no shirt. You can clearly see his hunchback. When the boy who climbs the beanstalk sees Mickie James he throws up his arms and screams.

The director comes back on the stage with his loudhailer and angles it at Mickie James.

'I TOLD YOU I WANTED UGLY BUT I THINK YOU HAVE GONE TOO FAR!'

At that point I leave the auditorium. I have tears running down my cheeks. This is Mickie James's theatre job. He is prostituting his hunchback. He is making a mockery of our dream.

For a number of hours I walked the streets with my package of cheese. I had become a black porno actor and Mickie James a freak in a panto. I wasn't sure if this was something we could ever get over, but if we didn't try to get over it then it stood to reason that we wouldn't. I decided I would go back to the theatre and I would take Mickie James out of there. It would be last time we would sell ourselves and from now on the only spiral we would make would be an upward one.

'Where have you been?' said the woman in the box office. 'You bring the cheese and then go again. With the cheese. That's a kind of takeaway service I haven't heard of before. Is there much money in it?'

'I'm looking for Mickie James,' I said.

'I don't –'

'He's the hunchback.'

'You're telling me,' said the woman. 'Through the foyer. Second door on the left. The changing room.'

The changing room was full of people. The two halves of the cow were sitting on opposite sides of a mirror. The director was sitting on a tall stool, flicking angrily through a script. The boy, whom I could now see was an ageing dwarf, was sucking hungrily on a long cigarette. Over in the far corner, by himself, was Mickie James.

'Ah,' said the director, 'the cheeseman cometh.'

'About bloody time,' said the dwarf, 'I'm parched.'

'Mickie James,' I said.

Mickie James looked up and saw me. His eyes went wide and he grabbed for a towel and draped it over his back.

'You got that job in the cheese shop,' said Mickie James. 'And I felt like a failure. I just wanted to get us some money.'

'There are more important things than money. We've got that gig with Showaddywaddy. We're going to be rich.'

'It's because of my hunchback. That's why we haven't got any gigs until now. That's why I didn't want to see Ivan Norris-Ayres. I didn't want to put him off.'

'You wouldn't have,' I said, and I went over to him. 'He loves our music. He loves us. He's a man of integrity. I promise you.'

There was a bit of a scene in the theatre when they realised I was taking Mickie James away.

'WHERE ARE WE GOING TO FIND SOMEONE AS GROTESQUE AS THAT TO REPLACE HIM?' shouted the director into his loudhailer.

I snatched the loudhailer from him and the cow went for me. I kicked it in what I hoped was a tender region and told Mickie James to run for it. He did and I followed him out the door.

'They didn't like the cheese?' said the woman from the box office as I went flying past.

When we were what I hoped was a safe distance away and in the vicinity of a Burger King I told Mickie James to stop running and that I would buy him a Whopper Meal.

'And about what you said,' I said. 'I like your hunchback.'

Mickie James shrugged at this as if to say I was talking rubbish.

'I mean it,' I said. 'And you know what, everyone else is going to love it too. This gig in Southend, we're going to knock them dead. You can blow me over with a feather if we don't.'

'You promise?'

'I promise,' I said. 'Now finish your burger and let's go and practise. I've been working on this song. I didn't want to tell you about it until it was finished but you might as well know now. It's called Hunchback Christmas.'

Mickie James looked at me.

'It's a feel-good song,' I said. 'And it's a real killer.'

Mickie James saw right away what was wrong with 'Hunchback Christmas'. He put in another verse and changed the words in the chorus.

We had only a week before the gig. With my first week's money from the cheese shop I bought us a new second-hand amp and every night after work we practised into the small hours.

In that week we wrote two new songs. One was called 'Monster Movie' and was about how kids don't grow up watching monster movies any more. It was full of these really dramatic moments. The other was a ballad called 'Last Train from Euston'. This one was about two people who meet on the last Silverlink train from Euston to Milton Keynes. The people could have been either a boy and a girl, two boys or two girls. A lot of our songs were clever like that. They were mainstream while still maintaining a certain cutting edge. In fact, thinking about it, the train could have been a Silverlink or a Virgin one.

On the night before the Southend gig Mickie James asked if I thought we were ready. I said we were and Mickie James nodded his head. I said that if 'Hunchback Christmas' was released right then, then it would definitely make it to Christmas number one. Mickie James nodded his head again as if he agreed with me and then he said he wanted to show me something.

'Wait,' he said, and he got out of bed. He flicked on the light and opened the window. I asked him what he was doing because it was bloody freezing.

'Watch this,' said Mickie James, and he took off his T-shirt so his torso was bare. He climbed out of the window and went out onto the flat roof and started to dance.

'What are you doing?' I said. 'Mind you don't fall off the edge.'

'I want to show you that I'm not ashamed of my hunchback,' said Mickie James. 'That's something that working in the theatre taught me.'

'You were playing the monster,' I said.

'They hated me,' said Mickie James, 'but it doesn't matter what they thought. I want *you* to see.' He stood up on his toes and did a pirouette right in the centre of the roof. 'Do you see?' he said. 'Do you see?'

'Come back to bed,' I said. 'You're a fool.'

'I want you to like me for who I am,' said Mickie James.

I shook my head. 'You're Mickie James,' I said, 'and there's no one like you. Believe me.'

As Ivan Norris-Ayres said, the trains to Southend went from Liverpool Street Station. The journey took fifty-five minutes and as we arrived I put my hands on Mickie James's arms and looked him in the face. 'We arrive here as nobodies, we will leave as somebodies. Tonight Showaddywaddy are supporting us. This is the beginning.'

There were a number of taxis outside the station. We jumped in the first one and I asked the driver to take us to the Astoria. He scratched the top of his head and turned round.

'The London Astoria?'

'The Southend one.'

'Problem there, mate, there isn't one.'

'There must be.'

'There isn't. We've got Talk, Storm, Ego, Chameleon, Zinc and the Palace Ballroom but we haven't got an Astoria.'

'What's going on?' said Mickie James.

I sat in the back of the cab and thought for a minute. Then I had an idea. I leant forward. 'Do you know if Showaddywaddy are playing in Southend tonight?'

'I fucking hope not.'

'Shit,' I said.

'Aren't they just?'

'Look,' I said, 'take us to all the clubs, one by one, there must have been a mix-up.'

'You're the boss, boss.'

The taxi driver rolled up his window and pulled out of the station.

At each of the nightclubs we got the same response. No Showaddywaddy. Sometimes as we travelled we got a glimpse of the sea, the waves were high, and clouds were gathered above them.

'I don't mean to be rude,' said the taxi driver as I returned from what he said was the final nightclub, 'but why are you so keen to see Showaddywaddy? I saw them once in the seventies and they were shit even then.'

'It's a long story,' I said.

'They had one good song,' said the taxi driver. '"Under the Moon of Love". I must admit I liked that one.' He started to sing. 'I wanna tell ya, That I love ya, And I want you to be my girl. Ooh yeah, under the moon of love.'

'Are you sure there aren't any more clubs?' I said.

'Positive. We've done them all. You want me to take you anywhere else?'

I looked at the meter. It said fifty pounds. Fifty pounds was all I had. 'It's OK,' I said, 'We'll walk from here.'

'Where to?' said the taxi driver.

'Good question,' I said.

It was Christmas Eve. We were in Southend and we were broke. I couldn't think of a worse situation, but then it began to snow, big angry flakes that went for your eyes.

Ivan Norris-Ayres had turned out to be a big con. When he saw me all he saw was a stand-in for his black porn star. You read about that happening in the music business but you don't think it will happen to you.

'Come on,' I said to Mickie James.

We took a left and a right past rows of terraced houses and found ourselves by a sea wall. Here the snow seemed to be coming down even thicker and it was settling on the cars, the pavements, the trees. There wasn't a soul around.

I was in front and Mickie James was behind. I could hear the Korg keyboard knocking against Mickie James's shins as he walked. The sound was a constant reminder. I had promised him a big gig before Christmas and I had failed.

I was on the point of turning and saying how sorry I was when I saw a figure up ahead. She was leaning against the sea wall and she was talking into a mobile phone and she was crying.

'Are you OK?' I said, going up to her. I was keen to find someone worse off than me to make myself feel better.

The figure slipped the mobile phone into a pocket and did something to her eyes with her fingers.

'I came out for better reception,' she said. A tear fell out of her left eye and then her right. 'I'm sorry.'

I looked out across the sea. It was snowing there. I looked back to the road. It was snowing there too. The snow, I imagined, was general all over Essex. Even Mickie James had an upside-down ice-cream cone of snow on top of his hunchback.

'I'm Abigail Pincet,' said the woman. 'I work there.' She pointed across the road to a gargoyle-fronted five-storey building. A large sign declared, 'The Southend Orphanage for Crippled Children of War'.

'We arranged a concert for the children. They were so looking forward to it. But . . .' Abigail's lip started to tremble '. . . the band haven't turned up. I don't know how to tell them.'

I looked at Mickie James and he nodded his head. I turned to Abigail.

'It just so happens –'

'You know of a band?'

'We are one.'

Abigail put her hands up to her cheeks. 'And what are you doing tonight?'

I smiled. 'We're performing at an orphanage.'

'Oh my,' said Abigail, and her whole face went pink.

'Take me to your leader,' I said.

As we walked through the door of the building a one-legged tow-headed boy ran up to Abigail and flung his arms around her.

'This is Olav,' said Abigail. 'He's from Bosnia.'

Then there was armless Olga from Herzegovina, toothless Amjad from Iraq, blind Quentin from Sierra Leone and many more besides.

'We have one hundred and fifty-seven,' said Abigail. She continued in a quieter voice. 'I shouldn't say this but Porl is my favourite. He wasn't in a war so technically he shouldn't be here, but his parents didn't want him. Here he is.'

Stepping through the doorway was a small black-haired boy. He was five or six. Unlike the other children he had all his bodily parts: two arms, two legs, teeth.

'What's wrong with him?' I asked.

'Why,' said Abigail, 'he has a hunchback.'

'Oh yes,' I said, 'I hadn't noticed.'

'Isn't he lovely?'

'Yes,' I said, 'beautiful.'

'Where do we set up?' said Mickie James.

We did the set we had planned: 'Slow Train to Havana', 'Monster Movie', 'Curve', 'Ain't It', 'Festival of Dreams', 'Last Train from Euston', 'Alien Amore', 'Manos Sucias' and 'Hunchback Christmas'.

'Hunchback Christmas' went down the best. All the kids got up out of their seats for this one and danced, and the ones that couldn't get up and dance danced in their seats.

There are some moments in your life that make you realise what life is about. Sometimes you forget that because you want to be famous and you want to make money. At the beginning it is the music that matters and connects you to people. I would like to say that this night the music mattered and I can say it because it did.

We did 'Hunchback Christmas' four times in a row and then Abigail wrote down the words on these big white cards and stood at the front of the stage and we did it four more times with all the kids joining in. It went like this:

Back in the days of old
When Quasimodo was of this world
Living in the Notre-Dame spire
Above the voices of the funeral choir
Christmas was a different thing
St Nick was a man not a commercial offering
And Quasimodo had his love Esmeralda.

Who says nobody wants a hunchback at Christmas?
Just ask that old guy from Notre-Dame
Who says nobody will love a hunchback this Christmas?

Nowadays if you're crippled or old
Infirm, diseased, or merely not bold
Don't hide away in your white tower
Come down from there sooner than nower
Christmas is the peace and love holiday
I beg you don't let the marketing men hold sway.

Who says nobody wants a hunchback at Christmas?
Just ask that old guy from Notre-Dame
Who says nobody will love a hunchback this Christmas?

It was a perfect night and when it was over Abigail said that Mickie James and I could stay at the orphanage. She fixed us a room on the top floor, at the end of five flights of stairs.

We were just about to get into bed when there was a knock at the door. I looked at Mickie James, wondering 'what now?' and I went to open it. Standing there, to my surprise, was Porl, the very small hunchback. In one hand he had a pen and in the other a piece of paper torn from a phone directory.

'I wonder,' he said. 'Can I have autograph? Mickie James's especially.'

Mickie James smiled and took a step forward. Outside I could see it was still snowing.

TROUBLE AT TIVOLI

Mickie James and I had been booked for the pre-spring season at Copenhagen's Tivoli Gardens. We were going to be famous. There was no doubt about that.

'I want you back by summer,' said Con. 'Summer is a big time for cheese.'

'We'll be back,' I said, although in my head I was already thinking that I would never step foot in that cheese shop again.

'Hang on,' said Con, 'I got you something.'

He nipped behind the counter and reappeared moments later holding a small package. 'I got you this. For the journey.'

The package was triangular-shaped, wrapped in shiny paper, sealed with a string bow.

'It's a piece of cheese,' said Con. 'I might as well tell you. It's Gorgonzola. It's for you and the hunchback.'

'I don't like being called "the hunchback",' said Mickie James. He put particular emphasis on the word 'hunchback'. His deformity was still something he was particularly touchy about.

'Everybody gets called something,' said Con. 'I get called "the cheese man".'

'Cheese dick is what they call you,' said Mickie James.

I put a hand on Mickie James's arm. 'Let's go,' I said. 'Our destiny awaits us.'

It was a corny line, but right then, corn was appropriate. I didn't want Mickie James and Con to start a fight.

We left Con standing in the doorway to the cheese shop and made our way to the first point on our path to fame and fortune. This was Russell Square tube station.

The journey to Denmark went well, although there was this one hairy moment when we got cornered by these three drunk lads in the bar on the ferry. They wanted to know if Mickie James's hunchback was real. Mickie James took a swig from his Corona, looked the tallest one right in the eyes and said, 'About as real as your tiny cock, big balls.'

It could have got out of hand if it hadn't been for these two old ladies sitting at the table next to ours. One of the old ladies had a hunchback too and she asked the lads if they thought her hunchback was a fake as well. This seemed to shame the lads into silence and they sloped off to order more drinks at the bar.

I said thank you to the old ladies, although I had been about to deal with the whole situation myself. Then I told Mickie James that when he was old his hunchback wouldn't be such an issue because people respect the old.

'When I'm old those lads will be old too,' said Mickie James. 'It'll be the same.'

'It won't,' I said. 'When you're old you'll be rich from being a famous pop star and everyone will love you. You'll be like John Lennon if he'd lived.'

Mickie James took another swig from his Corona. 'John Lennon didn't have a hunchback,' he said.

'But he did have Yoko. There was a lot of resistance to her at the time.'

'Maybe,' said Mickie James, but I could see that my

comment had cheered him up. He likes it when I make him feel better about himself and for the rest of the night we talked about how brilliant this whole pre-spring season was going to be. Every night thousands of holidaymakers would be listening to original Down by Law compositions. That couldn't fail to make us famous.

Our contact's name in Denmark was Mr Bixen and as planned he was waiting for us by a flower stand within Hovedbanegarden Station.

'Are you the band?' he said as we walked up, and then he asked if we had any ID. 'You can't be too careful,' he said. 'Last week I was waiting for a sword swallower from Brno and this man said it was him. I took him on good faith but it turned out that he had never swallowed a sword in his life. Everyone is trying to get on the bandwagon these days. Even no-hopers.'

'We're far from no-hopers,' I said, and Mickie James handed Mr Bixen our passports.

Mr Bixen held them almost up to his nose, flicked through the pages, then handed them back.

'Just one thing,' he said. 'It says under distinguishing features, "hunchback".'

Mr Bixen was looking at me.

'That'd be this,' said Mickie James, pointing awkwardly at his back.

Mr Bixen nodded curtly once, then turned and set off across the station concourse.

I expected that we would head towards where the exit was clearly indicated, but instead we seemed to be heading further in towards the centre of the station. Eventually we stopped at a door.

'We find it suitable to put up some of our performers right here,' said Mr Bixen. 'In the station.' Mr Bixen opened the door, revealing a box-like room with a cage in the centre. 'Here is the lift,' he said rather grandly.

'Great,' I said.

'But unfortunately it doesn't work. We will have to take the stairs.'

The stairs were behind the lift and there were one hundred and sixty-eight of them. I counted. As we neared the top, quite clearly from above us, we heard the sound of shouting. There was a man's and a woman's voice and these were accompanied by frequent loud crashes.

'That is your neighbours,' said Mr Bixen. 'A magician and his assistant. Magicians are always volatile. It is in their nature. I hope you will become friends. You will be working very closely with them.'

Mickie James gave me a look and I tried to smile in what I hoped was a reassuring way although it was the first I had heard about working with magicians too.

At the top of the stairs were three doors and a dirty window. Mr Bixen took out a large bunch of keys, opened the door nearest to us on the left and gestured for us to go in.

The room was smaller than we were used to and we were used to small. It had one stained single bed and a sink. Above the sink was a round mirror with rust marks around the edges.

'The toilet is outside,' said Mr Bixen. 'You will be sharing with your neighbours.'

A scream came from behind the wall.

'I will introduce you at a more appropriate time,' said Mr Bixen. 'Now, if you don't have any questions I will be off.'

'I have one question,' said Mickie James.

'Yes?' said Mr Bixen.

'When will we be performing?'

Trust Mickie James to get straight to the nitty-gritty. That's what I liked about him.

'Ah yes,' said Mr Bixen. He removed the pork-pie hat he was wearing, revealing pork-pie hair underneath. 'First rehearsal is tomorrow. Nine a.m. Please report to the main gate. They will be expecting you.'

'Great!' said Mickie James.

I knew what he meant. It was great. This was the start.

An hour later Mickie James and I had unpacked and we were sitting side by side on the bed. The noises from the room next door were still continuing. Some of the phrases were very choice. I wasn't even sure what 'the biggest illusion in your life is yourself' could mean.

Part of me wanted sex with Mickie James but another part of me thought I wouldn't be able to concentrate with all that noise going on next door so I suggested that we go out and explore. Mickie James was well up for it.

Coming out of the station, the first thing we saw was the entrance to the Tivoli Gardens. It was lit up with thousands of tiny bulbs and a crowd of people stretched away from it along the road. From inside the park came the sound of fairground rides and people screaming. It was a beautiful noise.

'So, what do you want to do?' I said to Mickie James. As I said this I was looking at the entrance to the park. Only I didn't see it as an entrance to a park, I saw it as the doorway to a new and fantastic life. This life would be full of fame and stardom. 'Well?' I said to Mickie James, and I turned to look at him. He was staring at the park entrance too. I knew he was thinking like me.

'Come on then,' I said. 'Let's go in.'

Sometimes you know when something is right and sometimes you know when it is wrong. As soon as I stepped foot in the Tivoli Gardens I knew that we had found our spiritual home.

Cars on hundreds of wheels whooshed on tracks above our heads, other cars moved in circles through the air and from little wooden stalls drifted smells of frying or ice cream. Everywhere lights sparkled and fizzed like fireworks that wouldn't go out.

We bought two clouds of candyfloss and drifted with the crowds that flowed from attraction to attraction. At some point we came to a large stage with hundreds of plastic seats in front of it.

'Do you think that's where we'll be performing?' I said to Mickie James.

'It's awesome,' he said.

'Of course it's awesome,' I said. 'This is going to be us.'

I held the candyfloss stick in front of my mouth like it was a microphone and belted out the chorus to 'Manos Sucias'.

'Come on,' said Mickie James, grinning, 'I want to go on the roller coaster. I love roller coasters.'

He moved his hand up and down in the approximation of a car flying across tracks and then he snatched the candyfloss stick out of my grasp and passed it to these small Danish kids who were standing near us. Actually they might have been Swedish or something else. It was difficult to tell.

It was late when we got back to the room. As we neared the top of the staircase I told Mickie James to go and warm up the bed while I went and had a piss.

I pushed open the door to the bathroom and had just

35

positioned myself in front of the toilet and undone my flies when I had this feeling that I wasn't alone.

I twisted around and, sure enough, lying in the bath, pooled in the moonlight coming through the window, was a man. He had dramatically spiky short blond hair and was wearing a black cloak that went all the way down to his feet. The man had his hands folded over his chest and for a moment I thought he might have been dead, but then the eyes opened and he spoke.

'I am Harlan Harlan,' he said in a deep booming voice, 'man of mystery and mayhem, surprise and audacity.'

'You surprised me,' I said. 'I didn't expect to find anyone in the bath.'

'Kazam!' said Harlan Harlan and raised both his hands above his head in an arc-like movement.

We both laughed at this and then I told Harlan Harlan my name and held out my hand.

'By the way,' said Harlan Harlan, as we shook, 'your zip appears to be undone.'

'I need a piss,' I said.

'Oh, don't mind me,' said Harlan Harlan. 'Go ahead. You'll often find me in here. Penelope, she is a dear but she can also be a firebrand.'

I positioned myself so that my back was to Harlan Harlan and I started to go. I was a little nervous. I guessed that Harlan Harlan was the magician and I had never been to the toilet in the presence of a magician before. At the back of my mind was the thought that he might make something disappear, so I went as quickly as I could.

'Goodnight,' I said as I zipped up.

'Goodnight,' said Harlan Harlan.

I knew that we would be meeting again.

*

In the morning Mickie James wanted sex and I was happy to oblige. I was washing myself at the sink afterwards when the door to the room opened and Harlan Harlan was standing there. He looked like someone who had spent the night in a bathtub.

'I wanted to let you know that the bathroom is free,' he said.

I placed both hands over my crotch and Mickie James pulled the covers up to his chin.

Harlan Harlan waved a hand in the air. 'Don't mind me. One season Penelope and I shared a train compartment with seven dwarves and a Iranian funambulist. We've seen it all.' He made an arc-like movement again with his hands in front of his face. 'And I'll be seeing you.' Then he left the room.

'Who was that?' said Mickie James.

'That was Harlan Harlan. He's the magician. He slept in the bath.'

'Why?' said Mickie James.

I didn't know the answer to that one so I turned back to the sink and finished washing my cock.

We found Mr Bixen sitting in the first row of the seats at the front of the open-air theatre. When he saw us he raised his pork-pie hat and nodded towards the stage.

'I believe you've met Harlan Harlan and Penelope,' he said.

'We've met Harlan Harlan,' I said.

I looked up at the stage. Standing next to Harlan Harlan was a thin woman in a sparkling one-piece costume. The most noticeable thing about her was her short blue hair and her enormous glasses. She was very pretty.

'Who's rehearsing first?' said Mickie James.

'Excuse me?' said Mr Bixen.

Penelope hopped down off the stage and came towards us.

'Hey,' she said, holding out a hand, 'are you guys the musicians? Harlan Harlan has told me a whole bunch of things about you. You'll forgive our little tête-à-tête yesterday? You can read music, right?'

Mr Bixen flipped open the top of his leather briefcase and held out a wad of pages towards me and Mickie James.

'What's this?' I asked.

'It's your music,' said Mr Bixen.

'We've got our own music.'

'We're Down by Law,' said Mickie James.

'You are the backing musicians, right?' said Penelope.

'Backing?' I said, and then it all came out. We hadn't been booked to perform our own songs at all. We were supposed only to provide occasional incidental music while Harlan Harlan and Penelope performed.

'There are some pretty neat bits,' said Penelope. 'It was written for us by this guy from Peru. We would have had him doing it on pan pipes but there was a mix-up with his visa. We were desperate until you came along. He played those pan pipes with his nose.'

At these last words Mickie James glared at me and stormed off as if the whole thing was my fault, which it wasn't. He's like that sometimes; a bit temperamental. It comes with being a musical genius.

I told Mr Bixen that we had some contractual differences to sort out and then I set off after Mickie James.

He hadn't gone far. I caught up with him by the Flying Trunk, one of rides in the park. He was crouched down by the sign that said 'Minimum Height 130cm'. He looked pretty sad sitting there, like a kid too small to be allowed to ride.

'I'm not doing it,' he said. 'It's only one step up from porn music.'

As I had recently done some music for a porn film I thought a step up from that was a step in the right direction, but I didn't use this argument on Mickie James. I hadn't told him about the porn film yet. Instead I took a different tack.

'Look around,' I said. There was a snake ride on one side, the women's toilets on the other, and a red-and-yellow pagoda loomed above us. 'This is the Tivoli Gardens. Every night we'll be performing in front of crowds of hundreds.'

'We won't be doing our own songs.'

'It's experience,' I said.

Mickie James shook his head. 'We do this now and we might be doing it forever. Who says we're good at it? An agent comes along and the next thing we're booked to do backing on *The Paul Daniels Magic Show*?'

'Paul Daniels doesn't do magic shows any more.'

'He does,' said Mickie James. 'He's just not on TV. My mother saw him last year in Wolverhampton. What's authentic about that? I want to be doing my own stuff. I'm not some kid thrilled to be offered anything. I'm good. I know it. I'm better than this.'

I sat down next to Mickie James and put an arm around his shoulders. I asked him if he'd enjoyed the previous night and he nodded. He said that he'd enjoyed the roller coaster. He said that whizzing up and down on the tracks, for a while, he had felt free.

'Sometimes,' I said, 'you have to concentrate on the here

and now. You have to forget the bigger picture. And besides,' I said, 'I don't want to go and work in the cheese shop again. Please, do it for me. Do it for the cheese.'

When we got back to the stage Harlan Harlan was pulling a dove out of Penelope's ear.

'Is everything OK?' asked Mr Bixen.

I answered that before Mickie James had a chance to open his mouth. I took the sheet music from Mr Bixen's hands and hopped up onto the stage. I winked at Mickie James and it was all systems go.

The rehearsal lasted for four hours. The music was easy to follow, it was mostly plinky, plinky, plonk bits with a few dramatic chords here and there, and on top of this, watching the magic act was fun. Penelope played it dorky, screaming when Harlan Harlan pulled out a sword, or pretending she was scared of the doves and hiding under the table. She was a real character, especially with her blue hair.

About halfway through the rehearsal Penelope came over to Mickie James and me and pulled us to one side.

'I'm sorry about the mix-up before,' she said. She touched her thick glasses and moved them up a bit on her nose. She looked over her shoulder at where Harlan Harlan was trying to coax a rat into a shoebox with a piece of cheese. She looked back at us and continued in a low tone.

'Can I ask you a personal question? You are bum-munchers, aren't you?'

'What?' said Mickie James.

'I'm sorry,' she said. She put a hand over her mouth like she had when Harlan Harlan pulled out a big sword. 'That's a term Dyson always used to use. Dyson was this giant we worked with. He used to say he was the biggest bum-muncher

40

in North Carolina. He was seven foot four. It sounded cute when he said it.'

'We're gay,' I said.

'Neat,' said Penelope. 'I asked for gays. At least they got that right.'

'We're ready,' shouted Harlan Harlan from the front of the stage.

'Recently . . .' said Penelope and stopped.

'Yes?' I said.

'Let's just say,' said Penelope, 'that after what has gone on it's better if we work with people of your disposition. I don't want any more trouble.'

'What kind of trouble?' said Mickie James, but Penelope was already halfway across the stage screaming at the sight of a large sword.

At the end of the rehearsal Penelope and Harlan Harlan came over. They seemed very pleased with our performance and asked us if we would like to come to their room for supper that evening. I remembered all that shouting and crashing we had heard the day before, but thinking that it didn't make any kind of business sense to piss off our new bosses I said OK.

Thus at seven o'clock on the nose Mickie James and I, in clean underpants, were standing outside the door across the corridor.

'We're going to have supper with a magician,' I said. 'This is better than being in London, isn't it?'

'Do you reckon they're going to fight again?' said Mickie James. 'And what was Penelope going on about?'

'They're artists,' I said. 'That's what they're like. This is the kind of environment we're moving in now, like Paris in the thirties only Denmark and now.' Then I knocked on the door. It was opened by Penelope. She was wearing a small black dress with two arm straps. Harlan Harlan was behind her lighting a candle on a table.

The room was larger than ours and packed with furniture. There was a wardrobe next to the window, a table set for dinner, a large bed with a tan duvet. Covering the floor space between these items were numerous black boxes inlaid with gold scrollwork.

Harlan Harlan passed us both a glass with white wine in it.

'To a magical working relationship,' he said.

'Abracadabra,' I said.

'Something smells good,' sad Mickie James.

Dinner was a fancy affair. There were two courses and a dessert and a whole range of knives and forks.

While we ate, Harlan Harlan and Penelope told us stories of places they had been – Istanbul, Dar es Salaam, Bognor Regis – and people they had worked with – the Mighty Thumb, Mohammed Ahmed Muscleman the Third, the Flexible Flucks from Finland.

Every now and then I looked at Mickie James and we smiled. At one point he put his hand under the table and squeezed my cock and I knew that he was glad that we had stayed.

After dinner Harlan Harlan stood and put a hand on Penelope's back.

'Why don't you show them your party trick?'

'Oh I couldn't,' said Penelope, immediately standing up and going to the far side of the room to retrieve a box.

'What you are about to see,' said Harlan Harlan, 'will both amaze and stupefy.'

Penelope pulled the black box to the centre of the room,

unclipped some latches on the top and the sides fell away to reveal a clear plastic cube. It felt as though this was something the pair of them had done many times before.

'Penelope will enter the cube,' declaimed Harlan Harlan. He was speaking in his booming stage voice and he had his hands raised in the air. 'It is exactly seventy-five centimetres square.' He put his hands down. He spoke more quietly. 'It used to be fifty centimetres square but recently Penelope has put on weight.'

Penelope pursed her lips. 'For his next trick Harlan Harlan will disappear up his own arse.'

After the previous night's palaver I expected Harlan Harlan to explode at this, but he didn't. He laughed and put his hands back in the air. 'It really is the most miraculous miracle, the most stupendous spectacle.'

This was Penelope's cue. She placed one foot and then the other inside the cube and then, by bending first her knees, then her back, then her arms and finally lowering her head into the last inch of space, she was completely inside the plastic square. Harlan Harlan went over and closed the lid. Mickie James and I both applauded.

'That's brilliant,' I said. 'Why isn't it in the act?'

'It isn't in the act now,' said Harlan Harlan, his eyes darkening, 'because of what happened during our last engagement.'

'Where was your last engagement?' asked Mickie James.

'India,' said Harlan Harlan.

'Istanbul,' said Penelope.

They both spoke at the same time. I had the feeling there was something fishy in their confusion. I couldn't believe they were unsure where they had been.

*

43

On the third day of rehearsals, during the climax to the magic show in which Harlan Harlan apparently rips Penelope to shreds with a jagged-edged sword, Mickie James added a whole series of extra trills to the music we were following.

While we were packing away, Penelope came up to Mickie James and asked him about those extra bits. I could see that Mickie James was on the point of apologising when Penelope held up her hand.

'Don't worry,' she said. 'I like them. We'll keep them in.'

As Penelope walked away I gave Mickie James a wink.

'OK,' he said, 'you were right.'

Mr Bixen had given us a sub against our first week's wages, so we decided to go out for a celebratory takeaway. Harlan Harlan had told us about this fantastic Chinese down from the entrance to the Tivoli Gardens. He said it was the bee's knees.

Mickie James ordered chicken in black bean sauce and while we were waiting for it to come he whispered to me that we should take the food back to our room and that I could rub the sauce on my knob and use it as a lubricant to fuck him.

Mickie James gets kinky like this when he is happy and I couldn't wait to get back to the station. However, the first thing I saw when I opened the door at the top of the stairs was this Chinaman sitting on the bed. It was quite a surprise.

'Did you order Chinese delivery?' I said to Mickie James.

'Who are you?' said Mickie James to the Chinaman.

The Chinaman rose and held out a hand. He was dressed in a neat black suit and from the corner of his mouth hung a thin stemmed pipe with a narrow bowl.

'What are you doing here?' I asked. 'If it's a train you're

44

waiting for then you need to be downstairs. You can't wait here.'

'I have been watching you,' said the Chinaman and gestured for us to sit down.

I looked at Mickie James and I guessed we were thinking the same thing. Many bands have a Svengali figure. After the Beatles went to India their music was full of sitars. It was a new direction for pop music and cemented their place in history. This Chinaman had been watching us and maybe he wanted to be our manager. I was unsure what kinds of instruments they used in China, but I was certain this was going to be our big break.

'I am here about your neighbours,' said the Chinaman.

'I think you should go,' I said.

The Chinaman took the pipe out of his mouth and blew smoke into the air. The movement was very precise. 'In Shanghai I know people. Influential people. Maybe I can help you. You are in a band, yes?'

'Yes,' I said.

'We're Down by Law,' said Mickie James.

The Chinaman nodded. 'I like it. Maybe I can do something for you. But first you must help me.'

I looked at Mickie James. He was looking at me, waiting for me to make a decision.

'OK,' I said. 'Explain to us what you want. But I'm not promising anything.'

The Chinaman shifted on the bed and crossed one of his narrow legs over the other. Already there was a fug of blue smoke from the pipe above his head.

'Shanghai is a special place,' he said, 'unlike the rest of China. The reverence for the imperial family remains strong. Since the time of Mao and the reign of the communists they have lived there, protected, sheltered.' The Chinaman took the pipe out of his mouth again. 'Perhaps you would like to sit down? This may take some time.'

As there were no chairs in the room we went and joined the Chinaman on the bed, Mickie James on one side, me on the other.

For a long time the story didn't seem to have any relevance, being largely about early Chinese history and the rise and fall of emperors, but it began to get interesting around the time Tripitaka fled the Mongol hordes, taking with him the symbol of Chinese nobility, the great ruby of Szechwan.

'This ruby is as large as the greatest elephant's foot,' said the Chinaman.

'It must be worth a fair bit,' said Mickie James.

'It's priceless,' said the Chinaman. 'Every seventy-five years, when the year of the dragon coincides with the eclipse of the phoenix according to the old Gung-Huoang calendar, a great celebration is held. Thousands come from all around to see the ruby and it is the tradition of the emperor to put on a show.'

'Is that why you're here?' said Mickie James. 'Are you going to book us?'

'The show was one month ago,' said the Chinaman.

'I don't understand,' I said.

'One act booked for the show was the great Harlan Harlan and his beautiful assistant Penelope. In retrospect, this was foolish. Magicians have a certain reputation and now I can only regret what happened.' The Chinaman sucked hard on his pipe and after a thin trail of blue smoke seeped from his nose. Slowly it ascended to the ceiling.

'The trick took place on the roller coaster in Shanghai's premier theme park, The Golden Dragon. On the night in question the park was thronged with people; millions had come from the provinces around.

'At the base of the roller coaster, to the accompaniment of fireworks and trumpet noise, Penelope folded herself into a clear glass box. Harlan Harlan placed the box within one of the cars on the roller coaster and the car was started.' The Chinaman took a deep breath. 'The car would accelerate to one hundred and twenty miles an hour in two point four seconds. It would climb to two hundred metres and then loop the loop. When it completed the circuit and returned to the start then Penelope wouldn't be in the box but the great Szechwan ruby would.'

'What happened?' asked Mickie James.

The Chinaman took a box of matches from out of his pocket. He pushed out the inner tray and removed a match. He struck it and relit his pipe, filling the air with the smell of sulphur and tobacco.

'When the car returned Penelope wasn't there. But neither was the ruby.'

Mickie James and I glanced at the wall, behind which we knew were Harlan Harlan and Penelope.

'I want that ruby back,' said the Chinaman. 'You are with them every day. Maybe they will let something slip. You have access to their room. If you are successful in this I can be of great help to you. The Chinese market is large and largely untapped by Western artists. I could be the key to opening the door. You have one week. Then I will return.'

The Chinaman gave a neat little smile, bowed from the waist and left the room, shutting the door carefully behind him.

'What shall we do?' said Mickie James.

'We have to make that choice that all internationally

47

successful artists make. We have to choose between our friends and "the deal".'

'Since when did Harlan Harlan and Penelope become our friends?'

I smiled slightly. 'I don't know, but I kind of like them.'

'Me too,' said Mickie James. 'But I also want us to be big. I don't know what to do.'

I shifted closer to Mickie James on the bed. 'We've still got that black bean sauce. I reckon it will be at just the right temperature now. Wasn't I on a promise?'

When we turned up for the next day's rehearsal we found Penelope, Harlan Harlan and Mr Bixen deep in conversation.

As we climbed up onto the stage Penelope turned towards us. 'We were just talking about you.' She had this big beaming smile on her face and I knew something major was up. 'After the rat-catcher trick and before the sword-in-the-ass trick we feel the show needs some kind of pause, otherwise it's all wham-bam-thank-you-ma'am. We were wondering if you would do a song? Me and Harlan could be on the stage setting up the next trick real slow. I could do some japing towards the audience every time I saw the sword.' Penelope swung around to the front of the stage, raised her hands to her cheeks and did a mime scream. 'We think it would work real well. What do you guys think?'

Mickie James was already nodding his head.

'Yeah,' I said. 'I can see it.'

Penelope and Harlan Harlan gave us five minutes to decide which song we would do and Mickie James and I had a conference. Actually it didn't take much deciding. We still both thought that 'Manos Sucias' was our best song, but as it had this whole flamenco section in it we knew that it wouldn't be right for either a magic show or the kind of international cross section we were expecting to make up the audience.

The song we decided on was one we had written just before we had left for Copenhagen. It was called 'Mermaids are for Life' and was inspired by the story of the Little Mermaid. It was basically a ballad, but it also had this jingly chorus that was influenced by the music of a merry-go-round.

We played it for Penelope and Harlan Harlan and at the end of it Harlan Harlan clapped and Penelope wiped this tear away from her eye and came over and hugged me and Mickie James.

'You know what?' she said. 'I am going to make that our song. It's just beautiful.'

That night there was a meal organised for all of the performers at the Tivoli Gardens to celebrate the start of the pre-spring season. The venue was the Jailhouse Restaurant on Studiestraede. The time was eight o'clock.

The Jailhouse Restaurant was down this side street near the Orsteds Park. The windows had black bars across them and inside everything was painted black.

'It's mostly a gay bar,' said Penelope, as a waiter in leather trousers with the arse cut out arrived at the table to take our drinks order. 'Have you been out on the scene much?'

I glanced at Mickie James. He kind of nodded and I knew it would be all right so I said that we didn't go out on the scene. I explained that people tended to stare at Mickie James because of his deformity.

'I used to get teased at school for being so bendy,' said Penelope. 'People can be cruel. The thing is, you have to find your niche. Once you're comfortable in your niche you can open yourself up more to the outside world. I think of it like being a boxer. You have to have your corner to fight from.'

They sounded like wise words to me.

'Now,' said Harlan Harlan, 'do you know everyone?'

I shook my head. There were eight of us at the table and I didn't know anyone except Harlan Harlan, Penelope and Mickie James, so Harlan Harlan did the introductions.

Andrei and Sergei were tumblers from Serbia. Chantelle had been the Eurovision entry for Andorra in 1982 and Angus was a tightrope walker from Glasgow.

'There's hardnay eny blokes like me in Glasgay,' said Angus. He nodded across the table to Penelope. 'What that lassie says is true. Fight the true fight.'

The food was nice but the evening was mostly about drinking. Every time our glasses neared the bottom one of the waiters with no arse in his trousers would appear and refill them. By the time the food was finished both Mickie James and I were more than a little drunk.

'I hope you'll no be too pissed ta perform,' said Angus, leaning across the table with a cigarette clenched between his teeth.

'What do you mean?' I said, but right then, as if on some kind of unspoken cue, Andrei and Sergei took off their tops revealing small white vests and bulging muscles underneath. They strode out from their chairs and did some tumbling down the central aisle of the restaurant. This received a round of applause.

Several men with large moustaches applauded extra loudly and asked for more and this time naked, but instead Angus stood, hefted Chantelle onto his shoulders, and nimbly traversed the floor of the restaurant on the backs of other diners' chairs while Chantelle sang 'Oh My Love is a Painted Rock'. This, Penelope explained, was a famous Andorran ballad.

'See, what did I tell you,' I whispered to Mickie James, 'Paris in the thirties.'

'Only Denmark and now,' whispered back Mickie James. As he was smiling I knew he was having a good time and not being ironic as he can sometimes be.

When Angus returned to his chair it was Harlan Harlan's turn to stand. He bowed several times. The eyes of the whole restaurant were on our table; even the waiters with arseless trousers had folded their arms and stopped to watch.

Harlan Harlan boomed out a few words about the marvellous nature of the magical act he was going to perform, and had just taken out a pack of cards when a shadow fell across the table, right across the cards he was holding.

Harlan Harlan looked up, me and Mickie James looked up and the whole restaurant seemed to go extra quiet. Standing right in front of Harlan Harlan was the biggest bloke I had ever seen.

'Do you think it's part of the act?' whispered Mickie James.

'I don't think so,' I whispered back.

Harlan Harlan looked across at Penelope, turned whiter than the tablecloth, then shook his head, threw the cards so they scattered across the table and ran from the restaurant.

'Harlan Harlan!' screamed Penelope, leaping up. 'Come back! I didn't know. I swear I didn't know.' But Harlan Harlan had already gone.

Penelope turned to the figure who had cast the shadow, shouted, 'Get the hell out of my life, why don't you?' and ran out of the restaurant after Harlan Harlan.

51

Nobody said a word, not until Angus stood up and held out a hand to the figure.

'Gus, mate,' he said, 'I think mibbe the lassie is no pleased to see you. Sit doon anyhoo.'

The man grunted and sat down. He was a mountain of a man, with shoulders straining the seams of a huge green overcoat. He brushed hair out of his eyes and reached across the table for the glass that Harlan Harlan had left.

'Gus is our new roller-coaster guy,' said Angus. 'He comes to us via China. Beijing, wasnae it?'

'Shanghai,' grunted Gus and he downed the pint in one.

'I get it,' said Mickie James. It was later and we were in bed. 'Gus was in Shanghai. He was operating the roller coaster and he stole the ruby.'

'It all seems a bit easy,' I said.

'Seventy-five per cent of all murderers are caught standing next to the body.'

'Who's been murdered?'

'No,' said Mickie James, 'I mean, crimes are often easy to solve.'

'And what about all that between Gus and Penelope and Harlan Harlan?'

'I'm not sure,' said Mickie James, 'but it's to do with that ruby, it's got to be.'

'So we tell the Chinaman?'

Mickie James leapt out of bed. He didn't have his T-shirt on and I could see his hunchback. This was a fairly new thing for Mickie James. He never used to let me see his hunchback.

'We can't tell him. Don't you see? We've got no proof. I say we get that ruby back.'

I sat up on one elbow. 'What's got into you?'

'We're going onstage tomorrow for real,' said Mickie James. 'You know what, I feel alive.' He ran back over to the bed and leapt up onto it. 'I feel alive,' he shouted and then we heard the crash from next door and then a scream. Harlan Harlan and Penelope were up to their old tricks, not magical ones.

We slept late and then, when I went into the toilet for a dump, I found Harlan Harlan in the bathtub. He was sitting up and shuffling a pack of cards. As I entered he turned and looked at me.

'I'm a magician,' he said. 'I think like a magician. I think that one day she'll disappear.'

'You are a magician,' I said. 'You could make her reappear.'

'I thought of that, but I only have influence over things at arm's length.'

'You can't keep her close forever, you'll lose her.'

'Do you ever think you'll lose Mickie James?'

I sat down on the toilet. 'I used to think that the way he feels about himself would drive us apart, but I don't any more.'

'Why not?' Harlan Harlan plucked one of the cards out of the pack, looked at it, and tossed it on the floor.

'I don't know.' Then I said, 'The music; it gives us something to focus on.' I thought of a shadow looming over everything. 'This Gus?'

'It all started with a trick,' said Harlan Harlan. He took another one of the cards and threw it out of the bath. It landed a short distance from the other one. 'You've seen part of it. Penelope climbs into a small glass box and then I close the lid. That's the first part. Once the box is shut I get these huge sheets of wrapping paper – gold, silver, bronze, top-quality stuff – and I wrap the box up.'

'It sounds like a good trick.'

Harlan Harlan shook his head and another card joined the others on the floor. 'I walk around the box. I ask for a volunteer from the audience, preferably someone, I say, whose birthday is on that day. The volunteer comes onstage. I give them the box, all wrapped up. They open it, and hey presto, the box is empty.'

'Wow,' I said and crossed my legs. I still needed my dump and it wasn't helping matters that I was sitting on a toilet. 'That definitely sounds like quite a trick.'

'It was,' said Harlan Harlan. 'It was in Romania that it all went wrong. The traps in the stage didn't work. As I lift the wrapping paper over the first side of the box a trap is supposed to open below it. Penelope is supposed to slip out. That day I was distracted, I don't know why. I wrapped the box up. I called for a volunteer. The volunteer was Gus. When he opened up the box Penelope was still there. He thought that was it. He thought Penelope was his.

'From then on, everywhere we went, Gus was there. At first Penelope was flattered. She signed autographs. She had her picture taken with him. But it became an obsession.'

I thought of the screams and the crashes. 'You think she likes him?'

'Oh no,' said Harlan Harlan. 'But this, it puts a terrible strain on us. Imagine yourself in my shoes. If someone loved Mickie James and every time you turned round he was there, staring. It's not only the annoyance or the jealousy, it makes you question yourself. Do I love her that much? You lie awake at night and you wonder if you are worthwhile. It gets to the point where you snap. I don't trust anyone any more. Do you understand?'

'I think so,' I said.

54

'And the act has suffered too,' said Harlan Harlan. 'The box trick was once the high point of our act. But not any more. We performed it for the last time in China. We thought in China we would be safe. It was to be our most spectacular spectacular. But that went wrong too. This time for other reasons.'

I was on the point of telling Harlan Harlan that I knew about the Chinaman and the ruby when there was a knock at the door and Mickie James's head appeared around the frame.

'Have you been yet?' he said. 'I need to go as well.' He noticed Harlan Harlan. 'Is it a party?'

Harlan Harlan pushed himself up and stepped out of the bath. He bowed from the waist. 'Let me leave you boys to it. I must go and make my peace with Penelope. Again.'

Harlan Harlan left the room and Mickie James asked what we had been talking about. I said that I still needed my dump. Mickie James said not to mind him so I pushed open the little window and told him what Harlan Harlan had told me.

'Interesting,' said Mickie James when I had finished.

'What is?' I asked.

'You wipe your bum with your left hand, naturally you are right-handed.'

'Get out of here,' I said.

'No way,' said Mickie James. 'I still need to go.'

So he did and we tried to come up with a plan to get the ruby back. It was difficult. On top of everything else we were excited. That evening was our first night live onstage at Copenhagen's Tivoli Gardens. We were going to be famous.

*

Kids jostled for the seats at the front and it was standing room only at the back. Andrei and Sergei did their tumbling act and then Chantelle appeared from the wings. She sang a song about a seagull from Peru and then she introduced our act. She called us 'Harlan Harlan the Great and Penelope'. She didn't mention me and Mickie James but we were on anyway.

It was awesome being in front of so many people. To be honest, what with the lights and everything I couldn't really see them but I knew that they were there and that was what mattered.

Harlan Harlan whipped out his first sword, Penelope screamed and on cue from Mickie James I picked up the glockenspiel baton. My first note was a C.

The highlight of the show was definitely when we did our own song, 'Mermaids are for Life'. It seemed to fit in with where we were, the fairground atmosphere, the lights, the smell of candyfloss and stage lights and the low rumble of the roller coaster in the background.

When we hit the chorus for the third time and Mickie James started the swirling Wurlitzer succession of notes, I heard from the audience a number of reedy voices echoing my words in unison. I glanced across at Mickie James and already he was looking up at me and smiling and I thought we have a hit on our hands here and then the song ended and Penelope screamed and Harlan Harlan did the trick where he appears to rip her to shreds with a jagged-edged sword but the song was still going around in my head and I felt awesome.

At the end of the show while my heart was still buzzing Harlan Harlan came up to me and asked if we would like to come to the after-show party.

'The tumblers will be there,' he said, 'and Angus. Angus is going to do some naked tightrope walking. He holds the bar in a place where you wouldn't expect. He worked for a number of years in a freak show.'

I was just on the point of saying yes when Mickie James tugged my arm and hissed something in my ear. I missed it at first but he repeated it and pointed to an area away from the left of the stage.

There was no mistaking the shape. It was Gus. He was standing, with his hands in his pockets, looking up to where Penelope was putting away equipment.

'Come on,' said Mickie James. 'Let's follow him.'

'He's not going anywhere,' I said.

'But he will be,' said Mickie James.

I excused ourselves to Harlan Harlan and said there was something that we had to do.

There seemed no purpose to Gus's movements. We went past the Mine, the Odin Express, the Fun House, and more rides. At each of these kids queued, lights sparked and shrieks of laughter rose above everything. But Gus didn't look either left or right. He looked down at his feet and shuffled onwards.

'He's not happy about something,' said Mickie James.

'Look at the way people are looking at him,' I said.

Every so often some kid would notice Gus and they would tap another kid on the arm and they would both snigger.

'He's ugly,' said Mickie James. 'He's an ugly giant and that's why people are staring.'

Mickie James was saying that but I also knew he was saying something else as well.

'I thought you were feeling better about yourself these days?' I said.

Mickie James shrugged. 'In front of you. It's other people I have a problem with.'

Eventually Gus came to a stop. We were by the wooden struts of the roller coaster in the far corner of the park. High above our heads were the tracks, swooping and gliding through the air, silhouetted in the night sky by the moon.

At the base of the roller-coaster struts was a wooden fence and in the fence was a gate. Gus looked over his shoulders both ways and then went through the gate. He closed it behind him.

'I think we've struck gold,' said Mickie James. 'That must be where Gus lives.'

'Or something else,' I said, and we set off towards the gate.

We were in an open area, the dimensions of which were defined by the layout of the roller coaster overhead. There were wooden poles stretching up into the night, forming an eerie maze as they supported the tracks which twisted and turned high above us. The poles seemed to sing as roller-coaster cars rattled by on their journeys.

Exactly in the centre of this area was a shed. It had four wooden sides and one glass window. Mickie James and I crept up to the window and peered inside.

We found ourselves looking into a simple room. It had bare walls, the bowl of a toilet and a bed covered with a grey woollen blanket. There was nothing to indicate that the room was inhabited except for a large holdall at the base of the bed and Gus. Gus was sitting on the bed with his head in his hands.

'I bet the ruby is in that bag,' I said.

'He definitely doesn't look happy,' said Mickie James.

'Don't go feeling sorry for him,' I said.

'I'm not,' said Mickie James. 'I just know how he feels.'

Occasionally Gus stood up from the bed. He walked to one side of the room and then back to the bed again. We watched, time passed and I asked Mickie James if he would go out and get us both a coffee.

When Mickie James came back he asked what had happened. I said not much. At one point Gus had leant slightly to the side as if he had been breaking wind. This had been the highlight.

'It looks like the park's closing,' said Mickie James. 'They're shooing people out of the gate. The woman didn't want to serve me this coffee. She said I would have to drink it quick.'

I blew on the surface of the coffee and took a sip. I looked upwards. The cars that had been whizzing over our heads were not whizzing any more. The roller coaster had closed down for the night.

There was the sound of the gate opening behind us and me and Mickie James scooted over behind one of the pillars.

A tousle-headed boy had appeared. He pulled the door of the shed open and called inside.

'The park's all closed now, Gus. You can walk the tracks.'

There was a grunt in response and the tousle-headed boy headed back out of the gate. Moments later Gus came out of the door of the shed. He pulled it closed behind him and disappeared into the darkness.

'Where's he gone?' said Mickie James.

'Look,' I said and I pointed up at the sky.

It was a clear night. The moon was full and the stars were

out. Halfway up one of the roller-coaster struts was Gus; there must have been some kind of rungs inlaid into it to form a ladder. Gus was climbing up to the tracks.

'I've heard about this,' said Mickie James. 'Every night the tracks are checked for cracks. That must be Gus's job.'

Our eyes followed Gus as he made his way higher and higher up the strut. Finally he got to the top and we watched as he pulled himself up onto the tracks. He set off up the gradient, a lonely figure against the night sky.

'Now's our chance,' I said. 'Follow me and keep your eyes open.'

From the inside the shed didn't look any more hospitable than it did from the outside. I nodded towards the holdall which seemed to be the only place to hide anything and Mickie James nodded too and we lifted the holdall up on to the bed and emptied it out.

There were four pairs of underpants, unwashed. Two shirts, both blue, a pair of trousers and a towel. Apart from that there was nothing.

'It must be here,' said Mickie James.

'You're really into finding this ruby, aren't you?' I said. I had never seen Mickie James like this before.

'I like all these people. Harlan Harlan, Penelope, the tumblers, Angus.'

'You've hardly spoken to the tumblers,' I said. 'Or Angus.'

'I like them,' said Mickie James. He came over to me and put his hands on my shoulders. 'They make me feel like me. What Penelope said about finding a corner to fight from. She's right. I want this to last for a little while. I want this to be my corner. When I go back out into the real world I can take this with me. Do you understand?'

I nodded my head.

'I know Harlan Harlan isn't a real magician but for the moment I feel as if my hunchback has disappeared. That's probably as near as I'll get to my hunchback really disappearing. If the Chinaman does something bad to Harlan Harlan and Penelope then it will be over. We have to find that ruby.'

'But it's not here,' I said. I cast my arms towards the bed with the dirty underpants and large-size clothes on it.

'It must be,' said Mickie James and then from outside we heard this howl. It was mournful and dreadful. And most definitely human.

We rushed outside and the howl came again. We looked in the direction it was coming from. It was from up on the tracks. There was Gus standing with his head back with his arms raised to the moon. It was him. He howled once more and then set back off along the tracks.

'The ruby,' said Mickie James. 'It's up there.'

'How do you know?' I said.

'I just know,' said Mickie James.

'Do you think this is a good idea?' I said to Mickie James.

'Good ideas rarely seem like good ideas at their inception,' said Mickie James. 'That's what stops the majority of people from having them.'

'Don't fart,' I said.

We were climbing up the roller-coaster strut and Mickie James's bum was just in front of my face.

'It's getting windy,' said Mickie James.

'Now is not the time to joke,' I said.

'I'm not,' said Mickie James. 'Hold on tight.'

We advanced further up the ladder. As we got higher the park receded below us, the outer walls forming an area clearly

61

distinct from the streets around. It looked strange empty of people. Like a thing not in use, it was useless.

There was another one of those howls, piercing the night air. Mickie James reached the top of the ladder and he took my hand and pulled me up onto the tracks. Out on the lip of the second drop we could see the shape of Gus.

'This way,' said Mickie James and he set off.

The important thing when high up is not to look down, but we had to look down because we had to see where we were putting our feet. Between the sleepers of the track was open air.

'What are we going to do when we catch up with him?' I asked.

'I don't know,' said Mickie James. 'Play it by ear. Look, is that our room?'

I looked in the direction Mickie James was pointing. There was the station. At the top of the station a number of the windows were alight.

'Perhaps Harlan Harlan and Penelope are home,' I said. 'Do you think they appreciate what we're doing for them?'

'What about the other way around? It was great tonight.'

I thought back over the concert and agreed that great was the word to describe it. Then I remembered something. 'You said what we were doing was only one step up from porn.'

'You can't beat a good bit of porn,' said Mickie James and he laughed. Then he stopped laughing. 'It's Gus,' he said. 'He's coming towards us. Look.'

Gus was a big bloke even from a distance, and as he got nearer, he got bigger. The ground was a long way down and in my mind was the thought that we were only a push away from it.

'What are we going to do?' I whispered.

'It'll be all right,' Mickie James whispered.

'Did she send you?' said Gus. He was directly before us. His long hair was being whipped across his face by the wind and there were clear tracks down the dirt of his cheeks where tears must have run. 'I want you to take this.'

Gus reached into the pocket of his overcoat and his hand came out in a fist. He opened the fingers one by one to reveal a large red stone. 'She gave me her heart,' said Gus, 'and it is torturing me. Please. Take it.'

Mickie James stepped forward to take the ruby. At the same time Gus stepped forward. His foot must have missed the sleeper because the next thing I knew he was falling towards us. The whole gigantic form of him.

'Shit!' I said.

'Grab him,' said Mickie James.

My eyes were on the ruby. It flew up into the air and then came down in an arc against a background of stars, red against the black, black behind the red. I put out my left arm, opened my hand, and with a thump the ruby landed there and I closed my fingers around it.

'Got it,' I said. Then I looked up. The track ahead of me was empty. I spun round. The track behind was empty. I heard a scream. Then another thump.

'Nooo!' I screamed. 'Noooo!' And in my head I could see a hunchback falling from the sky, and with it, the death of everything that I had believed in.

'Mickie James,' I said, 'Mickie James.'

'Don't worry,' said a voice below me. 'I'm OK. But Gus. He's fallen.'

I looked down. Mickie James was there. He was hanging by one hand from the track of the roller coaster.

'Mickie James,' I said. 'Shit!'

I got down on my belly on the track. I gripped Mickie James by the wrist. Above us was sky, below us was ground. They both seemed as far away as each other.

'Don't drop me,' said Mickie James. 'I don't want to be a cripple *and* a hunchback.'

'You won't be,' I said.

'Have you got the ruby?' said Mickie James.

I nodded. 'What about Gus?'

'Didn't you see? He fell.'

'Swing your other hand up. And I'll pull you up.'

'We could write a song about this,' said Mickie James.

'Concentrate,' I said.

Mickie James's face was showing the strain. He swung his free hand around and I caught it. I wrapped my left leg under the outer track and, tensing the muscles in my stomach and back, I heaved.

Sometimes when you are onstage you can forget where you are. You can go into another world where it is just you and the music. This was like that except there was no music. It was just me.

A lot of songs are about love because love is what is important to us. I loved Mickie James. I wouldn't let him go. I closed my eyes and I pulled and I pulled until I heard a voice.

'You can stop now,' it said. 'I'm back.'

I opened my eyes and Mickie James was sitting there cross-legged on the tracks.

'We have to go and see if Gus is all right,' he said. 'I don't think he will be. He took quite a fall.'

We found Gus on the ground by the side of the shed. His left leg was bent up behind him in an angle from a school maths book. His left arm was crushed beneath him. But he wasn't dead. At least he didn't look it.

'Gus,' I said and his eyes flickered open.

'You're the guys from the stage,' he said. 'You know Penelope.'

I nodded my head.

'Will you give her back her heart?'

I thought of the ruby in my pocket. I nodded my head.

'Say you'll do it,' said Gus. 'Say it.'

'I'll do it,' I said.

'I'll go and get help,' said Mickie James. 'You stay here. Check he doesn't die or anything.'

'OK,' I said and I watched Mickie James as he left by the gate.

I went into the shed and I brought out Gus's clothes. I put them over him to keep him warm and I sat behind him and cradled his massive head on my lap.

'Will you explain to Penelope if I don't make it?' said Gus.

'You'll make it.'

'But if I don't.'

'OK,' I said but I didn't know what I was explaining. Until Gus told me, right there under the stars and the night shadows of the roller coaster.

His story started in a place far from the one either the Chinaman or Harlan Harlan had told me about. It started on a farm somewhere in a desert somewhere in Arizona in America. It started when Gus was fourteen years old and his daddy blew his own brains out with a sawn-off shotgun.

'You see,' said Gus, 'my mommy was a whore and Daddy couldn't take it any longer.'

'After Daddy died, Mommy said I would have to go away. She took me into town and put me on a bus. As I was getting

65

on the bus she gave me a parcel. "This is my heart," she said, "and if you always have my heart then you will know that I always love you and you are the most precious boy in the whole world."

'As soon as the bus pulled out of our dusty little town I ripped open the parcel and found in there this single tiny ruby on a chain.

'The people my mother was sending me to were my two aunts in South Dakota. They owned a shrimp farm and every morning they would prod me awake before the sun had risen and send me out to tend the shrimp ponds, all day long, for as many hours as the long days had.

'I could bear all this because my mommy had told me to, but in the third year, my older aunt, the one they called Celia, caught me pleasuring myself out by the shrimp ponds and she beat me with a stick and said I was no better than my no-good whore mother. I said my mother was a good whore and Celia and Carolina laughed cruelly at this and beat me some more. They said my mother would be for the ground soon anyway and good riddance to her.

'I asked what was wrong with my mother and Celia said my mother was as good as she deserved to be and Carolina said this was no good at all. They said she had this thing called Aids.

'The next day I walked the twelve miles back to the bus depot and I took the bus back to that little town where I had grown up. Only in my absence the town had grown down and our old house especially. It was all boarded up and outside was a little white cross with my mommy's name on and I knew what this meant. I sat down where I stood and I cried enough tears to make seeds grow if this were the kind of ground where seeds were scattered.

'That night I broke into my own house and found it empty except for that clear plastic box that I knew and remembered so well from my childhood, being the place where my mommy performed her special trick, folding herself into it like an oyster in a shell. I vowed that if I would marry anyone, it would be a woman such as my mother.

'I didn't have no schooling but in my town there was a theme park. I went there after work and they said they had one job but it was a job nobody wanted. I said that wasn't true because I said it was the job that I wanted and so I had it.

'"You have to walk along the tracks," said the guy they sent me to. He was an old man with only one eye and three teeth. He always chewed on the left side. "You must look for cracks and signs of wear," he said.

'When I wasn't working I would climb up the tracks anyway and I would take out my ruby and I would talk to my mommy. I could hear what she was saying and she would say that I was the best boy in the world and that she would always love me.

'One year I found myself in a country that called itself Romania and it was in Romania that the lady who calls herself Penelope first appeared in my life.

'Harlan two times over was on the stage with her and he was talking his fancy talk. He was asking someone to come up onstage and he was saying that it must be someone whose birthday was on that day and I put up my hand and said it was mine.

'Of course, after Harlan times two gave me the present and I unwrapped it and found her in that clear plastic box I knew that she must be the one that I would always love because that was the special trick my mommy used to do, fitting herself into a fifty-centimetre glass box.

'After Romania I learnt that Penelope was going to Brazil and then Argentina so they were places I went too.

'"Has she given you her heart?" said my mommy. "If she gives you her heart only then you will know that she truly loves you," and it was in China where it happened.

'Now this day they put these men with guns all over the roller coaster but that didn't matter because I knew roller coasters better than anyone so when that car with the box was doing the loop-the-loop I was in the car too and I reached in and meant to pull out Penelope and tell her once and for all that she was the girl for me.

'When I put my hand in it was if all my dreams had finally come true. Penelope was gone but she had left her heart. I took this heart and kept it for my own and it was from here that my troubles have started.

'You see, my mother's heart is a kind heart and it is has kept me company though all these years. It gives me advice when I need it and when I am down it tells me that I am dear and wonderful.

'Penelope's heart does none of these things. When I look into it I see only pain and I hear these millions of voices.

'I see death and destruction. I see people starving. I see limbs that are wasted and feel the slow decay that comes from no food, the body eating itself from inside out until it is all eaten up and the body is no more.

'The voices they cry out that they want me to help them and I am the one to cure them and they speak in a language that I don't understand or can't understand but I do understand it. There is one word that I hear again and again and this word is Mao. Mao.

'This evening I came up to the tracks and I have spoken to my mother about this and she asks how I came by this heart. I say that Penelope gave it to me and my mother asks exactly how did Penelope give it to me. And she asks over and over until I say that maybe I wasn't given the heart after all and that maybe I took it and my mother says I am a bad bad person. She says there are many things in life that you mustn't do but one of these is that you mustn't steal someone's heart. I say that I didn't mean to do it only I thought I was so much in love and when I think about it nobody has loved me not really not even myself.'

At this point Gus opened his eyes and gripped tightly onto my hand.

'You will promise to give Penelope her heart back and tell her that I am sorry.'

I nodded my head. 'I will.'

Gus coughed slightly and his massive body rocked with the pain of it. 'Do you think she will find it in her heart to forgive me?'

'I think she will,' I said. 'When she knows the whole story I think she will.'

Then Gus passed out.

Three days later when Mickie James and I come back into our room we find the Chinaman sitting neatly on the bed. Once more he has his thin pipe in his mouth.

'This is a private room,' says Mickie James.

'Do you have the ruby?' says the Chinaman.

With a flourish I produce it from the pocket of my jeans. The Chinaman's eyes light up and he snatches it from my hands. He turns it around, holding it close to his face. Then he deposits it in a small velvet pouch and slips it inside his jacket.

'I am a man of my word,' he says, 'the trip to Shanghai

will be arranged. Next week we are giving a large concert. A place, I am sure, can be found for you on the bill.'

'Next week?' says Mickie James.

'Is there a problem?' says the Chinaman.

I look at Mickie James and he nods his head.

'We are booked here,' I say, 'for the next four weeks.'

'Do you know how many people there are in China?' says the Chinaman.

'We want to stay here,' says Mickie James.

'Very well,' says the Chinaman and he rises from the bed. 'Thank you for the ruby,' he says. 'You don't know this, but we call it the heart of the Chinese people. It holds much mystery there.'

'Oh we know,' says Mickie James.

'Yes we do,' I say.

After the Chinaman leaves I tell Mickie James to get into bed and I will join him after I've had a piss.

In the bathroom there is no sign of Harlan Harlan and all night there is not a peep from the room.

The next morning we awake early and make the trip across Copenhagen to the hospital where Gus is recuperating. We find him sitting up in bed and when we ask him how he is he says that he is very well, very well indeed.

'Penelope came to see me,' he says. 'And Harlan Harlan. They gave me tickets to the show.'

'Do you need tickets for the show?' says Mickie James. 'It's free to all in the Tivoli Gardens.'

'Shh,' I say.

'I apologised for taking her heart and she said it was OK,' says Gus. 'They are going to Egypt after Copenhagen and have asked me to go with them. They have a lot of heavy boxes to carry.'

'That's great,' I say.

'And she said she has a surprise for you as well,' says Gus. 'She told me not to tell you. She has got you an agent who is going to represent you.'

'What?' I say.

'That's right,' says Gus. 'She has got you an agent who is going to make you famous but I am not going to tell you.'

'That's cool,' I say. 'Don't tell us then.'

I turn to Mickie James and I smile.

'Don't tell us anything,' says Mickie James. 'We're Down by Law. We go with the flow.'

WACKY IRAQI

Two days after returning from Denmark's Tivoli Gardens we were back in our room at the top of St Pancras Station. It was like going home. Actually it was going home, that was where we used to live.

As we were flush from our recent earnings at the theme park we decided to splash out on some things for the room. What we needed most was a toilet. Living in Hovedbanegarden Station we had got used to having our own bathroom even if more often than not Harlan Harlan was to be found sleeping in the bath.

Mickie James said the best thing for us would be one of those camping toilets so we went to the local camping shop. We explained to the female sales assistant what we wanted and she took us over to a corner of the showroom.

'This model is top of the range,' she said. 'It comes with its own deodoriser and there's also a slot at the back for storing spare toilet rolls. It can take up to four.'

'How much is it?' said Mickie James.

The sales assistant smiled. 'Two hundred and ninety-nine pounds and ninety-nine pence.'

What with the train fares back from Denmark and two weeks' rent in advance, forty quid, that was more money than we had.

'What about bottom of the range?' said Mickie James.

The sales assistant pushed out her lips. 'It's very basic,' she said.

'That's OK,' said Mickie James. 'We're arty types. One day we're going to be pop stars. Basic will look good in our future autobiography.'

'Fine,' said the sales assistant. 'However, I recommend that you keep it in a well ventilated room.'

'We're going to put it on the roof,' said Mickie James.

Outside our window at the top of St Pancras Station was a flat roof. We put the toilet near enough to the edge so as to give a good view but not too near so if you moved suddenly you would fall down to the station entrance eight floors below.

As the sales assistant had said, the toilet was basic. It was a round hole cut in a wooden chair. Under the round hole you attached a plastic bag. However, simple as it was, it was better than we'd had before. Before, we'd had to crouch. It hurt the leg muscles and we'd often argue over who would clear up the mess.

One day, a week after we'd bought it, I was sitting on the toilet-chair with my underpants around my ankles looking out over the British Library trying to think of a new song for our group Down by Law when Mickie James appeared next to me. It was a hot day and he had his T-shirt off.

'Do you want me to rub some sun lotion on your hunch-back?' I said.

Mickie James didn't answer. I could see that he had something on his mind and I asked him what it was.

'I thought when we got back things would be different,' he said.

'They are,' I said, 'I'm not working in that cheese shop any more. And we've got a toilet.'

'No,' said Mickie James, 'I thought we'd be famous.'

'Something will turn up. At least we've got an agent now.'

Mickie James sighed and sat down. 'I guess. I just miss the crowds. Performing every night.'

'Me too,' I said.

'Do you think it's because of this?' said Mickie James.

A bird landed on my underpants and started pecking at the crotch. 'Oi!' I said. 'That's my best pair.' And I kicked it away.

'My hunchback I mean,' said Mickie James. 'I heard about this place in Las Vegas. They do corrective hunchback surgery. Think what I'd be like if I didn't have this hunchback.'

Down below I could see people streaming across the Euston Road, motorcycle messengers nipping in and out of almost stationary cars and past all this, as far as I could see, the buildings that made up London.

I was just on the point of saying something profound that would change Mickie James's mood when there was a shout from behind. I twizzled round and saw poking through the window of our flat a head. It was Dave's. He was our landlord.

'You've got a visitor,' he shouted. 'Shall I send him through?'

As he said this his head disappeared and out through the window stepped a man. He was tall and handsome and had a muscular body that was packed tightly into green uniform.

This man set off across the roof towards us holding out a hand and fixing a grin on his face.

'Hey, you guys,' he said, 'are you Down by Law?'

'Pass me the toilet paper,' I said to Mickie James. 'I think our luck's about to change.'

After I had pulled up my pants we decamped to our room. There was nowhere to sit on the roof except on the toilet and we wouldn't have all fitted on there.

'I'm Lieutenant Reilly,' said our visitor. 'But you can call me Yankee Doodle Dan. That's what all the guys call me.'

Mickie James had pulled a T-shirt over his hunchback; he was quite self-conscious about it in front of strangers. I was just in my underpants. Outside, the sun slanted across the roof of St Pancras Station. It was a hot day.

'I hope you don't mind me turning up like this,' said Yankee Doodle Dan. 'Your address was given to me by your agent. We're in rather a tight squeeze.'

'You're looking for a pop group?' said Mickie James.

Yankee Doodle Dan nodded sharply. 'We need someone quick. We had booked the Drifters but they've pulled out citing musical differences. It's for a six-week stint. All board, lodgings and transport will be paid for and we'll even keep up the rent on this place for you. I took the liberty of speaking to your landlord. He hasn't got a problem with it.'

I looked across at Mickie James. His eyes were shining brightly and I knew he was up for it. This was exactly the kind of snowball effect we had been expecting since our stint in Denmark.

'We'll do it,' I said.

'Great,' said Yankee Doodle Dan. 'How does five a.m. tomorrow morning grab you?'

'Fine,' I said.

'We'll send a car to pick you up.'

75

'Great,' I said. 'But just one question. Where is it we're going?'

'Kirkuk,' said Yankee Doodle Dan.

'What?'

'It's in Iraq,' said Mickie James. 'Where they had that war.'

'Exactly,' said Yankee Doodle Dan. 'You'll be performing for the troops.' He pulled down the corners of his mouth. 'They're all a bit glum at the mo. You'll be going there to cheer them up. Have you seen *Auf Wiedersehen, Pet?*'

'I think you mean *It Ain't Half Hot Mum*,' said Mickie James.

'That's the one,' said Yankee Doodle Dan. 'You got it. Spot on. See you tomorrow then. Five a.m. sharpish. A word of warning though. Don't pack any jumpers. It's stinking hot out there.'

We woke at four and took turns on the toilet.

'Do you think it'll be OK?' I said to Mickie James as he came back in through the window.

'I don't think anyone would steal a toilet,' said Mickie James. 'Anyway, Dave said he would have someone keep an eye on it.'

'I meant in Iraq.'

Mickie James zipped the Korg keyboard into its travel case and hefted it onto his shoulder.

'Music is universal,' he said. 'Besides, it could be good for us. We might pick up some new sounds. It's about time the UK chart was bombarded with Arabic influences. We'll be a bit like Blur in Africa except we won't just be poncing around on our royalties doing in-depth interviews for the *Guardian*. We'll be doing it because we really want to be famous.'

76

That was one thing I liked about Mickie James. He was always so focused on the music. When I'd asked if we would be OK I meant would our feet get blown off by landmines or would we be killed in a surprise gas attack. That's what worried me about Iraq.

I picked up our rucksack, gave the room a final check, then told Mickie James to get a move on.

'In the words of George Bush,' said Mickie James, 'today Iraq, tomorrow the world.'

I laughed at this. It is not like Mickie James to make jokes. It made me realise how excited he was. He believed this would be our big break. I hoped he was right.

We went down the stairs. All 256 of them.

It was just light but already it was heating up. Across the road a group of lithe black kids were hanging around outside the Burger King, a couple of bums were curled up in the entrance to the station and there on the forecourt was a gleaming military vehicle. A tall soldier was leaning against it with a toothpick in his mouth. It was Yankee Doodle Dan.

He smiled when he saw us and held open the rear door. 'I hope you don't mind but to save some time I arranged for the doctor to give you the once-over en route.'

'What?' I said.

'Standard military practice,' said Yankee Doodle Dan. 'Just a formality.'

In the back of the car was a large man in a white coat. He had a black briefcase balanced on his knees. He opened it up as we got in and took out a cotton bud gripped tightly by a pair of metal handles.

'First we will do the rectal exam,' he said. 'If you would

like to lower your underwear and grip onto the front seat with both hands.'

'Who first?' said Mickie James. Suddenly he didn't sound so cheerful.

I was bleary-eyed when we finally pulled to a stop. That was partly due to tiredness and partly due to invasive medical procedures. I didn't like having things poked into me. That was more Mickie James's domain and even he wasn't happy.

We had dropped the doctor off at a small semi-detached bungalow in Chipping Ongar. He had waved goodbye and then we had gone past fields for a time until we had come to this long wire fence. A man who resembled Yankee Doodle Dan had opened a gate and let us in to what was obviously an airfield.

We got out of the car. In the distance were several squat beige huts with square windows. Next to the huts was a tall metal tower with a large head like a mushroom. Directly in front of us was an enormous aeroplane. Several groups of people were standing around in the shadow of the wings.

'Look,' said Mickie James. 'DD10.'

'I don't know much about planes,' I said.

'Not the plane,' said Mickie James. 'The dance group. DD10.'

'Do you know them?' said Yankee Doodle Dan. 'They'll be performing before you.'

'So they're kind of our support act?' said Mickie James. He seemed pleased by this thought.

'If you like,' said Yankee Doodle Dan. 'Come on. Chop-chop. This baby's ready to fly.'

The inside of the plane was like a shoe warehouse I had once worked in in Birmingham. It was massive. In the centre were two large tanks and down either side were benches where we had to sit.

There was some dispute over who was going to sit where. There were about thirty soldiers going and they all wanted to sit next to a member of DD10. DD10 were all women.

Mickie James told me that DD10 had got their name a) because there were ten of them and b) because they all had a double-D bra size.

'If it was in that order,' I said, 'then they would have been called 10DD.'

'They were originally,' said Mickie James, 'but it caused confusion. People going to see them thought they were going to see a 10CC tribute band.'

Just then one of the women bent over and another opened her shirt and her bra pinged off. It hit the far side of the plane. Several soldiers whistled and others gave a round of applause.

'They're nothing like 10CC,' I said.

'I know,' said Mickie James. 'We're more like 10CC. Except we have better lyrics. Do you think soldiers, in general, like a good lyric?'

It was at that point that I began to have my first doubts. The plane took off.

I woke up to find my head hitting the ceiling of the plane. As the ceiling was fifteen feet above me this hurt quite a bit.

'We're going through a bit of turbulence,' said Yankee Doodle Dan as I landed back in my seat. Actually he shouted this. It was pretty noisy in the plane. 'You'd better strap up.'

I pulled the seat belt across me.

'Where are we?' I said.

'About halfway to Iraq. You been there before?'

I shook my head.

'It's a beautiful country. If you like sand. We reckon this war could be the best thing that ever happened to them. Imagine, Iraq as the new Vietnam. People love to go and see those old Vietcong hideouts. Think what a money spinner Saddam's final cubbyhole could be. Plus you've got the benefit of Iraq being the home to the birth of civilisation, Mesopotamia, Babylonia, etc. People love that shit.'

Next to me Mickie James was snoring quietly. It was freezing in the plane. Wind whistled through it and outside the engines roared. I edged closer to Mickie James and rested my head on his shoulder.

'Don't forget,' said Yankee Doodle Dan, 'Iraq's not as far as Vietnam. That's a selling point too. I don't want to be in the army forever. I reckon I could make a killing as a consultant to easyJet. It's just a matter of changing the public's perception of the country. Get everyone to believe that this war was a good thing. That Iraq was fundamentally bad and we have changed it for the better. People won't go there if they believe that basically we fucked an innocent country.'

I nodded off. It was only later that I realised I should have been paying very careful attention.

I woke up. Opposite, several soldiers were stretching and several members of DD10 were adjusting their bras. Others were reapplying make-up.

'We're coming in to land,' said Yankee Doodle Dan. 'Hold on to your hats.'

'I haven't got a hat,' said Mickie James sleepily. He rubbed his eyes. 'They don't suit me.'

'Then just hold on,' said Yankee Doodle Dan. 'In my experience these things can get quite bumpy.'

The plane banked to the left, then to the right, then it lurched up and then there was a bang as it hit the ground. Several members of DD10 screamed, the whole shell of the plane vibrated and there was the roar of the engines outside as they were put into reverse.

Eventually the movement grew slower and the plane trundled to a stop. The back opened with a loud hydraulic noise.

'Blow me,' I said.

The effect was immediate and dramatic. The heat was like fire, the light almost blinding.

'I told you it was hot,' said Yankee Doodle Dan.

The land was flat, bleached white. We were on an airfield but it looked makeshift. The wire fence around it was ripped in places, almost hanging down to the ground. There were soldiers but they weren't in straight lines. Some were sitting at a distance, perhaps playing cards. A goat stood chained to a ring in the ground. The heat made it difficult to breathe, the air rippled.

Yankee Doodle Dan appeared looking at his watch. 'Where's that sodding bus? It should have been here to pick us up.'

I pointed at the soldiers sitting in a circle. 'Shouldn't they be on guard or something? I've heard about suicide bombers.'

Yankee Doodle Dan made a movement with his arm in front of him. 'Look around you. You could see a suicide bomber a mile off. We're in the middle of nowhere here. And I mean it.'

And then I saw something.

'Shit!' I said. 'Get down.'

Mickie James spun round, dropping the Korg onto the ground. Yankee Doodle Dan pursed his lips.

'That's our bus. We've got a four-hour drive to Kirkuk. Shift your arses. You're in the way of the tanks.'

I stepped to one side. The first of the tanks appeared from out of the back of the plane. Someone had hung a bra from its gun.

There was a lot of tears as DD10 said goodbye to the soldiers.

'They'll always have Iraq,' said Mickie James ironically and then he stepped onto the bus. I think he was angry that the soldiers hadn't paid us any attention. He gets like that sometimes. It's difficult when you desperately want to be famous and then ten women with big tits step in front of you and grab all the limelight. It had been different in the seventies. I mean look at Earth Wind & Fire, or Hawkwind. They weren't lookers and they'd been a hit.

'It's all about surface these days,' said Mickie James. 'What chance have we got when I look the way I do?'

'You're here, aren't you?' I said. I found this was the best way to deal with Mickie James, make him face up to the reality of his situation.

'I guess so,' said Mickie James and he looked out of the window.

There were these massive craters on either side of the road and bits of rubble around the craters.

'Excuse me,' called one of the members of DD10. They were sitting at the front of the bus. Mickie James and me were sitting at the back. Yankee Doodle Dan was sitting in the middle.

'Do you mind if we take our bras off? It's as hot as holy shit up here.'

I looked at Mickie James. He nodded his head.

'Go for it,' I said and this is how we ended up arriving

in Kirkuk naked. I mean, if they were going to take their clothes off, why shouldn't we? That woman was right. It was as hot as holy shit. Hotter I'd say.

It was dark when we entered Kirkuk. I mean, almost absolutely. London was all street lights and neon. This was different, there was nothing.

We could just make out squat two-storey white buildings on either side of the bus. Some would have a trestle table outside with an umbrella poking up from it. Others would have walls blown inwards. There was no set pattern to this. Mickie James and I had our eyes glued to the windows. We'd never seen anything like this. It was all new.

When the bus pulled to a stop Yankee Doodle Dan stood up. 'Girls, if you could put your bras on,' he said loudly.

This caused a lot of commotion. Several of DD10's members had fallen asleep and they didn't like to be woken in this way. They were even madder when the doors to the bus hissed open and two soldiers got on.

'Passes please,' said one of the soldiers. He said this in an official voice.

'This is the security checkpoint for the barracks,' said Yankee Doodle Dan.

'You might have woken us before,' said one of the women. 'Just let me get me bra on, love,' she added to the soldier who was waiting for the pass.

'Don't mind me,' he said and he laughed.

'What about you two?' said the other soldier. He was standing next to Mickie James.

'We're Down by Law,' said Mickie James.

'No,' he said. He sounded pissed off. 'Where's your passes? There's a war on, you know.'

83

'I thought it was over,' said Mickie James. 'I'd heard we'd won. It was in all the papers.'

The soldier sucked in his cheeks. I noticed he had a big cock. The high-waisted trousers they wore tended to show this off. I liked that about soldiers. I just didn't like their attitude very much. A lot of them seemed to be up themselves.

'Is there a problem?' said Yankee Doodle Dan.

'These jokers –'

'– have been sent to entertain you,' said Yankee Doodle Dan. 'Show some respect.'

The soldier nodded curtly and ran his eyes over our passes. As he turned I thought he said something. I thought it was 'Fuckin' yippee aye ai' but I wasn't sure.

'You'll be staying here in the barracks,' said Yankee Doodle Dan. 'I hope that's OK.'

We were in a corridor of a large building. We had dropped DD10 off further down the corridor. I was sorry to see them go. I'd kind of got used to them in a way. I'd liked it when they'd taken their bras off. It had seemed an authentic response to the heat.

Yankee Doodle Dan pushed open a door and stepped inside. There were bunk beds down one side, bunk beds down the other, bunk beds down the middle. Most of the beds had people in them. The room was filled with the sound of snoring.

'The toilet block's at the end,' whispered Yankee Doodle Dan. 'See that door?'

We both nodded our heads.

'If you need to go then go. Otherwise, find a bed and hop in. I suggest you get some shut-eye p.d.q. I'll be back here at ten a.m. sharp to pick you up. You'll be on at eleven.'

'In the morning?' said Mickie James.

'That's right,' said Yankee Doodle Dan. He nodded his head and was gone, pulling the door shut behind him.

Somewhere in the room a soldier farted loudly.

'It's not very glamorous, is it?' said Mickie James, giggling.

I was glad he could see the funny side of it. Sometimes with Mickie James it was either sink or swim.

'I don't know,' I said. 'It's a bit like a porn film. Can't you see it, "Down by Law star in *Iraqi Barracki*, also featuring Ken Schlong and Private Dong"?'

We both giggled at this and then got into the nearest bed. When we woke up there was a soldier in underpants standing over us. He had a thin waist and a smooth chest. He looked like someone who'd appear on the side of a box of Y-fronts in Matalan.

'Yankee Doodle Dan told me to give you a prod,' he said.

'Go for it,' I said, 'only don't tell my boyfriend.'

'Tell me what?' said Mickie James. He sat up and rubbed his eyes.

'I think it's time for us to get ready,' I said.

'Cool,' said Mickie James. 'Today is the day Down by Law make it big. Iraq won't know what's hit them.'

'Iraq has been through a lot,' said the solider. 'They might have a good idea.' Then he saluted, winked, smiled and went off to pull on some trousers. Or something else.

The room we were to perform in was like a big hall. Actually, it *was* a big hall. There was a low wooden stage at one end and some climbing ropes at the other. The soldiers sat cross-legged on the floor. There was hundreds of them, all in neat rows like dominoes.

DD10 were on first. They stepped from behind this big

red curtain and loads of the soldiers started to wolf-whistle and smack the floor with their hands. Mickie James and me were sitting on these wooden chairs by the side of the stage. Yankee Doodle Dan was next to us. It was freaking hot and sweat was running down my back. My heart was also beating fast. It always gets like that before a gig. The heat made it worse.

DD10 didn't do any of their own songs. What they did was sing along to backing tracks. They did Kylie and Sugababes covers and to mix it up the occasional Bee Gees or Celine Dion number. It was shit really. But the soldiers seemed to love them. Maybe it was because they all had big tits. Or maybe it was deeper than that.

Mickie James and I often talked about how bland our culture had got. That's why we thought we were good. We had something different to offer and it wasn't just because Mickie James had a hunchback, although that was the makings of it.

All the stars we loved came from a tough background. I knew it was bullshit but somehow it gave you something to say. If you say something and mean it people respond to that. People may like all this manufactured pop and I could dance along to it too but it was vile fluff, wasn't it?

For their last song DD10 did Beyoncé's 'Crazy in Love'. They danced like Beyoncé too, shaking themselves, and four of them popped out of their bras. This might have been accidental or it might have been just to titillate, but whatever, the soldiers loved it and went wild. Then the song finished and Yankee Doodle Dan went onstage to introduce us.

It's true what they say. You have to grab the audience by the bollocks by the end of the first hook line and if you haven't got them then then you won't get them.

We opened with Sigue Sigue Sputnik's 'Love Missile F1-11'. It was supposed to be ironic and I thought it would have gone down a storm but even as I got to the line, 'Missiles flying overhead. Shoot them up. Shoot them up,' and Mickie James did the cadenced effect on the Korg behind me, I knew we had lost them. You could tell, just by looking at their faces.

After that we couldn't get them back. It was dismal. Between songs I even resorted to making jokes about Iraqis. I reasoned that comedy is a male's equivalent of tits. I'd learnt this at a young age in the playground.

Reaching desperation point, I fixed a grin on my face and said, 'How many Iraqis have you killed today?' It was awful. I was overcompensating and trying to fit in; something that I hadn't done since I was eighteen. It was the worst day of my life except for that time when those three blokes had put my knob in a vice.

When we got to the end of our set, six songs, the last song being 'Alien Amore' which usually goes down a treat, the soldiers didn't even boo. There was just this stunned silence. I'd never experienced anything like it.

I shouted 'Thank you' into the microphone and exited stage right, closely followed by Mickie James.

We spent the next few hours hanging around the compound. Mickie James wanted to go out and see the real Iraq but there was a soldier with a gun at the camp entrance and I didn't fancy our chances.

We found this spot under a straggly palm tree in a quiet corner and stripped down to our underpants. I sat with my back against the tree and Mickie James sat in front of me. Mickie James started going on about it all being because of his hunchback. This is something he always turns to in times of trouble. I worry sometimes about what he will do if things get really bad.

Right then, I couldn't think of any words of reassurance so I didn't say anything. It was all still a bit weird. The day before we had been in London, having completed a successful season at a top theme park. Now this.

At some point the soldier we had seen in underpants that morning came over. He was in full uniform now.

'I've been looking bloody everywhere for you,' he said. He sounded quite angry but in an amused sort of way.

'We've been here,' said Mickie James.

'Yankee Doodle Dan'll have my bollocks for earrings. Come on. He wants you in his office.'

We pulled on our clothes and followed the soldier back into the building. It was cooler in there than it had been outside but it was still boiling. We went down some white-washed corridors lit by the occasional fizzing bulb and stopped outside a door.

'If it's any consolation,' said the soldier, 'I thought you were great. I like all that kind of stuff, Soft Cell, Heaven 17, Depeche Mode. My mum once slept with Tony James. In my opinion you shouldn't have opened with 'Love Missile F1-11'. Tony James was a cunt. So was Martin Degville. Sigue Sigue Sputnik were shit even in the eighties. If you had to do a cover, you should have done a Blondie one. That would have been different. I'd like to hear a Blondie song done by a man. You've got a great voice.'

'Thanks,' I said.

'What do you mean by "consolation"?' said Mickie James.

If the soldier heard he didn't answer. He opened the door and ushered us into the room.

Yankee Doodle Dan was there sitting behind a large desk. By the side of the desk was a chair. Sitting on it was a dark-skinned man with a large nose. He was wearing a ripped Michael Jackson T-shirt.

'There's been a change of plan,' said Yankee Doodle Dan curtly without standing up.

'What?' said Mickie James. 'You've booked us for six weeks. You can't just send us home.'

Yankee Doodle Dan held up a hand. He picked a piece of paper up off the desk, looked at it briefly and put it down again. Above our heads a propeller-shaped fan went around and around.

'Nobody's going home. To be honest this whole occupation thing is one hell of a palaver. We may have got their country but we haven't got their minds.'

Yankee Doodle Dan stood up, adjusted his flies and sat down again. He appeared agitated.

'To be honest,' he said, 'this is what we'd planned for you all along. Only now we're going to push it on a bit.' He coughed into his hand and looked up at the fan. 'You won't be entertaining the troops any more. You're going to be entertaining the Iraqis.'

'What?' said Mickie James.

Yankee Doodle Dan extended a palm to his left where the man in the ripped Michael Jackson T-shirt was sitting.

'I want you to meet Ishtar. He's going to be your guide. Tonight you'll be performing in Samarra. Be very careful that you do as he says. To avoid any confrontation you'll be travelling with him alone. You, of course, will be in mufti.'

'I don't like the sound of that,' I said.

The man who was Ishtar beamed brightly and took a step

forward. 'Oh, it will be very great. We Iraqis we love the Western pop. Come come. But watch out for snipers.'

And so we went, looking carefully around us.

Ishtar drove an old VW camper van. It had a triangular 'I've been to Mecca!' sticker on the front windscreen and the engine made a loud burping sound when he started it up.

The Korg went in the back and me and Mickie James were up front with Ishtar. He had these three mini-fans on the dash. They didn't make any difference. The windows were open and it was roasting.

'What you think of Iraq?' said Ishtar.

Apart from when we'd been in the bus and then it had been pretty dark we hadn't seen much of Iraq.

'It's very beautiful country,' said Ishtar. 'Ishtar, same name as me, he was Babylonian god of love. We have history. Come on. Put on tape. In there.'

Ishtar nodded towards a hole in the dash. There was a pile of cassettes. I picked up one and looked at the cover. There was a lot of squiggly writing, nothing that I could make out. I put it in the cassette player and pressed play.

'Ah,' said Ishtar. 'Mott the Hoople. You like?'

'Not bad,' said Mickie James. 'I like the Bowie-influenced stuff they did.'

'Bowie,' said Ishtar, 'you think he would come to Iraq?'

'Maybe when he was on heroin,' said Mickie James. 'He did *Panorama* and that was a big mistake.'

The white houses on either side gave way to a market. Hundreds of women in multicoloured shawls were bent over buckets balanced precariously on trestle tables. Ishtar slammed his hand on the klaxon and they threw their arms up in the air and slowly moved out of the way. One woman turned to look at us. She had one eye and no teeth.

'Hello, Mum, how do you do?' said Ishtar in English and waved out of the window.

After the market were more houses and after the houses empty fields. I was just about to ask Ishtar if it was all right if I climbed into the back for a snooze when he sat bolt upright and screamed.

'What is it?' I said.

'Sniper!' said Ishtar and he jolted the van violently to the left, swerving it off the road and up onto an embankment. Mickie James went up in the air and landed on my lap. We both put our hands over our heads.

'Heh heh,' said Ishtar, 'just kidding. No sniper.'

Mickie James went back over to his side of the seat.

'Don't do that again,' I said.

'Sniper!' screamed Ishtar again. 'Your faces. A picture.' His shoulders went up and down inside his ripped Michael Jackson T-shirt.

The setting sun greeted our arrival in Samarra. It hung, like a point, above a huge grey building that resembled a conch shell. Kids ran by the side of the van beating on the side of it with sticks and shouting wildly.

'That's a compliment,' said Ishtar. 'They are pleased to see you.'

'Great,' said Mickie James and he waved out of the window. 'I feel a bit like Princess Anne,' he said to me.

The first point of call was Ishtar's house where we sat on the floor around a low wooden table. Food was served from large earthenware dishes by a woman in a red-and-gold head-scarf. Apart from her there were Ishtar's two sons, Amjad and Nezzar, short for Nebuchadnezzar.

'They want to be like you,' said Ishtar. He spoke with his mouth open. 'They want to be pop stars.'

'What's this?' said Mickie James. He was holding up some of the food we had been served. It was this kind of tangy meat wrapped in a leaf.

'That is an Iraqi speciality,' said Ishtar.

'Love it,' said Mickie James taking a big bite.

'It's dog's bollocks,' said Ishtar. Then he did his laugh. Amjad and Nezzar did this laugh as well. They all sat there laughing. The three of them seemed to be a bit of a double act.

After dinner Ishtar said it was time for us to wash up and get ready for that evening's performance. He stood up and led us down this long corridor. We stopped by a wooden door.

'Whatever you do don't go into this room. It's very important, yes?'

We both said OK and Ishtar led us on to the bathroom.

'I wonder what all that was about,' I said after Ishtar had left us alone.

'It's probably a religious thing,' said Mickie James.

'Or maybe he keeps his wives in there,' I said. That was a joke. I liked Ishtar and I knew Mickie James did as well. He was about the best bloke we'd met.

We didn't give that secret room another thought.

Ishtar flicked a switch and some lights came on.

'Shit,' I said.

'Fucking hell,' said Mickie James. 'We're going to be playing here?'

'It's a basketball stadium,' said Ishtar.

'I can see what it is,' said Mickie James spinning around.

'Basketball is very big in Iraq.'

'We're playing in a fucking indoor stadium,' said Mickie James.

Ishtar clapped his hands. 'It's very good, yes?'

'Yes,' we said together, 'very good.'

We set up using the equipment Ishtar had got for us. He said he had borrowed the sound system from the local imam, whatever that was. It was a pretty good kit.

Mickie James said that he hoped nobody would bring a camel with them to the concert because if they did and we turned up the sound then it could blow the hair off a camel. Then he added, 'or a dog'.

I knew he'd added this because he didn't wanted to appear to be stereotyping the Iraqis by lumping them all together with camels. It's easy to slip into that kind of thing when faced by the unknown. Mickie James knew that because he had a hunchback. Besides, Ishtar was a lunatic and nothing like a stereotype.

While we were setting up Ishtar was playing basketball with his wife and two kids. The wife looked funny playing basketball with that shawl on her head. One time she put the basketball under the shawl so she looked like she had two heads. Ishtar and the kids laughed at this and almost couldn't stop.

At bang on eight o'clock Ishtar's wife put the ball away and Ishtar asked us if we were ready. We said we were and Ishtar went to open the doors.

I'd seen plenty of pictures of Iraqi people on TV and they always seemed to be wailing or pulling down statues so what happened was pretty unexpected. As soon as Ishtar opened the doors people came flooding in. It was a flood of biblical proportions only bigger. There were people of all ages, shapes and sizes and they were all talking and laughing like they were pretty happy to be there. You could tell it was to do with us because people kept staring and pointing.

'This is mad,' I said to Mickie James.

He shrugged his shoulders and smiled. 'This is how I always thought it would be.'

'Yeah, right,' I said.

And then Ishtar was back.

'I told them all you were the Beatles re-formed,' he said.

'You didn't,' I said and then I noticed his shoulders going up and down.

'Sniper!' shouted Ishtar as he made his retreat. He sat down in the front row where his wife and two kids had saved him a seat.

Before the show Mickie James and I had discussed what song we should open with. 'Love Missile F1-11' was definitely out. It wasn't that good a song anyway and we felt that the machine-gun sound effects would be inappropriate.

We remembered what that soldier had said about Blondie and as it happened her song 'Denis' was one we knew so we decided to go with that.

We liked it because there was an ambivalence about it. It was about a bloke but because 'Denis' was a French name we thought that English people might not know that. We didn't know what the Iraqis would make of it but we decided to go for it anyway.

By the time I had got to the first 'do-bi-doo' I knew we had them. The place was rocking. It was as if coincidence had forged a happy meeting of paths. We were thrilled to be doing our first massive concert; they saw us as a heady respite after months of bombing.

We ran through our full set, 'Alien Amore', 'The Curve', 'Ain't It', 'Hunchback Christmas' and we even included a few new ones, 'Dreaming of Uriah' and 'Kinky Goggles', but the one that went down the best was 'Manos Sucias'. That was the one with the flamenco bit in it and I don't know if the Iraqis knew what flamenco was but they were up out of their seats dancing during that one. Four little kids came down to the front and they did this hand-jiving in front of one of the speakers.

I was sorry when it came to an end.

Ishtar came up to us with an arm around each of his children.

'We're having a party back at the house. You will be our guests of honour.'

'Brilliant,' I said.

'You know what?' said Ishtar. 'I think you are better than the Beatles.'

'It was playing Hamburg that made the Beatles,' said Mickie James. 'That's in Germany,' he added for Ishtar's benefit and then we went out to the car.

There were about ten people at the party. Ishtar's wife brought snacks out from the kitchen and we all sat around the table where we had eaten earlier. Nobody spoke English but Ishtar and as everyone wanted to ask us questions Ishtar was busy translating.

At one point he held up his hand, got up from the table, and came back with a bottle. It was long with a large round bottom like an onion.

'In Iraq we don't drink alcohol but we drink this drink which happens to have alcohol in it.'

Small brown cups were produced and liquid was poured into the cups. Upon the sign from Ishtar we knocked them back.

Ishtar's face turned from brown to red and his eyes bulged.

'It has alcohol in it and nothing else really. You'd like another one?'

'Yes, please,' I said and I watched the liquid being poured into the glasses. Several people applauded.

'In Iraq,' said Ishtar, 'we call this stomach fire.'

We knocked the drinks back in one again.

More drinks were produced.

I remember that at some point I needed to go to the toilet and Ishtar recommended that Mickie James go with me.

The corridor was darker than before. It must have been a combination of the lack of sleep, the adrenalin and the alcohol but I couldn't remember which was the right door. It was only as I turned the handle and stepped through the door that I remembered there was a door that Ishtar had said that we weren't to go through.

We were in a kind of courtyard. The moon was out and around it the stars. Bang in the centre of this courtyard, unmistakable, was a long missile. It had a cone-shaped nose, fins at the end and lots of squiggly writing on the body. It was about twelve feet long.

'Shit,' I whispered to Mickie James.

'It's a missile,' he whispered back. 'What are we going to do?'

'I don't know,' I whispered. 'But let's get out of here.'

I turned round and there in the doorway was Ishtar. He looked serious.

'This is very bad,' he said and shook his head.

Standing behind Ishtar were four of the men from the party. They all looked serious too. Ishtar said a few words in his own language and this started what seemed to be a heated debate between the men. Arms went up into the air and then down again.

Finally a decision seemed to have been made.

'Come,' said Ishtar, and he led me and Mickie James further down a corridor. He opened a door and told us to step inside.

We were in a windowless room with two thin mattresses on a dusty floor. They had blankets thrown on them.

'You will sleep here,' said Ishtar and without further to-do he closed the door. We heard the sound of a key turning a lock.

'So are they going to kill us now?' said Mickie James.

'I don't know,' I said, 'but I still need that wee.'

'Go in here,' said Mickie James and he passed me a pot from a low shelf.

I took it with little feeling of satisfaction.

I didn't sleep all night then I was woken by the sound of the door opening. Ishtar was there and the same four men from the night before. There was no sign of the wife and the two children.

Ishtar motioned for us to come with him and we all went out to the van. Ishtar drove and the men divided themselves between the front and the back. Mickie James and I were in the back, sitting on a bench.

Through the windows we could see early-morning Samarra. We passed the pleasant bustle of a market with women poring over colourful baskets of spices and fruits and then there were houses again, the occasional one with roof caved in or missing a wall so you could see inside.

Ishtar slipped a tape into the player only this time it was some kind of Iraqi music or at least Arabic. In other times

I would have asked Ishtar what it was because I liked the sound of one of the instruments and I didn't know what it was.

The houses outside disappeared and gave way to sand dunes and the van bumped as it pulled off the road and then came to a stop.

'Where are you taking us?' I said, which was the first thing I had said in quite a while.

Ishtar shook his head and motioned for us to get out of the back of the van.

There was an area of empty space here that contained two more men and five large camels. Ishtar greeted the men. One of them took an electronic device out of his pocket and the other pointed into the distance across the desert. The sun was up forty-five degrees and I could see very little because of the glare. It was hot and my tongue was dry.

'Have you been on a camel before?' said Ishtar bluntly.

'No,' said Mickie James and I together.

'Then this is the first time. At one time camel was our preferred mode of transport. Times change.'

Mickie James was directed onto one camel and me onto another. We each rode clutching onto the back of one of the Iraqi men. Mine smelt of sweat and I could feel his taut body beneath the thin robe he was wearing. He wasn't much older than sixteen, just a child really.

The movement of the camel was like it was taking one step forward and two steps back. The whole thing was awkward because apart from anything else, squeezed together around the shape of the hump, all I was thinking was that my balls were getting squashed. That and the heat. It was hot.

We stopped, dismounted, and were offered water from a leather pouch. All around was sand. I remembered those shots from the first Gulf War with all the bodies in the desert. It was like that but without the bodies.

Yet.

I hoped we wouldn't have to get back on the camels. We got back on the camels.

Ishtar shouted something from the front and one by one the camels stopped and we got down. The sun was high and it was desert all around.

'They are going to shoot us and bury us in a mass grave,' said Mickie James.

'There's only the two of us,' I said.

'Kneel down and turn round,' said Ishtar.

'You know what my one regret is?' said Mickie James.

'I know,' I said. 'We never had a number one.' Then I said, 'I love you.'

'I know,' said Mickie James.

I felt something being placed around my neck. I took a deep breath and looked down.

Hanging by a strap was a pair of binoculars.

'Take a look,' said Ishtar. 'This is our big problem. Saddam is gone and now this.'

Ishtar pointed into the distance and I brought the binoculars up to my eyes.

I scooted the binoculars around until I happened on something. It was a house compound, seemingly in the middle of nowhere. Parked directly outside the compound was a green army truck. Soldiers were jumping out of the back of the truck. I adjusted the focus and got a surprise.

'Yankee Doodle Dan,' said Mickie James. And then he

added, 'He's got another one of those missiles. With the Arabic writing on the side.'

It was at that point that I understood everything.

'Why didn't you tell us?' I said to Ishtar.

'The West doesn't have a good record of believing the Iraqi people.'

We were in the camper van. Mickie James and I were in the front. Ishtar's four friends were in the back along with the missile.

As soon as we had seen Yankee Doodle Dan and the truck leave we had gone up to the house compound and retrieved the missile from where it had been left.

'We have a mole in the base,' said Ishtar. 'He tells us when one of the missiles is going to be dropped. We get it. It is cat and mouse. One day the cat will win. That is nature's way.' Ishtar added, 'Your army is the cat,' although I had understood what he meant.

I remembered Yankee Doodle Dan's words on the plane. Iraq had to be seen to be the bad guy. He had said so himself. Iraq needed to have WMD, so Yankee Doodle Dan was going to plant them.

'Why don't you go to the press?'

Ishtar shrugged. 'We have. We even have a video to prove we are not making the whole thing up. They told us to get lost. The BBC, NBC, CNN. Even our Arabic TV channel. That is now in the hands of your cat. It is the will of Allah maybe. What will be will be. You will perform again tonight?'

'At the basketball court?'

Ishtar nodded. 'Yes. You don't know how many people we could have got in there. You are the talk of the town. That is one good thing.'

'I guess,' I said but my thoughts were elsewhere. I had the beginnings of an idea. It came from something Ishtar had said.

We only had to get back to Ishtar's quickly.

Ishtar was sitting by the phone. Amjad and Nezzar were playing dinosaurs beside him until Ishtar shooed them away.

'Just call,' I said. It was five hours to the concert and counting. 'What have you got to lose?'

'My children,' said Ishtar. 'My wife.'

I sat down. 'You think it will come to that?'

Ishtar nodded. 'Exactly. That's what Saddam would have done.'

'You'll be OK,' I said. 'Once it's out in the open our government will put a spin on it, find a scapegoat. They won't hurt you. That's how they operate.'

'You want me to trust them after all these bombs?'

'That time Iraq was the scapegoat,' I said. 'This time you couldn't be. You're a nobody.'

'Thanks,' said Ishtar.

'I . . .'

'I think I understand. It is different times and we have to learn to adapt.'

On saying that Ishtar picked up the phone.

Half an hour later a slick 4 × 4 pulled up outside the house. One man in a neat black suit got out and came towards the house. Two fat men with moustaches stayed in the vehicle with a pile of equipment.

The man in the neat suit talked briefly to Ishtar and then he turned and held a hand out to me and Mickie James.

'I'm Zarife,' he said, 'and you must be Down by Law. It's all been a bit hectic but we've managed to boot some Iranian minor league football off the schedule. The concert will go out live. It's just the sort of feel-good story we need after everything that has gone on. After the concert we'll do an interview, if that's OK?'

'Fine,' I said, but for the first time before a concert I wasn't only thinking about the concert. I had other more important things on my mind.

Zarife and his two cronies set up their equipment and me and Mickie James set up ours. This time Ishtar and family didn't play basketball. They were busy doing something else. I hoped it would all work out.

At eight o'clock exactly Ishtar opened the doors to the stadium and the people came flooding in. It was only as the last seats were filled that I realised something.

'We're going to be on TV,' I said.

Mickie James nodded his head and didn't say anything. I knew what he meant.

We opened with Blondie's 'Denis' again. It was strange for me having a camera and an audience there. Usually I don't like to keep in one place. Zarife had told me though that I had to stand still. The camera they had could only move so far and not at any great speed. That made me think I would have to work on my static performance. To be honest, TV was a whole new ball game.

After 'Denis' we did 'Alien Amore', then 'Hunchback Christmas', then Duran Duran's 'Rio'. The audience seemed to love 'Rio' and quite a few of them held lighters up in the air. This would have been more effective if all the stadium lights had been turned off. They had to be on full because of the TV cameras.

Once I had finished singing 'Rio' I nodded to Ishtar and

he nodded to his friends and they snuck up behind Zarife and his two companions and put sacks over their heads and dragged them off. They were careful to leave the camera running.

Ishtar came up next to me and took the microphone. He spoke into it and the audience went quiet. He spoke some more and the audience went even quieter. Then he nodded to little Amjad and Amjad pushed the button on the video in front of me and some images flashed up on the projection screen that Ishtar and family had set up behind us earlier.

Ishtar didn't speak into the microphone now as he didn't need to. What was going on was very clear. There was Yankee Doodle Dan and the other soldiers. There was the missile being taken out of the back of the truck.

The images finished and Ishtar went over to the TV camera and switched it off. The sacks were taken off Zarife and his companions and the audience filed out without making a sound.

The concert was over.

It was ten o'clock when we got back to Ishtar's house. The stars were out again and with them the moon. The heat of the day had barely abated.

We went and sat around the table in the living room. Ishtar pulled a sheet from off a square shape in the corner and there was a TV. He switched it on.

He came and sat next to us and worked his way through the channels with a remote. On every channel was the same thing. It was the video he had shot. Catching an English voice I told him to stop. It was BBC News 24 and there was Tony Blair.

We only caught the end of the statement but we got the gist. A rogue element of the British army had been acting independently from British and American wishes. Someone in Yorkshire had committed suicide and a full inquiry would take place. Right at the end there was a clip of me and Mickie James. We were performing 'Rio'.

'It could have been one of our own songs,' said Mickie James.

'Never mind,' I said.

Ishtar poured some liquid from the onion-shaped bottle.

'I want to propose a toast. To my new friends, Down by Law.'

It was quite embarrassing having a toast to yourself but Mickie James and I held up the glasses and downed the liquid in one.

One week later it was the day Mickie James and I were due to leave Iraq. We were sleeping when Amjad and Nezzar rushed into our room and pulled us out of bed.

Ishtar was sitting in the living room looking very pleased with himself and opposite him was Zarife, the man from Iraqi TV.

'Zarife has a proposition,' said Ishtar.

'Let me speak,' said Zarife and he stood up and brushed down the front of his shirt. 'Ishtar tells me you have been working on a song.'

'"Wacky Iraqi",' said Mickie James.

'That's right,' I said.

'We have this new talk show, *At Home with Hayat*. We were wondering if you would like to be on it?'

'We're leaving today,' I said.

'You have time,' said Ishtar. 'If we go now.'

Five minutes later Mickie James and I were in the front seat of Ishtar's camper van following Zarife's 4 × 4 through the streets of Samarra.

The studio was smaller than I expected, one large room on the second floor of a three-storey office block. Hayat, the presenter, was a glamorous woman with ruby lips. We were on after a cooking slot about sheep's intestines.

I had been practising my static movement and had rehearsed a dance. Ishtar had helped me with this and had even taught me some arabesques.

It was a different feeling not having an audience directly in front of you but I could imagine them out there glued to the screens as I hammered out the chorus.

> He's a wacky Iraqi
> Driving in his VW van.
> He's a wacky Iraqi
> From Samarra to the temple of Goran.
> Wa-Wa-Wa-Wacky I-I-I-Iraqi.
> Wa-Wa-Wa-Wacky I-I-I-Iraqi.

'What did you think?' I said to Ishtar as we stood on the courtyard outside the TV studio.

'We have to get you to bloody Baghdad,' said Ishtar. 'We have to make your plane.'

It was only as we were saying goodbye under the watchful gaze of the soldiers at the temporary airport that Ishtar mentioned the song.

'It was about me, wasn't it?' he said. 'That song.'

'A little bit,' I said.

'Silly bloody Westerners,' he said and then it was time for me and Mickie James to get on our plane. Ishtar, his wife,

Amjad and Nezzar all stood on the tarmac and waved goodbye to us.

As I ducked inside the doorway I saw Ishtar mouth a word. I knew what it was.

'Sniper!'

I wouldn't miss the heat of Iraq but I thought I would miss everything else pretty badly.

TOAST OF TOKYO

Summer was in full swing and our room at the top of St Pancras Station was as hot as a twirling dervish's crack, sac and back. Heat-wise, it was like our time in Iraq all over again except this time there were no cute soldiers in white underpants or major concerts looming on the horizon to distract attention. Things were bad.

Mickie James had taken to moping about on the roof muttering how everything would be different if only he didn't have a hunchback and I spent most of my days holed up in the practice room trying to write the songs that would launch us into international pop superstardom. This wouldn't have been a bad thing except the songs I was writing reflected my current state of mind. Even I could see the Leonard Cohen inspired 'Suicide Would Be the Sensible Choice If It Didn't Involve So Much Pain' would never make it to the top of the charts. It wasn't the sixties any more and besides, who had ever liked Cohen anyway?

Things came to a head one Thursday. I had just penned the verse, 'I used to have hopes, like latter-day Popes. Now any chance of happiness, is as likely as a dose of nappy rash,' and was seriously considering taking my pride between my legs and going to Bloomsbury Cheeses to ask Con for my old job back palming Parmesan to ladies of leisure when Mickie James burst into the room.

'Shouldn't you be polishing knobs?' I said. This was in reference to Mickie James five-hours-a-week job wiping the door handles on Midland Mainline's upgraded fleet of 125s.

'We got a telegram,' said Mickie James.

'People don't send telegrams any more,' I said. 'The Post Office cancelled them about the same time John Taylor left Duran Duran.'

'John Taylor is back with Duran Duran now,' said Mickie James and he did a jump in the air and started waving the piece of paper he was holding like it was a flag and he had been paid to wave it. I knew something was up.

'Our agent wants to see us,' said Mickie James. He stopped jumping and read out the telegram. '"Major interest in Down by Law. Stop. Tried to call but you have no phone. Stop. Please drop by the office at your earliest convenience. Stop."'

I could see why Mickie James was so excited. In my limited experience agents didn't go bandying words like 'major' about unless they meant it.

'What are we waiting for?' I said, throwing down the sheet of lyrics I had been working on. 'Let's go.'

I started down the 256 stairs that led from our room to the station below. It wasn't until I was at the seventy-fourth, or it may have been the seventy-fifth, step that I realised I was wearing only my briefs. I didn't mind. It was the kind of amusing anecdote that would go down well in the future chronicles of Down by Law. They would describe how we struggled for years before finally making it big one Thursday very shortly after receiving a telegram. That was the kind of story that people liked.

I started back up the stairs to slip into something more suited to this important event.

Our agent had two rooms above a remaindered shoe shop in Canning Town. At one time Mickie James and I had gone there daily. This had stopped when Betsy Wong, our agent, had slammed her hands down on the desk and said that we weren't her only clients you know and if something turned up she would be in touch pronto pronto. She had a point. If we were always there then how could she engage herself fully in scouring the trade papers looking for work for us?

There was one other person in the reception, a man with a nose like a carrot, and we took a seat next to him. This was under a large photograph of the *Titanic* sinking.

After several minutes the door to Betsy's room opened and a woman carrying a large hen came out. She looked like she had been crying. The door shut behind her and the woman rushed down the stairs making loud wailing noises. Or it might have been the hen.

'I hope I have better luck than that,' said the man.

'What do you do?' I said.

'I lift weights with my penis.'

The door opened and Betsy called the man with the weightlifting penis into her room.

That was one of the things that attracted me to having Betsy as an agent. She could spot individual talent. She wasn't one of these people who only wanted to put together five good-looking lads, get them singing covers and then send them off round the gay clubs showing off their arses. She understood that there was more to life than having a good arse. It was about integrity of talent.

The door opened and the man with the nose like a carrot came out of the room.

'How did it go?' I asked.

'Not bad,' he said. 'She wants me to work on my routine. She says lifting weights with your penis is old hat. If I lift metal moulded figures of famous people she thinks she can find me work. She suggested Kylie Minogue for starters.'

'Kylie is big at the moment,' said Mickie James.

'Come on,' I said and we went into the room.

Betsy Wong was an extremely large woman, especially in the upstairs department. She had started out as a novelty model for certain diverse clients in her native Beijing and from there she had worked her way up to being one of London's most sought-after agents. She knew the trade inside and out.

'So what's this major interest?' said Mickie James, cutting right to the chase.

Mickie James and I were sitting on one side of the desk, Betsy Wong was on the other. She was smoking two cigarettes. This was a habit of hers.

'Down by Law,' said Betsy, 'you guys are going to be big.'

'What's going on?' I said.

'You remember that TV spot you did?'

Mickie James and I both nodded. It wasn't something we were likely to forget. It had almost been the highlight of our time in Iraq.

'Well, that broadcast was picked up by some DJ. He does shit like that, scours the airwaves looking for new sounds. He came across you, played it on his show.' Betsy put her elbows on the table and leant towards us. 'It's totally against copyright conventions of course. But if it works it works and who am I to bite the ass that feeds.'

'Exactly,' I said.

'So he played our song?' said Mickie James.

'Now where is his bloody name?' said Betsy scattering papers everywhere. 'Ah, here it is.' Her hand clutched a paper-thin piece of paper. 'He didn't play it once, Mickie James, my dear,' she said, blowing smoke from her nostrils. 'He's played it over twenty-five times. "Wacky Iraqi" has become the most requested item on his show.'

I looked at Mickie James and he looked back at me. We were grinning like that time when we'd been on *Jim'll Fix It*. That had been our first taste of stardom.

Betsy took a long drag on both of her cigarettes. 'He wants you to appear on the show. Do an interview, the whole kit and caboodle. There's even talk of them cutting the song onto disc.'

'Wow,' said Mickie James.

'When are we going to be on the show?' I said.

Betsy looked down at the letter. 'A week today. You're scheduled in next Thursday. I've said yes on your behalf. I hope you don't mind the liberty. All you have to do is present yourself at the radio station and give them hell. This could be it.'

'This is definitely it,' said Mickie James.

'Where is this radio station?' I said.

'Tokyo,' said Betsy. 'Capital of Japan.'

'Cool,' said Mickie James clapping his hands. 'Cool cool cool.'

'There might just be one incy-wincy snag,' said Betsy. She put down her cigarettes and smoke came out of her nose.

'Which is?' I said.

'Airfare is not included. If you want to go you are going

to have to pay your own way.' Betsy held up both of her hands like she wanted to stop a truck. 'If I were you, I'd go. But it is a long way and it won't be cheap.'

Mickie James was out on the roof sitting on the toilet with his underpants on his head. He had been there for quite some time.

Shortly after leaving Betsy Wong's we had checked out the airfares to Tokyo. The cheapest we had found was five hundred pounds each via Moscow with Aeroflot. On top of this we would need money for hotels and food.

'Two thousand easy,' said Mickie James. 'Where are we going to find two thousand? We haven't even got two hundred.' Then he had gone out to the toilet and hadn't come back.

I was sitting on the bed with a guitar across my knees quietly strumming the bridge to Nirvana's 'Smells Like Teen Spirit'. I was thinking that Kurt Cobain had probably made a mistake in killing himself when I suddenly had an idea. Ideas happen to me like this sometimes and it was one of the things that I believed set me apart from Westlife. Westlife's ideas are all management-sponsored.

My idea was that I would go to the cheese shop and ask Con if he would like to make an investment. I would tell him about our imminent impact on the cash-hungry Asian Tigers, clearly stating how we already had a well-established fan base.

Con was a businessman and I knew that when I put this gift horse in front of him he couldn't fail to blow up its nose. Besides, he always said he was fed up with bloody cheese and if somebody could show him the way out he would leap at it like a goatherd on a virgin. That was his expression,

Con was Greek by birth if not by inclination. I shouted a farewell to Mickie James and ran down the stairs.

Ten minutes later I was standing outside Bloomsbury Cheeses. I took a deep breath, said, 'Tokyo here we come,' and stepped inside. A bell rang above my head.

'Hello, boy,' said Con, looking up and wiping his hands on his apron. 'If you are wanting your bloody job back you are out of luck. I have new staff now.'

On cue from out of the back stepped a lanky youth with massive ringleted red hair and pale thick lips.

'This is Marmalade,' said Con. 'He can juggle cheese. The punters like that. It's something other cheese shops don't offer.'

Marmalade smiled sycophantically and began to loop three pieces of oak-aged Roquefort through his hands and into the air over his head.

'It isn't about cheese,' I said, 'I have a proposition for you.'

'Mickie James not bloody giving you any?' said Con and he laughed.

'A business proposition.'

'Well, you better come round the back then.'

I followed Con through to the storeroom and took a seat on an upturned prize-winning Gorgonzola. I started with the telegram and quickly moved on to our meeting with the inimitable Ms Wong.

'So you see,' I wound up, 'a CD single is almost certainly in the offing. You know how much money that could make the right backer?'

Con stood up and pursed his lips. 'You are like a son to me,' he said. 'You know that.' Then he shrugged. 'I would help you but right now I am in a struggle. This bloody war in Iraq has pushed the price of cheese sky-high.'

Because Con and I went back a long way I felt that I didn't have to beat around any bushes. 'Last thing I knew,' I said, 'there weren't any famous Iraqi cheeses. Nor, for that matter,' I added for good measure, 'is Iraq famous for its fields of cows.'

'It is not the cheese itself,' said Con, 'it is the method of transport. My cheese comes from a dealer in Italy. It is transported by boat and boats use oil. It is the oil that has gone up in price and ipso facto so has the cheese. It is a dire time for us cheese-shop owners. This is something I am sure that Mr Blair has not considered. I cannot help you. I am sorry.'

'Me too,' I said, and not wanting to go back to our room at the top of St Pancras Station empty-handed, I set off towards the centre of London.

Something had to turn up. I figured that if it had worked out for Dick Whittington it could work out for me. After all, he didn't even have the added bonus of being able to play the guitar.

Four hours later I was sitting cross-legged on the green in the middle of Leicester Square, trying to remember exactly how it was Dick Whittington had made his money. Come to think of it, was he famous for being rich or was it something else?

That's the trouble with these fables, unlike great pop usually they don't have a catchy tune to help you along with the words. I was on the point of giving up the goat and going sheep-like home when I spotted a face I recognised coming out of the Häagen-Dazs shop. Actually it wasn't the face I recognised, it was the hat – a large pink fedora.

I wasn't pleased to see it. I had a large bone to pick with the person under it.

'Ivan Norris-Ayres,' I said, standing in the man's way, 'what the fuck happened to Showaddywaddy?'

'Still going, I believe,' said Ivan Norris-Ayres. 'Performing in the smaller discos of provincial England. What of it?'

Then I think he recognised me. He made a sound like a penguin mating and put his hands up to his face. 'Let me explain,' he said.

'Over an ice cream?' I said threateningly.

Ivan Norris-Ayres nodded and we headed into the Häagen-Dazs.

I ordered the largest item on the menu and as I spooned it down Ivan Norris-Ayres tried to give his side of the whole Showaddywaddy scenario. This involved a lot of hand movements and plenty of words either beginning or ending in 'ism'. Whatever, I could clearly see that the whole line he was feeding me had more holes than one of Con's prime Swiss cheeses.

I would have got up and left but a) the ice cream was nice and b) this was the type of managerial fracas any aspiring pop group had to go through.

'So you see,' said Ivan Norris-Ayres as I pushed my empty ice-cream bowl away, 'it was all a simple misunderstanding. When I said Southend, I actually meant Basingstoke.'

This kind of rubbish might have washed it when I had newly arrived in London but not now. After all, I had been in war-torn Iraq. I nodded curtly like Elvis Presley probably wished he had done that last time he had stood from the toilet and was about to leave when Ivan Norris-Ayres put a hand on my arm.

'Our meeting like this might actually be fortuitous for both of our natures.' He twizzled his head and leant in closer to me. 'You might be exactly the person I am looking for.

115

You see, I am putting together another little montage of the European bent and once more I find myself with a little problem.'

'Your leading man has gone AWOL?' I said.

'Gone flaccid, more's the point,' said Ivan Norris-Ayres sourly. 'Langston recently OD'd on Viagra at Chessington World of Adventures and is no longer able to stand up to the job. I wonder if you would be able to step into his trousers?'

'How much?' I said.

'A grand,' said Ivan Norris-Ayres.

'Make it two and I'm in.'

Ivan Norris-Ayres smiled slyly and held out his hand. 'It's a deal. But for two, we might have to go for something a little out of the extraordinary.'

I knew Mickie James wouldn't be too happy about me being a hot item on the European porn circuit so I told him that Con had come up trumps in the cash department and more or less exactly six days later we found ourselves jet-bound for Tokyo's Narita Airport.

'It's not many people who break Asia before Europe, is it?' said Mickie James.

I agreed with this and I pressed the call button for the air stewardess. Drinks apparently were free for fare-paying passengers.

This whole gig was already turning out better than Iraq although Iraq had probably been good for us in that it had sharpened our cutting edge and looked good on the résumé.

When the drinks came Mickie James and I knocked them back in one and then ordered another one before the lady went away. We were both kind like that. Having worked at the bottom rung for a number of years we knew what it was like when arseholes take advantage of you.

'I'm sorry if I've been down a bit lately,' said Mickie James.

I said I didn't mind because after all everybody gets a bit down sometimes. Some people have even made a career out of it. Look at Morrissey and that one who never talks in Busted.

'When I get depressed then I always go on about my hunchback. Somehow it's easier to blame that than anything else.' The air stewardess arrived and put down our drinks. Mickie James downed about half of his drink. 'I should learn to think of it the same way you do.'

'We're going to be famous,' I said.

'All those people looking at me, I don't know if I could cope.'

'We could be the next Pokémon,' I said. 'He was blue.'

'Do you think?' said Mickie James.

'Yeah, he was definitely blue,' I said.

'No,' said Mickie James and then he laughed.

'Or that egg-shaped computer where you have to keep the chicken alive. What's that called?'

Mickie James said he wasn't sure although he knew that it wasn't Pac-Man. Pac-Man was another big craze in Japan. Japan was pretty much full of them. I pressed the call button for the air stewardess again and asked if she wouldn't mind bringing an extra cushion for Mickie James. Having a hunchback meant his head was too far forward away from the seat.

I put the cushion behind Mickie James and ordered us another one of those drinks and then we both looked out of the window.

117

I couldn't see much down there. It was dark. But somewhere far below I guessed there were houses and in those houses were mums and dads, boys and girls who were just waiting for the next big thing in pop. Even if they don't know it, people are always waiting for the next big thing. It's one of the things that life is about.

I believed we could make a difference. We wrote songs that had stories. We believed that every song must have a tune. We'd had a hard life and in that life there was meaning. I believed that Mickie James and me loved each other. Somehow we belonged together and that made our music special. Like the Carpenters or the Osmonds.

I ordered another drink but before it had even come I had fallen asleep and then at a certain point in the darkness we were landing in Tokyo.

I'd seen Tokyo on the news once when they had this big disaster so I was expecting it to be all neon-lit and there to be geisha girls with their feet wrapped in bandages coming in and out of revolving doors on tall buildings. Instead the scenes slipping by outside the taxi window looked more like the outskirts of Dagenham on a Sunday morning. But in a good way because, after all, Mickie James and I were in Tokyo and we were going to be famous. This time there was no doubt about that.

Our taxi dropped us outside a hotel that was shaped like a pyramid. Inside it was all chrome. I put my hand on a shining metal counter.

'Not bad,' I said. 'I should have brought my sunglasses. Like Bono.'

'I wonder how you check in,' said Mickie James, and then a Japanese man with a large flat face appeared from behind a tank of large flat green fish. He bowed and Mickie James bowed and Mickie James said that we would like a room for the night.

The Japanese man pulled back his lips. 'We don't have rooms,' he said. 'Only capsules. This is a capsule hotel.'

'Then we'll have a capsule,' said Mickie James.

The Japanese man pulled back his lips again. 'Will that be one capsule or two?'

'Just the one.'

I expected the Japanese man to pull back his lips a third time but this time he didn't. Obviously they were as far back now as they would go now. 'Two people in one capsule would be a tight squeeze, sir.'

'That's OK,' said Mickie James, 'we've been in a few tight squeezes in our times.'

I laughed at this. The Japanese man didn't. Instead, from somewhere he produced a card, told us this was for entry, and nodded goodnight.

We found our capsule on the fourth floor. It was above one capsule and below another one. Mickie James slid the card in and the door clicked open.

'It's not very big,' I said.

'It's a capsule,' said Mickie James. 'What did you expect?'

'We should have got two,' I said. 'Or eight and knocked them through.'

As the capsule was only about three foot high, four foot wide and eight foot long, I came up with the idea of getting undressed outside and then climbing in. Mickie James said that the idea was a good one.

Just as we had simultaneously removed our underpants and I had linked my hands to give Mickie James a bunk-up about fifteen of the capsule doors on the left-hand side of

119

the corridor opened and out of each one popped a teenage Japanese ballerina dressed in a pink tutu.

The one nearest to us screamed and then all fifteen of them screamed and they all began running up and down the corridor. I lifted Mickie James up, pushed him into the capsule and quickly followed him in, slamming the door behind me.

'That was close,' said Mickie James. 'Do you think they saw us?'

'No,' I said and we both laughed.

'Hey,' said Mickie James bunching up his knees and pulling the covers over him, 'don't you think it's like some cryogenics chamber.'

'We'll wake up in three thousand years to a brave new world.'

'Do you think there'll be Down by Law memorabilia in that world?'

'Definitely,' I said. 'There'll be puppets, and school bags, T-shirts and underpants.'

'What about the music?'

'Oh,' I said, 'everyone will listen to the music.'

'Cool,' said Mickie James and with that he fell asleep closely followed by me.

I woke up to find a sharp object inserted into my ribs. It was Mickie James's finger.

'What's up?' I said.

He held up the receiver of a telephone that was hanging from the roof of the capsule by a curly wire. 'I couldn't sleep. I called the radio station. They want us there in thirty minutes.'

'Shit,' I said.

'Don't worry, they're sending a car. It'll be here in five.'

'Shit,' I said. 'We better get ready.'

Remembering the faux pas with the teenage ballerinas I suggested getting dressed within the capsule. Mickie James agreed. Then he pushed a button by his side of the wall. A toothbrush popped out.

'Cool,' I said and I pushed a button on my side of the wall. A tissue slid out. 'Cool,' I said and took it and blew my nose.

'That was a mistake,' said Mickie James. 'That was a moist toilet tissue for wiping your bum. Look.' Mickie James held up a small slim book. 'I found this. *Capsule Living* by Wakanai Hitogata. It's an A to Z.'

'What's it say under Z?'

'"Z,"' read Mickie James. '"equals Zanzibar. Not many people know that Zanzibar has more capsule hotels than any country outside Japan."'

'I didn't know that,' I said.

Above Mickie James's head the phone started to bleep. The car had arrived. It was time for our inaugural appearance on Japanese radio.

On the way to the radio station we discussed our game plan. We both felt it was important to be ourselves. We decided that if we put on a front now then we would have to maintain it and that would lead to problems later.

'Like Robbie Williams,' I said.

The radio station occupied two floors above a hundred-yen shop. We were met by a small man wearing a silver shirt with a button-down collar. He had his hair in a Mohican and funky shoes.

'I'm DJ Kenji,' he said in an American accent. 'I think you guys are great.' He jumped up and down on the spot

121

and then from side to side. He stuck his thumb up and grinned. 'Fuckin' A.'

DJ Kenji took us up a narrow staircase to a room that was like a radio station. Actually it *was* a radio station. There were lots of sliding buttons, a glass partition and some big headphones.

DJ Kenji explained the format of the show. He would play some songs, then he would interview us, then he would play our song and then he would take some calls. He said that he would translate our questions and answers into Japanese.

'Is that OK?'

'That's great,' I said. I could feel Mickie James rocking backwards and forwards next to me. I knew this meant that he was excited.

'How many people listen to your show?' asked Mickie James.

'About five millions,' said DJ Kenji and then he drew a finger across his lips and spoke into the head of a microphone.

The first song DJ Kenji played was called 'Shake Your Boom Boom'. It was by a Latvian singer called KY Jelly. Next it was an American song by a group called Siddharta. The song was 'I Wish You Were a Dog But Even Then I Wouldn't Kiss Yoo-Da-Laa-Hoo-Hoo'. Then there were some Japanese songs and then it was us. DJ Kenji counted down in the air with his fingers and nodded that we were on.

'Down by Law are in the studio,' he said. 'The ones you have all been waiting for.'

I grinned at this and touched Mickie James on the knee. This is the sort of thing you can do on the radio and one of the things that makes it such an exciting medium.

Mickie James and I both understood that as DJ Kenji was translating it was necessary to keep our answers as short as possible. At the same time we wanted to get our personalities across. It was good really that we had the opportunity to learn our trade in a foreign country. That meant when we got home we would be pretty slick.

DJ Kenji's questions were wide-ranging and it was obvious that he had done this before. He asked us what our names were, where we were from, how old we were, and what was our favourite colour. Then it was time to play our song.

I think that was my favourite part of the whole show. The interview and meeting and greeting people was all hoopla. The music was the important thing.

Apart from the demo tapes that we had made ourselves I had never heard our music properly. Listening to it through the hi-tech earphones I thought we sounded great. My vocals reminded me of early Jesus and Mary Chain, Mickie James's keyboard playing was up with Yazoo at their best.

During the last chorus I found myself singing along, 'He's a wacky Iraqi, driving in his VW van, he's a wacky Iraqi, wa-wa-wa-wacky I-I-I-Iraqi'.

Whatever happened in the future I knew that I would remember this moment forever. It was magical.

As the song finished a light started flashing on the console and I knew that this meant we had a call.

'What do you think about Blair's stance on Iraq?'

We had decided to be ourselves so the answer to that was easy. Mickie James said it sucked and I said with bells on. In translating our answer DJ Kenji made a sucking noise with his lips, then he pushed a button on the console and a bell rang. He was a good DJ.

After that it was all Mickie James. It turned out that in the recent publicity for the radio station they had used our pictures. Everyone wanted to know about his hunchback.

I thought this would upset Mickie James. Usually he does his best to hide it. But there was something about the directness of the questions that seemed to gel with him. Besides, the general consensus appeared to be that he was *kawaii*. Translated by DJ Kenji, this meant cute.

'I'm cute,' said Mickie James. He had a grin on his face as large as a side of beef.

'I know you are,' I said.

'I think I like it here.'

'Me too,' I said and then as the radio show ended I asked DJ Kenji about the disc we were cutting and when we were due in the studio.

Dj Kenji pulled an ignorant face and goggled his eyes so I told him what Betsy Wong had said, about us recording our song for the Japanese market.

A cloud passed over the sun of DJ Kenji's face. 'I think there is some misunderstanding. I don't make records. Only play them. Thank you for coming. It's been fuckin' A.'

He showed us the door. It was the way we had come in.

We had a problem. Banking on our success I had booked only single tickets to Tokyo. Without the money I had counted on getting, we had no way of getting home.

The radio-station car dropped us back at the capsule hotel. Mickie James was walking like a pop star on acid after the radio appearance and he wanted to go out and explore Tokyo. I said I thought we should get shut-eye first as we had only had about two hours' proper sleep and I was pleased to see that Mickie James agreed. While he slept I would come up with a plan of action. Mickie James didn't yet know of our single-ticket status.

As with songwriting I do my best thinking while pacing. However, pretty soon I discovered that it was difficult to pace in a capsule. Being careful not to wake Mickie James I clicked open the door and dropped down into the corridor.

'Aaaaiiiii!' came a voice behind me somewhat resembling a scream.

I spun round. Standing there was a very fat man, six feet tall, six feet wide. He had long hair in a ponytail and he was wearing nothing but a very thick leather G-string. He looked extremely angry about something.

As I watched he reached into one of the capsules and pulled out a tiny man. He shook this man violently causing him to open his eyes momentarily. Then the tiny man slid to the floor.

The very fat man glanced along the corridor at me. 'Pissed as a fart,' he said. Then a smile crossed his face. 'I wonder if you could help me,' he said. 'I need someone quite desperately to manipulate my intestines.'

I didn't want to get into a huge fight about it so I said yes.

It turned out the man's name was Koji and he was a sumo wrestler which pretty much explained his get-up straight off. He told me he had a big tournament that evening against a bundle of other sumo wrestlers and he needed his intestines manipulated sooner rather than later.

'You speak English very well,' I said.

'Three years at Cambridge,' said Koji. 'I majored in philosophy. Nietzsche. Schopenhauer. Freud. I love your fish and chips.'

125

Koji led me up to a large room at the top of the hotel and lay down on a white hospital trolley.

Manipulating intestines is not all it's cracked up to be. Koji said it was like kneading bread. It might have been. I didn't know. I had never kneaded bread.

'So what are you doing here?' asked Koji.

On the off-chance I sang the opening lines to 'Wacky Iraqi'.

'Hey,' said Koji, 'I heard you guys this morning. I thought you were great. Everyone's been talking about you.'

'Thanks,' I said.

'It's the major intestine that's giving me gripe,' said Koji. 'If you could give it a real good squeeze.'

'Sure,' I said. I pushed in my knuckles like Koji had shown me and did a swift one-two moment with my wrists.

At the far end of the room was a large window. We were practically at the top of the world and from it I could see the sprawl of Tokyo. It seemed to go on forever.

'So what are you up to now?' said Koji.

'Not much,' I said and as Koji seemed like a nice chap and not about to go anywhere until I had finished with his intestines I told him what had happened.

I thought he had fallen asleep, but when I got to the end of my story Koji sat up.

'That was great,' he said, rubbing his massive stomach with both hands. 'And as you say in your country, one good turn deserves another. I may be able to help you.'

'What do you mean?' I asked and Koji explained.

It was like sunshine on a rainy day. It was even better than that. After all, 'Sunshine on a Rainy Day' was a crap song.

*

This time it was me who woke Mickie James up with a sharp finger.

'What time is it?' he said, sitting up and rubbing his eyes.

'Get dressed,' I said, passing him his underpants. 'We've got an appointment.'

Koji had given me a map of Tokyo's subway system and he had even written in Japanese symbols the station we were to get off. This symbol looked like a man going off to war while eating a banana. It was easy to spot.

Mickie James kept asking me what was going on. I told him he would find out soon enough and I patted him on the hunchback. My mind was going everywhere. I was on the tube in Tokyo. I had been on the radio. There was more to come.

When we reached the correct station I hustled Mickie James off the train and up an escalator. As Koji had said, there was the restaurant, the Lotus. I couldn't read the words but that was what Koji had told me it was called.

In the restaurant a lot of people were sitting on the floor around tables with short legs and as we went in an old man with side-parted grey hair and thick glasses stood up and bowed.

'Down by Law?' he said.

'That's the baby,' I said.

We started towards him but were stopped by a round Japanese woman with chopsticks in her hair who wanted our shoes.

'I am Mr Takahashi,' said the man once we were shoeless. 'Koji tells me you are the big thing with the sumo wrestlers.'

'Who's Koji?' whispered Mickie James.

'He's a sumo wrestler,' I whispered back.

The woman with the chopsticks in her hair arrived at the

table and placed a steaming bowl in front of each of us. Then she put chopsticks next to each of the bowls.

'Can I have a fork?' said Mickie James.

'It happens,' said Mr Takahashi, 'that I am looking to move away from the sumo management status. A novelty pop act is the kind of thing I am looking for. Would you be interested in having me represent your interests?'

'Brilliant,' I said.

'Hang on,' said Mickie James.

A mobile rang in Mr Takahashi's pocket and he excused himself and moved away from the table to answer it.

'It's brilliant, isn't it?' I said.

'He said novelty act,' said Mickie James. 'I don't want to be a novelty act.'

Sometimes with Mickie James although I knew where he was coming from I couldn't see where he was going to. He didn't understand the front end of the pop market in the same way that I did.

'In one way or another,' I said, 'everything leads to something. Look at Geri Halliwell. She started off by appearing topless on a Turkish game show. Everything depends on how hungry you are. That's what agents and scouts and producers are looking for. It's not just about talent. It's hunger.'

'What about the Cheeky Girls?' said Mickie James.

'That was a TV show,' said Mr Takahashi, sitting back down. 'I put some feelers out. They want you.' He placed some papers on the table. 'This is the contract. I need you to sign.'

Mickie James and I glanced at the papers. They were full of the symbols like that man eating the banana while going off to war.

'It's all in Japanese,' said Mickie James.

Mr Takahashi reached across the table and turned the top page over. 'Actually, this side is in Chinese. I am thinking of the international market. That TV station want you this afternoon.'

I looked at Mickie James and he was kind of rocking backwards and forwards again. This wasn't only his excited rocking, there was something else there too. In a way this was what we had always wanted and in a way it wasn't too. Sometimes you have to go ahead and make the decision.

'Where do we sign?' I said.

'Here,' said Mr Takahashi and he pointed at the international symbol of a dotted line.

After Mickie James had received his fork we ate our meal and then Mr Takahashi said it was time to go to the TV studio.

We were picked up outside the restaurant by a sleek car. It wasn't a limo but it felt like one and I'm sure even the Beatles didn't get taken to a TV studio in a limo the first time.

'Look,' I said to Mickie James, 'it's got electric windows.' I pressed a button on the door and the window went down. I pushed it the other way and it went up.

'How do you do that?' said Mickie James so I showed him.

We both lowered our windows together and without planning it or anything we started singing the opening verse to 'Wacky Iraqi'.

'If you don't mind,' said Mr Takahashi, turning round from the front and looking sharply at the windows. 'The car has air con . . .'

I expected the TV studio to be bigger but somehow it wasn't. It was full of people though. We had make-up stuck to our faces by a woman with eyes like a salamander and then we were taken to a tall white room with lots of cameras and men holding clipboards. Down the centre of this room were rails like for a narrow-gauge steam train.

Mr Takahashi explained the set-up to us.

'You will sit in these two wooden carts,' he said. 'The wooden carts will be pulled along the rails by those two monkeys.' Mr Takahashi pointed to two monkeys leaping around in a small cage. 'While you are being pulled along questions will be fired at you from loudspeakers situated at various points in the studio. Meanwhile up above,' Mr Takahashi pointed to a wire running the length of the room just under the ceiling, 'a man naked except for a posing pouch and angel wings will be pulled along the wire doing a simultaneous translation of everything you say. Any questions?'

'When do we perform the song?' said Mickie James.

'Good question,' said Mr Takahashi. 'When the trucks reach the end of the tracks this will release a lever that will cause two cages to fall from the ceiling. On top of each cage will be a podium on which you will stand to perform the song. While you perform the monkeys will dance below you. They like dancing. They have been trained.'

I looked at Mickie James. When we had talked about it in the past he had always said he would like his first TV appearance to be on *Parkinson*. He liked the sensitive way in which Parkinson treated his guests and he wanted the chance to talk about how difficult it had been growing up with a hunchback. I was worried that he wouldn't like this, especially the dancing monkeys, so I waited nervously for his answer.

'The monkeys,' said Mickie James, 'they don't get injured at all, do they?'

'As I said,' said Mr Takahashi, 'the monkeys are trained. They do not get injured. In fact, they rather enjoy it. It is either this or working with children. They know they are onto a good thing.'

'Cool,' said Mickie James. He moved his eyes around the studio and he gave his head a little nod. 'It looks cool.'

The TV show started. There was some chat between the two hosts. Then a man and a cow were brought on. The man had some crocodile clips attached to his nose. The other end of the clips were attached to the nose of the cow. Then a light bulb was put in the cow's bum. It started to glow. The clips were taken off the man's nose. The bulb went out. There was a round of applause. Then we were on.

It went exactly as Mr Takahashi had said. As the monkeys reached the end of the tracks, the cages rattled down and we leapt up on top of them and the opening bars to 'Wacky Iraqi' boomed out of the studio speakers.

It was awesome. There must have been five hundred people in the studio audience. Apart from that time in Iraq when we had performed in the basketball stadium this was only the second time we had performed the song live. Well, this time we weren't actually live because we were miming along to the backing track. That's one thing you have to learn when you are performing, how to mime well.

As the song ended the audience were up out of their seats. Some of the girls were even screaming. I could have stayed on that podium forever drinking it in because it was such a perfect moment but then the cow was brought back on and this time the crocodile clips were attached to the man's genitals and our turn was over.

*

That night neither Mickie James or I could sleep. It was either him or me that kept remembering highlights from the day.

'So you don't mind being a novelty group?' I said.

'I don't feel novelty,' said Mickie James. 'This feels real.' He stopped talking for a second and then said, 'Do you think Mr Takahashi will rip us off?'

I shook my head. 'These Japanese are pretty honest, I think.'

'Look,' said Mickie James, '*Godzilla.*'

Mickie James had been flicking through the channels on the TV that was fitted into the side of the capsule.

'Shall we watch it?'

I was going to say that it was in Japanese but then it struck me that most of the people who listened to our song wouldn't understand the lyrics. These days it was an international market. You either had to go with the flow or against it.

'We'll watch it,' I said, and we watched as almost single-handedly Godzilla destroyed a large Japanese town.

Perhaps this was an omen. Not of things to come but of how things always are.

In the morning we were woken by the beep-beep of the capsule phone. It was Mr Takahashi. He said that he was sending a car to take us to the recording studio. He had arranged for us to cut a CD. It was due to be released the following week.

I put the phone down and told Mickie James what Mr Takahashi had said.

'Next week,' said Mickie James, 'I'm going to have to buy some new underpants. I only brought two pair.'

We both laughed at this and then got dressed. I was beginning to get the hang of it now, getting dressed lying down.

The recording studio had a completely different feel to the TV studio, but it was fantastic nevertheless.

The sound engineers and mixers all seemed like very serious blokes. They explained that because of time constraints they were going to more or less use the track from the Iraqi TV show. What they wanted us to do were to lay some harmonising vocals over the top and for Mickie James to tidy up the keyboard playing at the end.

Before we went into the recording section of the studio Mr Takahashi appeared.

'After yesterday's TV show the studio have hundreds of calls.'

'Really?' said Mickie James.

'Some people like cow with the light bulb up bum but most people prefer you.'

'Cool,' said Mickie James.

'Do you think we've got a hit on our hands?'

'You remember Right Said Fred?' Mr Takahashi put his hands above his head. The jacket of his suit rode up above his waist. 'I'm too sexy for my shirt-o-wa,' he sang. He put his hands down. 'I think you be bigger than them.'

One of the sound engineers appeared. He had jeans hanging very low on his arse and in his hand he was holding a stopwatch.

'They're ready for you now,' he said and he opened a door.

The first thing I noticed in the room were the ten sumo wrestlers.

'Hello,' said one of them, lifting an arm.

'Who's that?' said Mickie James.

'That's Koji,' I said. 'I manipulated his intestines the other morning. You were asleep.'

Mr Takahashi put his head through the door. 'The sumos are going to sing backing. They do the "Wa-wa-wa-Iraqi". I think it give you Japanese flavour. Help you go to number one.'

'You think we'll go to number one?' said Mickie James.

'On five,' said the sound engineer and he held up a hand, his fours fingers and thumb extended.

I remembered seeing this documentary about Mariah Carey where day after day she is doing TV appearances, radio spots, signings, interviews. At the end of all this she goes mad and takes her clothes off while performing on a children's show. Our week was like that except we didn't go mad at the end. It was great.

Mickie James had always had this thing about people looking at him. He didn't like it. The space behind the keyboards had always been a hiding space for him and if I was honest with myself then I had been worried about what it would be like if we ever made it. I thought it would freak him out.

But that week in Japan he surprised me. He loved it and was even prepared to talk about his hunchback on TV. He explained it by saying that growing up he had always been scared of being singled out, noticed, pointed and laughed at. This was different, he said. There was no fear of being singled out because he was already singled out. He was the centre of attention already and that made it easier to deal with.

Sometimes I didn't understand Mickie James and that was good because it kept our relationship fresh.

*

134

The final highlight of the week was our performance on Japan's most prestigious pop show. Unlike our other appearances, on this one we would be actually singing live. The producers had got Mickie James a Korg keyboard just like the one he used back home and we had done a final soundcheck.

'The single is in shops tomorrow,' said Mr Takahashi. 'Do well here and sales go through the roof, yes?'

'Yes,' I said.

The first group on were Japanese. They were kind of a Japanese cross between Guns N' Roses and the Sugababes but to be honest I wasn't really concentrating on them. I was thinking about our performance. This time we didn't have any monkeys and carts to hide behind. It was just us.

Their song finished and the lights came up on our section of the studio. Mickie James hit the opening notes to 'Wacky Iraqi'.

I remembered what I had learnt from my appearance on Iraqi TV. Don't move around too much or the camera will lose you. Be aware of where the camera is but don't gawp into it like a zombie. A small gesture on the TV is like a big one in the theatre.

But by the time I'd got through the first chorus I'd forgotten all that. I was only enjoying myself.

'Wacky Iraqi' had been written for fun. We'd knocked it off one afternoon. Mickie James had the hook line and I did the lyrics. Sometimes it can be difficult to judge your own music but this time I knew we'd got it right. It was three minutes of pop perfection.

I hammered out the second verse and moved towards the audience. Most of them were up out of their seats and dancing. I got in amongst them and started dancing too. I could see Mickie James on the stage concentrating on his

135

keyboard work. I could see the cameras pointing towards me. I could feel my heart beating and the music coming out of me and I thought right then that I was the happiest I had ever been and on top of the world.

One problem of being on top of the world though. It's a long way to fall.

We were up late that night and the next morning I woke early to hear someone tapping on the door of the capsule. I moved carefully to avoid disturbing Mickie James and slid it open. Standing in the corridor was Koji the sumo wrestler.

'I thought I'd better warn you,' he said.

'Of what?'

'We should go somewhere private.' He did this thing with his hands where he kind of wrung them together and then beat his chest three times and I knew something terrible was up.

I followed Koji up to the room where I had massaged his intestines. As before, the window looked out over Tokyo. The previous night I had thought it was my oyster. That had felt pretty good.

'What's going on?' I said.

Koji took a newspaper from where it had been stored in a pocket in his leather G-string and spread it on the table. He pointed to a picture on the front page.

'That is you, isn't it?'

'Shit,' I said.

'I didn't know you were an international porn star. Apparently you have a massive following in Japan.'

'Shit,' I said again and looked at the picture more closely.

It was from the video I had made for Ivan Norris-Ayres. In the background a woman is holding the penis of a donkey and in the foreground I am wearing nothing but a Stetson hat. Mine and the donkey's penises have been blacked out but you can still see that they are penises.

'What does it say?' I said.

Koji put his finger on the large symbols next to the picture. '"Down by Law Star Goes Down on Donkey."'

'I didn't,' I said.

'This paper is like your *Sun*,' said Koji. 'A lot of people read it.'

I put my head in my hands. 'Do you think this is going to affect sales?'

Koji slapped his hands against his sides. 'I don't think there are going to be any sales. Come with me.'

We went out of the capsule hotel and down the road. Here there was a Virgin Megastore.

At the front there was a Down by Law merchandiser. Kneeling in front of merchandiser was a shop assistant. She was taking out our CDs and putting them in a box.

'Ask her what she's doing?' I said.

Koji spoke to the girl and then he turned to me. 'She's taking the CDs out of that merchandiser and putting them in that box.'

It was as bad as I thought.

'She says she's taking them off sale.'

'I got that,' I said.

'She says you can have one if you want,' said Koji. 'For the memory.'

'Tell her thanks,' I said and I took one of the CDs.

On the cover were me and Mickie James. He was standing behind a Korg keyboard and I was holding an Iraqi flag with the words 'Wacky Iraqi' written on it. It looked really great.

*

When I got back to the hotel Mickie James was awake and sitting up in the cubicle.

'We had a call from Mr Takahashi. He wants to see us now. He's sending a car. I wonder what it's about.'

I didn't say anything.

'It's probably about our sales strategy.'

'Yes,' I said.

'Are you OK?'

I nodded my head and passed Mickie James the CD. I wanted to see him happy. Just for a minute I wanted to see him happy.

It's not true that all publicity is good publicity. If the video hadn't had a donkey in it then we probably would have been OK. Apparently having sex with a donkey is something the Japanese frown heavily upon.

Ivan Norris-Ayres had said that if he was paying me two thousand pounds for one day's work then he wanted something a bit special. For the record, I didn't have sex with the donkey. I made it clear to Ivan Norris-Ayres that I wasn't into donkeys but in the end me and the donkey were having sex in each other's vicinity and that was what counted.

You read about it all the time. Young stars are taken advantage of but you don't think it will happen to you. You believe you are wiser than that. Besides, Ivan Norris-Ayres had told me the video was going to Belgium. He had said Belgium quite a number of times. It was the Southend and Basingstoke incident all over again only this time it was on an international level. That was one positive: the circle of our disasters was getting bigger.

I shouldn't have trusted him but he had me over a barrel. If I hadn't done it then me and Mickie James wouldn't have been able to come to Japan at all. None of all the wonderful things that had happened would have happened at all.

You can't judge everything by the outcome alone. Life is a journey. I hoped Mickie James would understand that.

The interview with Mr Takahashi went very quickly. He said in light of the newspaper story then he had no choice but to release us from our contract. Mickie James asked what story and Mr Takahashi put the paper on the table.

Mickie James didn't give me time to explain. He was up out of the room and gone.

I tried to reason with Mr Takahashi but he was firm and what I'd heard called indomitable. He took out our contract. He told me to read clause 7. Was it about donkeys? I asked and he said it was about scandals particularly of the sexual kind.

So that was it. We were back to where we had been a week before, only things were worse. With no single there was no money and with no money we were stuck in Tokyo. I didn't even have the money for a return ticket home.

Mr Takahashi's office was in Yokohama. I found Mickie James outside sitting on a bench in the shadow of a wheel as big as the London Eye only not quite as big. The bench had a view of the sea. Out at sea a number of liners were coming in and out of the harbour. They were white and sleek and spoke of endless wealth. I sat down next to Mickie James.

'I'm sorry,' I said.

'What I don't understand is that you didn't tell me.'

'I was trying —'

'You think, "Oh Mickie James has a hunchback and he has enough things to worry about so I'll keep him in the dark".'

'It wasn't like that,' I said.

'If you don't give me the option of coping then I can't.'

'And if I'd said that the only way we could get to Japan was by me being in a porn film would you have let me?'

'So some things are best left unsaid?'

I shrugged. 'It's more complicated than that. The thing about secrets is that they have to remain secret to be secret. It's OK to have secrets in relationships. I was trying to do the right thing.'

'Did you have sex with that donkey?'

I shook my head. 'No, I didn't.'

'Right now,' said Mickie James, 'I'm on a high. All those things that happened, still happened. But one day this video will come back to haunt me. You. That woman. The donkey. And when they do, it's the hunchback I'll blame. I hope you'll be there to pick up the pieces.'

'What pieces?'

Mickie James took the CD out of his pocket and turned it over in his hands. There was some writing in Japanese and then a track listing. There was the version we'd recorded in the studio with the sumo guys and the original recording from Iraqi TV. There was also an interactive bit but I didn't really know what that was.

Mickie James drew his hand back as if he was going to throw the CD into the water. Then he stopped.

'You know,' he said, 'I like this CD but to be honest I didn't want to have a novelty hit. If this had gone through we would have been pigeonholed. What you said about Geri Halliwell, you were wrong. That whole Turkish thing could have ended badly. She was just lucky, that was all. We might look back on this and see it as some kind of escape.'

'So it's not over?' I said.

'Oh no,' said Mickie James. 'It's not over.' He stood up and shouted. 'It's not over. We're Down by Law. It's not over.'

He shouted this over and over again until I was standing up too and shouting too.

We both stood shouting over and over again. It was like a bad thing hadn't happened at all. I wondered if we should write a song about it.

PACIFIC PLUNDER

'How much have we got?' I said.

Mickie James counted out the green oblong notes onto our bed. Then he looked up at me. 'About twenty thousand yen.'

'How much is that in real money?'

Mickie James shrugged. 'No idea. Not enough though. At this rate we're never going to get home.'

Just then the door to our room opened and Takuma came in. Takuma had black hair, a lopsided smile and one leg. The other he had lost in an accident that, as far as we could work out, involved a helicopter and a banana.

Takuma nodded at us, sat on his bed, unzipped his flies and started to masturbate. He was in the habit of doing this. Both Mickie James and I were people of the world but it was beginning to bug us. He didn't even turn to one side.

'Come on,' I said to Mickie James. 'Let's go.'

Mickie James had found a job washing dishes in the bowels of a Japanese noodle shop and I had taken to busking down at the port. There were often tourists around there who were liable to stop and listen to a bit of sophisticated street music with a cutting European edge. I pulled on my comedy busking hat, picked up my bongos and made my way down the stairs.

The room we shared with Takuma was in the rafters above Shinjuku Station. I counted the stairs as we went down. There were seventy-two.

'Don't worry,' I said to Mickie James as we reached the bottom, 'I'm going to make a big pile of money today.'

'I hope so,' said Mickie James. 'Japan is OK but I wouldn't call it home. I want to go back to England. If we're going to make it big I want it to be there. I've realised one thing, I want to be famous in the eyes of the people who used to tease me. I want them to see me, Mickie James, the hunchback, live on *Later* with Jools.'

The position I always stood in was in front of the big wheel that was like the London Eye but not as big. It was a good spot because here I appealed to not only people coming on and off the wheel but also to people using the port. That's one of my top tips for busking: do it in a busy place.

I put the strap of the bongos around my neck and figuring that a job half finished was one already commenced, I started to bongo.

The bongos we had purchased from a music shop in Shinjuku. Mickie James had wanted me to go for this little portable keyboard but I said that if we fell on harder times than we were already in, then how would we afford new batteries? Nobody was going to pay anything to watch my hands move over a silent keyboard, were they?

I think Mickie James was quite pleased that I was being assertive like this. He could see that I wasn't letting the fiasco that had landed us penniless in Japan get to me.

This morning I started with 'Manos Sucias'. All things considered I still felt this was our best song. Moreover, I really liked doing the flamenco bit in the middle on the bongos. It was something you could get your teeth into. During a typical day busking I would do this song about eight times. That's another top tip: play the same songs over and over. Familiarity with your music breeds cash thrown in your bucket.

After 'Manos Sucias' I did 'The Curve', 'Ain't It', 'Hunchback Christmas', 'Dreaming of Uriah', 'Kinky Goggles' and Duran Duran's 'Rio'. Then I stopped for a breath and looked in my bucket.

There were four one-yen coins, one five-yen coin and a flyer for a Zen meditation class. The flyer was in English and it had a picture of a bo tree on the front. I put that in my pocket. I thought I would show it to Mickie James later. He was into shit like that. He said that meditation helped him get in touch with his inner hunchback. I didn't understand exactly what he meant but if it made him happy then I was happy too. All in all we'd been through a lot together and it had to be said, we usually came out flying.

When the sun hit the sea I packed up my bongos and went back to the room at the top of Shinjuku Station. Mickie James was already there. We sat side by side on the bed and counted out our wages for the day; Mickie James's came to five thousand yen, mine, two hundred and twelve yen.

'I think you might need to get another job,' said Mickie James.

I took the Zen flyer out of my pocket and showed it to Mickie James. He nodded his head silently for a few moments then said, 'There's a job going at the noodle shop. The guy who divided the noodles into even portions left this morning. The job's yours if you want it.'

'I'm a musician,' I said.

'So am I,' said Mickie James. 'But sometimes you have to bite the bullet.'

I didn't say anything to this. I took my clothes off and got into bed. After a while I felt Mickie James get in next to me. I turned away from him and stared into the open room. It was lit brightly from the neon lights that were streaming in through the window. The lights flashed off and on, on and off. They seemed to have some meaning, I wasn't sure what.

After a while Takuma came back. He sat on his bed, unzipped his trousers and started to masturbate. I turned towards Mickie James.

'Just give me one more day,' I said.

'OK,' said Mickie James.

I put my arms around him, felt his hunchback press against my chest, and eventually I fell asleep.

The next day started off formidably. These two small Japanese kids came up and stood in front of me. They were clapping along with the music and doing this little dance with their feet.

They seemed to like 'Kinky Goggles' so I did this one twice. I changed the words though because they are rude in the middle. 'Kinky goggles on a kinky boy' didn't seem right for them so I changed it to 'Dinky goggles on a pinky boy'. When you've got a good tune it doesn't matter what you sing.

At some point the boys' mother came up and pointed at the big wheel and took a hand of each of the boys. The boys said something to this and nodded at me. The mother then took a note out of her wallet and got one of the little boys to put it in my bucket. It was a thousand.

When I saw this I did a little dance, like the ones the boys had been doing, and they both laughed. The mother laughed too this time and then they all went away.

'I'm going to have a great day,' I thought, and then the sun went up in the sky, boats docked and undocked and not even one bugger came up to me for three straight hours in a row.

This sort of thing can happen sometimes. It's the Sod's Law of busking. Just when things are going really well, you can trip over and smack your nose on the ground.

However, what I didn't realise was that when your nose is smacked on the ground, this is the point that you may find out that the ground you have been standing on has been made of gold all along. This is another Sod's Law; a different kind of one that doesn't involve any Sods.

I had just come back from a dump behind a large rhododendron bush and bashed out 'Denis' by Blondie when I saw a blond-haired man in a sailor suit approach and come to a full stop in front of me. He looked at me like he had something on his mind.

I had been approached by sailors on shore leave before so I thought I should get in there sharpish before he got the ball rolling.

'Sorry, mate,' I said, 'I'm here only for the busking.'

'You're pretty good on those things,' he said, meaning the bongos. 'People think it's easy but it's not. You've got quick hands. You might be just what I'm looking for.'

'I don't do anything kinky,' I said.

'Whoa,' said the sailor and held up his hands. 'You see that boat?' He pointed at this big liner parked just down the way. It was half the reason why no one had been to see me. There were big crowds all around it and metaphorically speaking it had been out-bongoing me all morning, but not really, because nobody plays the bongos like me.

'You know what that is?' said the sailor, 'It's a floating opportunity for people with the right talent. We need guys like you.' He took his hands out of his pockets, looked at his fingernails, then put his hands back in his pockets. 'To cut it short, I'm offering you a job.'

I'd heard about this sort of thing. These boats are a playground for the rich and famous and if it's one thing that these rich and famous like more than anything then it's entertainment. What had I told Mickie James? Something would turn up. It looked like we were going to be the next Jane McDonald. She had been plucked from obscurity too and look at her now.

'I have to tell you,' I said, 'I come as part of a package. My friend plays the keyboards. We're a pop combo.'

The sailor clapped his hands. 'Great! Believe it or not, that makes my life even easier. Tell you what, you and your mate come to my office tomorrow morning 0800 hours. I'm on deck C, room 414. Just ask for Jim the Corset. That's my name.'

'You sure about this?'

'Absolutely. I've seen you on the bongos, haven't I?'

I did a quick riff using the tips and palms of my hands. 'Cool,' I said. 'It's a deal then. You get top-class performers and we get our ticket back to England.'

Jim pulled a face. 'Actually, we only need you as far as Ho Chi Minh City.'

'Where's that?'

'Vietnam.' Jim the Corset held up his hands. 'But hey,' he said, 'it's the journey that's important, right? Not the destination.'

147

I looked over at the ship. It was white and immaculate in the midday sun and towered out of the water in what seemed like a miraculous fashion. It felt right, the miraculous part of it.

'Sure,' I said. 'The journey. We'll see you tomorrow.'

Jim the Corset smiled, saluted, spun on his heel and was off. I couldn't wait to get back to Mickie James and tell him the news.

When I got back to our room at the top of Shinjuku Station Takuma was sitting on the edge of his bed and Mickie James was kneeling in front of him bobbing his head up and down in Takuma's lap. I knew a blow job when I saw one.

'What's going on?' I said.

I can only guess that my words caused Mickie James to clamp his teeth in surprise because the next thing Takuma had leapt up from the bed and was hopping around the room on his one leg clutching at his crotch in obvious pain. This went on for a few minutes until he managed to hop right into the bucket we all used to wee in and bucket and man both went crashing to the floor.

'I'm sorry,' said Mickie James.

'I don't understand,' I said.

Mickie James was looking at the ground. 'You were in a porn film,' he said. 'With a donkey. How do you think that made me feel?'

'I never touched that donkey.'

'I hate you sometimes,' said Mickie James. 'You always turn things around. And I've got a hunchback.'

'Help me,' said Takuma.

Somehow in trying to get the bucket off his leg Takuma had managed to get the bucket handle twisted around his

148

arm and from there the bucket had somehow ended up on his head. His pants were still around his ankles and his one leg was pointing straight up in the air.

'We'll talk about this later,' I said. Then I said, 'I know you've got a hunchback and I'm not bothered. I love you.'

Mickie James removed the bucket and I helped Takuma pull up his pants. That was the thing about me and Mickie James, not only did we go well together musically, we made a great team.

Pretty soon we had Takuma back on his bed and me and Mickie James were on ours. There was a pool of wee on the floor between us.

'About before,' said Mickie James.

'I've found us a job,' I said. 'It's on an ocean liner. We'll be entertaining the rich and famous.' And then I explained to Mickie James what had happened. I even told him about the two dancing boys who had liked 'Kinky Goggles'.

'I told you to trust me,' I said. I said 'trust me' but it was obvious that I meant trusting Mickie James himself.

'I'm sorry,' said Mickie James. 'You can kiss me if you want.'

I remembered that his mouth had recently been between Takuma's legs, or rather leg, and I shook my head.

'There's no need to be like that, you were unfaithful first.'

'But I did it for money.'

'And that makes it better?'

I wasn't sure if it did or not and that night I had trouble sleeping. It was like when you get a new CD and you have this music going round and round in your head only this time it wasn't about music it was something else.

It is always relationships that break up the best bands.

I had believed me and Mickie James were different to that but look at what had happened. Maybe Takuma would turn out to be our Yoko Ono. After all, they were both Japanese and I had read somewhere once that she was into this open masturbation thing. Who knew how it could affect a man?

I eventually fell asleep. The next day we would be leaving Japan. That was probably for the best. It was one of those experiences that could either make or break us. I hoped it would make us.

We had weathered the novelty hit single episode with panache, we would also get through this infidelity situation. From now on the only direction we would move would be forwards, together, heading towards that number one we definitely deserved.

The following morning there was still a bit of an atmosphere between me and Mickie James but when he saw the ship his eyes lit up like Shanghai rubies and I hoped things might work out after all.

There were these sailor-type people milling around everywhere on the ship all acting like they owned the shop. I noticed that most of them were wearing high-waisted trousers which showed off their knobs, but in light of the current situation I thought it best not to make too much of this.

We asked the way to deck C room 414 and eventually we found the right place at the end of a long white passage with endless amounts of white steel doors. I knocked loudly, heard a yes and we stepped inside.

Jim the Corset was sitting with one leg over the other behind a small plastic desk. In front of him was what looked like a mountain of paperwork.

'We're here,' I said. Then I said, 'Down by Law,' and smiled and spread my arms like they do in those London musicals.

Jim the Corset put the end of a pen in his mouth and began to suck.

'We met at the port,' I said. 'You said I had quick hands.'

'Ah yes,' said Jim. 'You were filling the spot to Ho Chi Minh, is that right?'

'That's right,' I said, although it was the first I had heard of filling any spots. Mind you, these showbiz impresarios are often a law unto themselves.

'Well, if you'd like to follow me, I'll show you to your boudoir.'

Jim led the way and Mickie James and I traipsed behind along white corridor after white corridor. The general direction seemed to be down and after about four floors the stairs turned into ladders and the ceilings got lower above our heads.

'Not much further,' said Jim the Corset, running a finger down a map stuck to a wall. 'In fact, I think this is it.'

Jim took four steps down the corridor and stopped outside a door. There were other similar doors all around it. Water dripped from the light fitting above our heads.

'Where there's water, there's drips,' said Jim. 'That's one of the first laws of the sea.' He put his hand on the handle of the door and swung it open.

Inside there were three narrow bunks on the left-hand side and on the right-hand side a mirror fixed to the wall with a slops bucket below it. Sitting on the lowest bunk was a man. He had his trousers down and he was masturbating. It was Takuma.

'Oh my God,' I said.

151

'There's no need to take offence,' said Jim. 'There's a lot of that on ships. That and farting. After all, boys will be boys.' Jim scratched his head and then looked pleased with himself. 'That's the second law of the sea.'

'I don't believe it,' I said.

'It's true,' said Jim. 'And the third law –'

'I didn't know a thing about this,' said Mickie James. He put a hand on my arm. 'Concentrate on the bright side of the sun, that's what you're always saying. At least we'll be performing every night to a crowd of the rich and famous.'

'Performing?' said Jim.

'Yes, performing,' I said. I did that thing with my hands again. 'We're Down by Law, that's what we do.'

'I hope there hasn't been some misunderstanding. You boys will be working in the galley.'

'Is that a small theatre?' said Mickie James.

'It's the kitchen,' said Jim.

'Shit,' I said.

'Aiieee,' said Takuma. He gave a final jerk and his come shot across the room and splattered on the wall just below the mirror.

'Come on,' said Jim. 'Dump your bags and I'll introduce you to your new boss.'

The kitchen was about two and a half miles at the other end of the ship. If what Jim said was true about water and drips there must have been a lot of water because there was a lot of drips.

While walking Mickie James and I whispered possible courses of action to each other. I said we could throw Takuma overboard, Mickie James said we could stay in Japan and go back to our old jobs but the best idea we had was that a) there were likely to be performers on the boat, b) we could worm our way into their community, c) we would dazzle them with our talent and they would be begging us to perform.

'It would be galley slaves made good,' said Mickie James. 'We'd be a bit like Spartacus.'

'I don't know their music,' I said. 'Is it indie rock?'

'We're here,' said Jim, coming to a stop.

The room we went into was larger than a ballroom but certainly contained more steam than would be suitable for any kind of ball.

Down one side was row after row of double hobs, down the other were dozens of overflowing sinks. There were chrome appliances everywhere and the air was filled with the noise of whirring, scraping, shouting.

'It's a bit like a war zone in here,' said Jim. 'You'll get used to it.'

Suddenly out of a cloud of steam appeared a massive red-faced man. He had blond curly hair and a badly broken nose. He shook hands vigorously with Jim.

'This is Jürgen,' said Jim. 'He'll be your new boss.'

'There's two things you need to know about me,' said Jürgen, holding up three fingers. 'One, I drink my own piss. Two, you do wrong by me, I'll make you drink it too. With a straw . . .'

'I'll leave you guys to it then,' said Jim.

'Great,' I said. I didn't mean it.

'Come on,' said Jürgen. 'This way.'

'Do you think he's taking us to the toilet?' whispered Mickie James.

'We haven't done anything wrong yet, have we?'

'This whole thing feels wrong.'

We went past a bench where a boy with pimples was cutting lobsters down the middle. At another bench a girl was cutting the heads off fish. And then Jürgen moved to the right and opened a door.

'That's where you'll be working,' he said. He had this way of talking that was like one step away from the toilet and all that it implied.

'Thanks for showing us,' I said. 'We thought we'd go and watch the ship leave. Have you got a number to ring in case we can't find our way back here again?'

Jürgen scowled. 'You were supposed to start work two hours ago.'

'We weren't here two hours ago.'

'Then you have a lot of catching up to do, don't you? I want two hundred pounds of potatoes washed and peeled by midday.' Jürgen reached into his apron, pulled out two potato peelers and told me and Mickie James to get to work. As he left the room I was sure I heard the sound a man makes while standing at a urinal. On the other hand, it might just have been water dripping from the ceiling.

After the second hour we got some kind of system. Mickie James gave the potatoes a quick all over scrape and wash and then I polished up the bits he missed.

'It's not that bad,' I said.

'My fingers have turned to mush,' said Mickie James. 'I read it in Paul McCartney's autobiography, it's not good for them to be constantly immersed in water. If I had to play the keyboards right now then I couldn't.'

'Listen,' I said. 'I've got this line going around my head, "Potato peelers of the world unite," and I think I've got a bit of a chorus.' I put down the potato I was holding and hummed the few bars I had.

'That's not bad actually,' said Mickie James, 'but I think we'd have to change the words 'potato peelers'. The repetition of the p sound is a bit obvious.'

'I know what you mean.'

'Shut that door,' said Mickie James, 'it'll give the room better acoustics.'

That's what's good about Mickie James; musically no one can touch him. With the door closed the room had a kind of haunting dull echo to it. The echo was further given a dampening effect by all the potatoes over the floor. We couldn't have wished for a better studio.

Pretty soon we had the whole of the first verse worked out and a title. We called it, 'The Uniting of the Potato Two'. The song was kind of a working-class anthem, the sort of thing Elvis Costello usually writes. What was genius about our song though was that Mickie James worked out this whole staccato bass beat backing that pushed it into Kylie territory.

'That's the problem with most working-class anthems,' said Mickie James, 'they don't appeal to the working classes.'

Some songs take days to write and some are like bolts of lightning. This one was the latter. Within only a few minutes we had worked out a second verse and then a third. I had this feeling straight away that it was going to be big; if only we could get it out there.

'Brilliant,' I said, as Mickie James added a final hook and I tweaked the chorus a little. 'We make a great team.'

Mickie James nodded. 'Yeah, we do.'

Then the door opened and Jürgen put his head in and scowled.

155

'What the bloody hell's going on here? That pile is nowhere near high enough. Is it that you like the taste of piss or something?'

I don't know what time it was that Jürgen finally let us go but in terms of hours it was late. Mickie James asked me if I could remember the way back to our cabin but I said I had another idea and I told him to follow me.

I wasn't exactly sure of the way but I had an idea of the general direction. This was up and forward.

'Mind the step,' I said as I pushed open the door that led out onto the deck.

'Bloody hell,' said Mickie James, 'it's cold out here.'

The wind hit us like a shovel and almost ripped the door out of my hands. In the distance I could see the pinpricks of light that must have been the shore and between them and the ship was the undulating mass of blackness of the sea.

A chain separated the forward area of the ship and there was a sign which read, 'Authorised Personnel Only Beyond This Point'. I climbed over the chain myself and helped Mickie James over after me.

We passed a number of large funnels and the boat narrowed to the point of the prow and the air was filled with spray and the boom of water on metal. Above our heads a searchlight ranged the sky.

'What are we doing here?' shouted Mickie James and I loudly hummed the opening notes to the *Titanic* theme song.

'Very funny,' shouted Mickie James.

'I mean it,' I shouted back. 'Come here.'

I positioned Mickie James against the rail at the front of the boat and lifted his arms so they were horizontal and then I put my own arms around him and gripped onto the railing.

'There was never anything between me and that donkey,' I said.

'You're quite the romantic, aren't you?' said Mickie James.

'That's what pop has in common with popular movies,' I said. 'It goes for the heart.' In front of us was the ocean, spread out as far as we could see. 'And it works,' I said, because whether we like it or not, we all have a heart. Mickie James, I'm sorry about the porn thing.'

'And I'm sorry for sucking Takuma's knob. I didn't mean anything by it.'

Mickie James pushed back his bum so it was nestled against my crotch. The wind was whipping our hair, the boat was cutting the water before us and I know we could have stayed like that forever if it wasn't for the fact that it was freezing and we were both knackered from washing and scraping potatoes all day. I gave Mickie James's balls a tweak and said that we had better be going to bed.

Mickie James nodded and we turned and it was then that we noticed the two men.

They were at the opposite end of the rail. One was standing with his arms out like Mickie James had been but the other one, he was balanced on the other one's head; palm flat, arm straight, feet pointing up to the sky.

'Show-offs,' said Mickie James and that would have been that if I hadn't recognised them.

It was Andrei and Sergei, the tumblers we had met while working at Copenhagen's world-famous Tivoli Gardens.

'Shit,' I said, 'what are they doing here?'

Andrei and Sergei were as pleased to see us as we were them. We told them about Iraq, Tokyo and peeling potatoes and they told us how for the past six months they had been doing performances on various cruise ships.

'We performed for the Queen of Sweden once,' said Andrei. 'She wanted sex with Sergei.'

'I said no,' said Sergei. 'I mean, what was in it for me?'

'We're going to a party now,' said Andrei. 'Would you like to come? All the entertainers on the ship will be there.'

Mickie James and I were both as tired as dogs but we knew when not to turn down a chance to attend a party that might take us that bit nearer to international fame and fortune. A lack of sleep is one of the sacrifices you have to make if you want to get to the top.

We could hear the party even before we came to the room. Inside, it was packed.

'That's Humphrey,' said Sergei. 'He's a magician.'

'Those people over there in the evening suits,' said Andrei. 'They're the string quartet. Although because of the union we've got six of them.'

'The lady with the wine glass and the big baloomers is the hostess. She worked her way up from third-class cigarette sales. And that man over there with the round stomach is Octavio.'

'He's v famous,' said Andrei. 'He's a tenor and has sung in all the top venues around the world. He was almost one of the three tenors. As it is, he's definitely the fourth.'

'The rumours about his voice going are just jealousy. Grab a drink and make yourselves at home.'

A fug of smoke hung below the ceiling, people were pressed almost cheek to cheek. Mickie James and I made our way to a table in the corner with a bucket and plastic glasses on it. We smiled at a dwarf-like lady standing hard by.

'You may be thinking I'm a dwarf,' she said. 'But in fact,

I'm a giant very tiny person.' She laughed for about a minute and then asked us what we did on the ship.

'We peel potatoes,' said Mickie James.

'Great!' she said and excused herself and went to speak to a tall man balancing a sword on his nose.

Mickie James and I stuck pretty much next to the bucket for the next couple of hours. The truth of it was that neither of us was much good at schmoozing, Mickie James especially because he still worried about what people would think of his hunchback. Although he was getting better; it was ages since he had referred to it as 'his cross to bear'.

That was our biggest problem, getting people to listen to our stuff in the first place. The right people, I mean, because sure enough we had a whole army of fans; just look at all those people in Tokyo and Iraq. They couldn't be wrong, could they?

I was on the point of suggesting to Mickie James that we call it a day for the night when Sergei and Andrei did some dramatic tumbling which got everyone's attention.

'And now for the moment we have all been waiting for,' said Sergei. 'It's time for the entertainers to entertain the entertainers.'

There was a round of applause and someone flicked the lights on and off.

'But remember,' said Andrei, 'we want to see something a bit different from your stage show.'

First up were the six members of the string quartet. The one with the biggest nose stepped forward and said they were going to do *Rhapsody in the Nude* and then they all took off their clothes.

The tune was rather like *Rhapsody in Blue* but every time there should have been the saxophone bit the one with the big nose made out like he was playing the saxophone on his knob. It could have been tacky but somehow it worked as a piece of entertainment. As it finished there was another round of applause and someone flicked the lights again.

Next Humphrey, the magician, took centre stage.

'Tonight, ladies and gentlemen,' he started very grandly, 'you will see me disappear up my own arse.'

He had just produced a large top hat and a tube of KY jelly when I felt a tugging at my arm and Sergei and Andrei were there.

'You can go on next if you want,' said Andrei.

'Something that you've never done before,' said Sergei.

I looked at Mickie James and he looked at me and we both nodded at the same time.

'We've got this song about potatoes,' I said.

Sergei did something with his face and then Andrei put his fingers in his ears.

'We do it with a pint of beer balanced on my hunchback,' said Mickie James.

'Brilliant,' said Sergei and Andrei together and clapped their hands.

When we turned back to the stage Humphrey had disappeared and that meant that it was our turn.

Someone passed Mickie James a keyboard and someone else passed him a pint of beer and we were off.

During the first verse I could see that people didn't know how to take us. They were kind of glancing at the beer on the hunchback and wondering what the gimmick was but when we hit the chorus and Mickie James sent out that funky bass beat people began to see that what we were was a tight pop combo.

By the end of the second verse we had them in the palm

160

of our hands. I could see the dwarf lady jumping up and down and Octavio the tenor had his head on one side and he was beating the air with his finger. If we could please the musos, I thought, then everything else is bound to fall into place.

As Mickie James released his fingers from the final dramatic chord the whole room burst into a round of spontaneous applause and cheering.

'We'll be performing tomorrow in the kitchen,' I said and I passed the mike to the man with the sword who was waiting at the side. Obviously he was next on but what he was going to do with the sword I didn't like to think. Off the top of my head the only alternative use for a sword would be if he put it up his bum and I wasn't sure that I wanted to see that.

We were making our way back to where the bucket and glasses were when Octavio appeared in front of us and held out his arms like a welcoming dignitary.

'If you don't mind, may I have some little words with you, yes?'

He pulled us to one side and produced a bottle of champagne from out of a large pocket in his jacket. He looked quite excited about something and it wasn't just the bottle of champagne in his pocket.

'Brilliant,' he said, 'I thought you quite brilliant.' He kissed his fingers and flicked them into the air. 'More than brilliant. Brilliantissimo as Lech Walesa used to say to me!'

Both Mickie James and I took an instant liking to Octavio, especially when he cracked open the bottle of champagne and suggested we have a little seat.

'I have contacts all over the world, yes?'

This seemed to be a question so both Mickie James and I nodded our heads.

161

'A little bird tells me you are leaving the boat at Ho Chi Minh City. Wait, I have here. Yes.' Octavio had been patting his sides and now produced a small black notebook. 'Quan Hi Truc. He runs the Ho Chi Minh Rock City. It's quite the place for up-and-coming bands. Tell Quan I sent you with special recommendation. He will book you in a flash. More than a flash.' Octavio was scribbling away on a small piece of paper which he tore with a flourish. 'This is the address, yes?'

'I don't know what to say,' I said.

'Fantastic,' said Mickie James.

'No,' said Octavio, 'it is you who are fantastic.'

Around us there was a round of applause and from the stage area Sergei announced Octavio would be next to perform.

'Oh dear, oh dear,' said Octavio, going suddenly pale and clutching at his throat. 'I am performing a highly erotic aria, in Latin, but the voice, you know? I am having this little problem, yes?'

A path had been cleared in the crowd and people were slow-handclapping. They were shouting the name Octavio, Octavio.

Octavio gave a final bow to us, brushed down his waist-coat and made his way elegantly towards the stage. He adjusted his tie, placed both hands flat on his belly and the crowd went silent.

Mickie James has always said that you can't make blind distinctions about music. There is little to be gained by arguing that pop is good and classical is bad. Mickie James has always said that there is good and bad music and that is that.

As soon as Octavio opened his mouth in an O and the

words came forth we were in no doubt that we were hearing good music. I closed my eyes and could almost see the Mediterranean lapping against white stucco buildings on a rocky coast. And this was despite the fact that Octavio had told us the lyrics were mostly about slippery vaginas and Roman soldiers with wooden dildos.

It seemed that Octavio was reaching a climax, his voice soaring across the room, when two things happened at once.

Number one was that all of a sudden Octavio's voice, while hitting the highest note he had yet tried, missed the note and then seized up and died completely, and number two was that the door to the room burst open, the lights came on, and Jim the Corset was standing there looking none too pleased.

'THERE'S BEEN A THEFT ON BOARD,' he shouted. 'DUCHESS OSTRAVIA VILLAMOND HAS HAD HER DIAMOND NECKLACE LIFTED FROM AROUND HER THROAT. SHE SWEARS IT HAPPENED WHILE SHE WAS MINGLING WITH THE ENTERTAINERS BEFORE THIS EVENING'S SHOW. THAT WOULD MAKE YOU LOT PRIME SUSPECTS.'

There was a lot of gasps and shrieks at this.

'HER LADYSHIP HAS OFFERED A REWARD FOR THE SAFE RETURN OF THE DIAMOND,' shouted Jim the Corset. 'FIVE THOUSAND POUNDS, NO QUES-TIONS ASKED.' He held his hands up in the air. 'THIS PARTY IS NOW OFFICIALLY OVER. I WANT YOU TO GO BACK TO YOUR ROOMS. NOW.'

'It's over for me anyway,' said Octavio, who had appeared silently at our side. 'You heard my voice. It's gone. Gone, yes?'

'Worse things happen at sea,' I said and put a consoling

arm on Octavio's shoulder. At the same time I heard Mickie James speak quite clearly.

'Five thousand pounds,' he said, 'that would be more than enough to get us home. And there'd probably be enough left over to make a demo tape. We have to find that necklace.'

Somehow day had dawned while we had been at the party. Morning light scuddered off the tops of gentle waves.

Mickie James said he could remember the way back to our room. We went down corridor after corridor until finally he opened a door. Behind it was a small cupboard containing about twenty-five yellow life jackets.

'I don't think this is it,' I said.

'Sorry,' said Mickie James, 'I've got a lot on my mind.'

'Come on,' I said, 'this way.'

Sometimes I know when I have to take charge and this was one of those times. It was all very well Mickie James having a bee in his bonnet about rewards but what we needed now was some sleep. By my reckoning we had been awake for a straight twenty-four hours.

When I opened the door to the room the first thing I saw was Takuma.

'Shitfuck,' he said, 'Shitfuck. I'm going to be late.'

Then he jerked towards the door, tripped over the bucket and went sprawling on the floor of our cabin.

'Shitfuck,' he said again.

I helped Takuma to his foot while Mickie James retrieved the bucket.

'I oversleep,' said Takuma, 'I am supposed to be cleaning entertainers' rooms but I oversleep. Wank!'

'Not now,' I said.

'What did you say?' said Mickie James.

He got Takuma to sit down on the bed and repeat his story and then he nodded his head and said he had a plan.

'We'll help Takuma clean the rooms and while we're doing that we can look for that necklace. Jim the Corset said himself, it is the entertainers who are the prime suspects. What do you reckon?'

'I'm tired,' I said.

'This is our big chance,' said Mickie James. 'Remember the reward, five thousand pounds. How many potatoes do you think we'd have to peel to earn that much?'

Takuma was more than pleased for us to help. First he found us both an apron from the cleaning supplies cupboard, then a bucket each with various cleaning products.

'I like do toilets myself,' said Takuma. 'The rest we split, yes?'

The first room we did belonged to the six members of the string quartet. I knew this because they were all there asleep, evenly divided between the two bunks.

'Their toilet very dirty,' said Takuma. 'You sweep floor.'

There weren't many places in the room to hide a necklace. By the time Takuma came out of the toilet we had been through all the cupboards and drawers and come up with nothing except several magazines of animal porn. Luckily neither me nor the donkey featured.

The next room we did belonged to the dwarf-like lady. She watched our every move so we had to be more careful in our search. Still, we came up with nothing.

'What time are we due in the kitchen?' I said.

'Shit,' said Mickie James, 'in five minutes. What do you think we should do? I say we should carry on here. Look at my hands, they're still fucked.'

'OK,' I said.

165

Next we did Humphrey the magician's room.

'Did you like the way I disappeared up my own arse?' he said.

'I missed it,' I said.

'Good point,' said Humphrey, 'and it's been said before.' He ran a finger through his moustache. 'Perhaps I should go up there more slowly.'

'Could you lift your feet while I do under the bed?' said Mickie James.

At midday we stopped for a break. We had done twelve rooms and there was no sign of any necklace. On the plus side Takuma had yet to masturbate. This was the longest time we had been in his company without that happening. It was a shame really. Cleaning with a compulsive one-legged masturbator might have made a good story for our future biography.

After we had eaten, Takuma said that we were still behind and that it would be better if we split up. He passed us a skeleton key and a list of the rooms he wanted us to do.

'Do toilets properly,' he said. 'I like a clean toilet.'

'Come on,' whispered Mickie James to me, 'it's time to rumble.'

The first room we were to do was at the far end of a long white corridor. I put the key in the door and pushed it open.

The room was slightly bigger than the others we had been in and more opulently furnished. It had a proper bed, not a bunk, and over against the wall was a chest of drawers and a cupboard.

'I'll do the toilet,' said Mickie James, 'you check those drawers.'

'Yes, sir,' I said.

To be honest I didn't think that Mickie James and I had a chance of finding the necklace so when I opened the top drawer and saw it sitting there I was more than a little surprised.

'Bingo!' I said.

'Shh,' said Mickie James, 'what's that?'

From the corridor outside was the sound of someone whistling and then we heard the sound of a key in the lock of the door.

'Quick,' whispered Mickie James, 'hide.'

He pulled me over to the toilet and we had just got inside as the door to the room opened.

'Fuck!' I whispered.

'What is it?' whispered back Mickie James.

Mickie James was behind me. I was standing next to the bathroom door with my eye against the crack.

'Who is it?' whispered Mickie James.

'It's Octavio.'

'Shit!' whispered Mickie James and I knew what he meant. We hadn't said anything to each other but I knew that we thought the same. We didn't want the thief to be Octavio. He had been nice to us.

Through the gap in the door I watched as Octavio crossed over to chest of drawers and scooped up the necklace. He pressed it to his lips and held it up to the ceiling.

'You are not only going to change my life,' he said, 'you are also going to change me.'

Then the phone over by the bed began to ring.

Octavio quickly put the necklace back down and went over and picked up the receiver.

'Yes, I've got the goods,' he said. 'No one suspects a thing. I've completed my side of the bargain and now you have to do yours. I'll meet you as arranged, 2200 hours, deck F, room 806.'

Octavio replaced the handset, came back over to the chest of drawers, took the necklace and left the room.

'What are we going to do?' I said.

'There's more to this than meets the eye,' said Mickie James. 'I say we go to that room later and get to the bottom of it. But first I reckon we should go and check in with Jürgen. He's going to be fuming.'

The kitchen was as we had left it, full of noise and steam. As soon as we entered Jürgen came steaming over.

'Where've you two bloody been? We're crying out for potatoes in the stroganoff.'

Jürgen was holding a glass of yellow liquid. Both Mickie James and I looked at it nervously.

'Don't count your chickens,' said Jürgen. 'This is mine.' He knocked back the liquid and wiped his top lip with the back of his hand. 'Now get to bloody work.'

Mickie James and I were about ten pounds in before either of us said a word and then it was Mickie James who spoke.

'If there's one thing I'm sure of, it is that you don't crap on the people who have treated you well. Octavio gave us that contact in Ho Chi Minh. I'm not going to turn him in.'

'But what are we going to do?'

'I think Octavio is in some kind of trouble, you heard the way he spoke. Here, pass me a potato.'

We slipped into our routine from the day before. When we had a pile of sufficient height Mickie James closed the door and we went through 'The Uniting of the Potato Two' and that kind of led to a full-blown practice session. That's the thing with Mickie James and me, we always have our music to fall back on.

'Do you ever think that we might not make it?' I said.

'I always think we won't make it,' said Mickie James, 'but at the same time I always think we will make it.'

'I know what you mean,' I said. 'Pass me a potato.'

Mickie James passed me a potato.

'If we're not going to turn Octavio in,' I said, 'what are we going to do?'

'That, I'm not quite sure of,' he said.

At 2100 on the nose we were standing outside room 806 on deck F. We were wearing our pinnies and we had a plastic bucket each. That was our cover; if anyone asked, we would say we were cleaners. We had even come up with fake names; Phil and Steve.

I knocked once on the door, waited, knocked again and there still being no answer, I inserted the skeleton key Takuma had given me earlier into the lock and twisted. The door swung open.

'It's not what I expected,' said Mickie James.

I knew what he meant. A bare light bulb hung from a ceiling dripping with water. In the centre of the room was a gurney covered in a dirty blue sheet and next to the gurney was a trolley holding a range of surgical-looking knives.

'What do you think's going on?' said Mickie James.

'Let's hide over there,' I said.

Over there was another door. I opened it and it led to a kind of broom cupboard. At least, it was a cupboard and there was a broom in it.

'We could write a song about this,' said Mickie James.

169

'"The View from the Closet",' I said. 'That could have two meanings.'

'It's a bit clichéd,' said Mickie James. 'How about "Va Va Broom"? The verses could work in the story and the chorus could be the sort of thing they would sing on the football terraces. That way we'd be pleasing two sets of audiences and give ourselves more chance of having an authentic hit.'

We continued talking like this for about an hour and then we heard loud footsteps outside, the sound of the key in a door and we both saw the door to the room open.

'Shh,' I said, 'the party's started.'

The man standing in the room was small, about five foot tall. He had only one eye and his head was completely bald. There was something sinister about him and it wasn't only his empty eye socket.

He walked over to where the trolley was, picked up one of the instruments, tested it against his thumb and when blood appeared, he put his thumb in his mouth and sucked. He folded his other arm under his elbow and waited.

Mickie James and I were both at the crack of the door watching. I could feel Mickie James's breath on my neck. I reached behind and placed my hand on his left buttock. I squeezed it tightly as there was a knock at the door and Octavio stepped into the room.

'Have you got the necklace?' said the bald man.

'It's at the designated place,' said Octavio. 'After the operation you can have it. Are you sure you can make me look like this?'

Octavio held something up. Because of where the bald man was standing we couldn't see it but we could see his head moving.

'First I'll do your bollocks, then your voice box. I can't

foresee any problem. Take off your clothes and get up on the table.'

'What's going on?' whispered Mickie James.

'I'm not sure,' I whispered back.

Octavio removed his shoes, socks, trousers and under-pants. Then he climbed up onto the gurney. The bald man bent and came back up holding some leather straps.

First he put one around each of Octavio's arms and tied them to the rail on the gurney. Then he took another two and attached one end of each to Octavio's ankles and attached the other end to some eyelets in the ceiling. He pulled on the straps and Octavio's legs were hoisted into the air.

'This one goes around the top of the scrotum,' said the bald man. He seemed very pleased with himself.

The strap was thinner than the others. The bald man lifted Octavio's penis out of the way and tied the strap around Octavio's balls. The balls bulged against the skin, looking like two eggs in a duck's bladder.

'What shall we do?' whispered Mickie James.

'Maybe this is what he wants,' I whispered back.

'I'm sorry I don't have any anaesthetic,' said the bald man. 'This may hurt a little.'

The bald man picked up one of the scalpels off the trolley and moved towards Octavio's balls.

'No,' said Octavio. He made a gargling noise in his throat.

'The pain will be sharp,' said the bald man. 'But it won't kill you. You want me to stop?'

The bald man held the scalpel in the air.

'You want me to stop?' said the bald man again.

'No,' said Octavio.

'I can't let him do this,' said Mickie James. 'I can see

myself and my hunchback on that table,' and he gave me a big push.

The door was ajar and offered no resistance and I went flying into the room.

'Stop what you're doing!' shouted Mickie James.

'Down by Law,' said Octavio.

'I don't know why you are here,' said the bald man, 'but we have a procedure to complete.'

'We know you have the necklace,' I said.

'Oh how wonderful,' said the bald man. 'But as you see I do not have the necklace.'

'I want to be a castrato,' said Octavio. 'If I don't do something, then my career will be over.'

'The procedure is simple,' said the bald man. 'I cut through the sac and remove the balls. I have done it countless times. You would be surprised.'

'Imagine the headlines,' said Octavio. 'Former tenor becomes boy soprano. All the opera houses around the world would want to book me.'

'I've heard about these backstreet clinics,' said Mickie James. 'Growing up with a hunchback you consider all the options. They promise the world but invariably they go wrong.'

I looked at Mickie James and we both nodded. It was one of those moments where we knew exactly what the other was thinking without having to say a word.

'There's a five-thousand-pound reward for that necklace,' I said. 'No questions asked. Give it back and you can use the money to get the operation done properly. If you're serious.'

Octavio shifted his body on the table. His penis flopped to one side and bounced off the surface of his tightened ball sac.

'You are not going to turn me in?' said Octavio.

'You were very kind to us,' said Mickie James.

'I've been a fool,' said Octavio. 'You might be right, this is all wrong.' Then he twisted his head and looked around the room. 'Where has the doctor gone?'

'The necklace,' said Mickie James and I together.

It took some time to undo the straps and for Octavio to pull on his clothes.

'I'm sorry I can't go any quicker,' he said. 'My balls are sore.'

'Just be thankful you still have them,' I said.

Octavio told us that the plan was that the doctor would complete the operation and then he would go and collect the necklace from Octavio's room so we figured that that was where he would be headed.

'It's been in my head for a long time,' said Octavio as we ran. 'Me as a castrato. It became an obsession.'

'I've thought about getting rid of my hunchback,' said Mickie James. 'Most days I believe you have to work with what you've got. That way, if you are successful you know you've done it on your own terms and it is more meaningful. Look at Jordan and those enormous fake breasts. You can tell when you look into her eyes that even she knows it's all a sham.'

'Who's Jordan?' said Octavio.

'But other days I just want to go for it,' said Mickie James. 'And by getting rid of my hunchback I think I would just feel better. It's not cosmetic.'

'This is the right room, isn't it?' I said.

We all stopped running and Octavio nodded his head. 'Yes, this is it.'

We went in, Octavio pulled open the top drawer on the dresser and banged down his fist. Then he looked in all the other drawers. He banged down his fist again. The meaning was obvious, we were too late.

'Now, I have my balls and no necklace,' said Octavio. 'This is where I started.' He sat down on the edge of the bed and put his head in his hands.

'Don't worry,' said Mickie James. 'I think I have a plan.'

The Duchess's suite was on deck A. At first the butler who answered the door was reluctant to let us in but when we said we had news of the necklace he did something with his lips and ushered us straight through.

The room had crystal chandeliers hanging from its high ceiling and all the furniture had red velvet covers.

'This is the style,' said Mickie James as the Duchess glided into the room, clutching a glass of champagne in one hand and a Pekinese dog in the other.

'Seward tells me you have news of my necklace,' she said. She looked at Octavio and her face went white and she lifted her hands to her mouth, dropping both the dog and the champagne glass. The dog squealed as it hit the floor and went to take shelter under a large golden pouffe.

'Octavio,' said the Duchess, 'it really is you. I am your biggest fan.'

Octavio rolled his hands dramatically in the air and bowed from the waist. 'Duchess,' he said, 'we come with news of the necklace. A great crime has taken place. Unbeknownst to all, a master criminal has secreted himself aboard this ship. His name is Dr Fu. He was seen by the pop duo on my left in possession of your necklace. I can vouch for their utmost veracity.'

174

'We must put out a search for this Dr Fu,' said the Duchess, 'but first will you sign the CDs I have of yours? I never travel anywhere without them. They are like my third hand.'

Seward was called to fetch the CDs and we were all made to sit and take some champagne. It wasn't until Octavio had signed each and every one that the Duchess took a description of Dr Fu and called security to go and look for him.

'While we wait for his capture,' said the Duchess, 'would you do me the honour of listening to your music with me. I am rather partial to *Rigoletto*.'

'Duchess,' said Octavio, 'the pleasure would be mine.'

Seward inserted the CD and more champagne was brought for us all. The Duchess knocked hers back almost in one and asked for more champagne and more volume.

'I like it to boom,' she said. 'Good music should always be louder than a bad war. That is a saying in our family.'

Octavio's voice was like a dream. As they were in Italian or Flemish or something, I didn't know what the lyrics to *Rigoletto* were about but there was great passion there. I thought of Octavio and how he was willing to have his balls cut off to achieve once more this glorious fame. That seemed to me to be the story of *Rigoletto*.

A young shepherd boy is heard by a musical agent singing in the hills and is whisked off to the opera palaces of the world. He misses his goats but he becomes drunk on fame, he wants more and more, and when his voice goes one day, he decides to have his balls chopped off. He is about to go through with the procedure when suddenly he is overwhelmed with the images of goats.

He realises that, after all, this was his happiest time, but the knife has already gone in and his ball has popped out never to be put back. That is the tragedy of Rigoletto.

'It's beautiful, isn't it?' said the Duchess as the piece came to an end.

'Yes, beautiful,' I said.

There was a knock on the door. It was Seward.

'We have Dr Fu,' he said, 'and we have recovered the necklace.'

'Oh bravo,' said the Duchess and clapped her hands. 'Now, there is the small matter of the reward. To whom do I owe this five thousand pounds?'

Mickie James and I had already agreed on this matter. The money was for Octavio. If that was what he wanted, he could go through with the operation, or perhaps like Rigoletto he would realise the path to true happiness lay elsewhere. Whatever, that would be his choice.

The Duchess wrote out a cheque, and as she handed it to Octavio she said, 'I would be honoured if tonight you would sing for me at my birthday ball.'

Octavio coughed into his hand. 'There is a problem. The high notes I can no longer reach.' Then Octavio frowned. Then he smiled. 'But I may sing a song that requires no high notes. Down by Law,' he said, turning to Mickie James and me, 'will you grant me the pleasure of singing with you tonight?'

'Oh yes,' said the Duchess, 'that sounds wonderful.'

'Down by Law and the Fourth Tenor,' said Mickie James, smiling.

'Brilliant,' I said.

We didn't have long to rehearse but Octavio was a genius when it came to picking up a tune. We ran through a few songs and Octavio decided that the best one we could do together was 'Kinky Goggles'.

'I'll come in over the chorus,' he said, 'then I'll do the third verse in Latin. Those Romans were kinky buggers so it's right that a song about kink should by sung in Latin. It'll be a classical/pop fusion.'

We were slotted in to perform after Humphrey, the magician. That evening, he wasn't disappearing up his own arse. He said that it wouldn't be right for a duchess's birthday party; instead, he was sawing a rabbit in half.

'Normally I do a whole person,' he said, 'but what with the luggage allowance I couldn't fit a human-sized apparatus in.'

As Humphrey rejoined the two halves of the box he waved his wand over the top and then brought the rabbit out by its ears. Miraculously it was in one piece. It was also wearing a pink tutu. There was a massive round of applause, Humphrey bowed and we were on.

We had performed in some places but there was no doubt this ballroom was the most opulent and the audience the most prestigious. Some of them were even wearing tiaras and there can't have been many pop duos who had performed to people in tiaras.

Octavio had sorted out me and Mickie James a dinner suit each and we had on clean underpants so we looked the part, no question.

'Kinky Goggles' had undergone some changes since we'd first written it. Playing it every day down at the port on the bongos had given me a new angle on it.

Originally it had been about this guy who put on these special goggles and his whole view of the world changed so that every item he looked at, even normal run-of-the-mill ones, took on a kinky aspect.

It had said something about the pornography latent in

everyday life. But with the changes I had made it became more obvious that not only was it saying something about the latent pornography in the objects but also how that reflected back on the man. It had an altogether darker, more urban edge while still retaining an upbeat pop sensibility.

Whatever, the people in the audience seemed to love it. By the end of the second verse a couple had got up out of their seats and were dancing and others were holding their Martini glasses high in the air like they were Bic lighters which they weren't.

The killer thing though was when Octavio started to sing in the third verse. As soon as he opened his mouth the whole atmosphere in the room changed. It was like someone had cranked up the electricity button and attached wires to strategic points in the air.

I looked at Octavio and he looked at me and spontaneously we air-guitared each other and did the third verse all over again. It didn't seem to matter that it was in Latin. I could tell by people's reactions that they got it.

When we finished the song the audience made us do it again and then we went off the stage and the dwarf-like lady came on.

'How can I follow that?' she said sourly and took off her jacket to reveal a naked stomach and an enormous cone-shaped bra with small flags on each of the nipples.

'Let's go out on deck,' said Octavio. His face was red and sweat was pouring from his temples. 'I think we're arriving in Ho Chi Minh.'

Octavio was right. Near and getting nearer were the lights of a port. It was humid hot out here and I undid the top button of my shirt. I also wished I wasn't wearing my thickest underpants.

'I want you to have this,' said Octavio. He was holding out the cheque.

'What?' I said.

'It's not in our name,' said Mickie James.

'It's a banker's cheque,' said Octavio. 'You can cash it anywhere.'

'I don't understand,' I said.

'What Mickie James said was right,' said Octavio. 'I would be cheapening myself if I became a castrato. Any future success would be because of that and not because of my talent. And anyway, after tonight, I've realised my career lies in pop. You've opened my eyes to that.'

'I wish you all the luck in the world,' I said, and I meant it, and then I saw a figure I recognised coming along the deck. It was Jürgen. He was holding a glass of yellow liquid in his right hand and he looked furious.

'Oh shit,' I said to Mickie James.

'This time it is for you,' said Jürgen, coming to a full stop. Over his shoulder I could see the lights of the port getting nearer and brighter. 'Where have you two bastards been? I had to get Chas and Dave on the potatoes. They're not happy.'

Octavio was still holding out the cheque. I took it and turned to Jürgen.

'You can shove that piss up your arse,' I said.

'With a funnel,' said Mickie James.

There was a loud bang above us and a firework spread itself across the sky. From somewhere came the sound of cheering.

'This is Ho Chi Minh City,' I said, 'and we're getting off here. We won't be peeling another potato, no, sir.'

'Not unless it's for personal use,' said Mickie James.

'These people are artistes,' said Octavio. 'How dare you speak to them like this. I will have words with the Duchess. She is my biggest fan.'

Jürgen looked at his glass of piss, then up at the firework in the sky, then at the three of us.

'Ho Chi Minh is a cut-throat place,' he said. 'There isn't no use for artistes there, believe you me. After one week you'll wish you begged me to let you back in my kitchen. But by then it will be too late. Me and my potatoes will be long gone.'

He turned and stomped off back down the deck.

'What do you think he meant by cut-throat?' said Mickie James. Then he said, 'You think there'll be an airport in Ho Chi Minh City? I want to go home.'

'Oh, bound to be,' I said.

I put the cheque in my pocket and caught sight of a flotilla of little boats heading towards the liner. I could see head after head after head leaning out and even from here I could see the smiling faces.

'You fancy *Titanicing* our way into the port?' I said.

'I don't get you,' said Octavio.

I put my arms out like wings and shouted at the top of my voice, 'I'm the king of the world.'

'Oh, I get you,' said Octavio.

Above our heads another firework exploded. Then another. Then another. Then another. We made our way purposefully to the prow.

DOWN BY LAW IN HO CHI MINH

It took us ages to find a bank. We went into this one official-looking building and joined a queue and it wasn't until a small lady in a white coat asked us to drop our trousers that we realised we might be in the wrong place.

'You have the lice, yes?' she said. 'Everywhere this summer. Even the bloody foreigners. Down the pants please.'

'Actually,' said Mickie James, 'we want to cash a cheque.'

'You need a bank,' said the lady and ushered us out the door like lost and annoying children.

'We need a bank,' I said.

'Never thought of that,' said Mickie James and we set off again, laughing.

We had been in Ho Chi Minh City for twelve hours and already we had learnt a few things. Number one, it was a very hot place. Number two, very many Vietnamese lived here. Number three, a lot of them had lice.

'How did we end up in Vietnam again?' said Mickie James.

'Not sure,' I said and then I saw the sign.

Inside, overhead fans cut the air, white walls stretched into the distance. Mickie James took the cheque out of his back pocket and slid it across the counter to a neat woman with almond skin and a smile like a piece of cheese.

'One moment,' she said, making a bow, and she took the cheque and disappeared across the floor.

Ten minutes later Mickie James tapped me on the arm and asked me how long I thought a moment was in this country.

'They move at a different pace in Asia,' I said. 'That's a well-known fact.'

After another fifteen minutes the woman appeared again. She still had the almond eyes but her smile like a piece of cheese had gone.

'I am so sorry,' said the woman. 'This cheque is forgery.' She held up the cheque for us to see and then she tore it repeatedly so that soon it was in tiny pieces. She threw the pieces up into the air and they fell around her like snow. Or confetti.

'Nooooo!' said Mickie James.

A security guard in a hat several times too large for him and with a gun on his belt appeared behind us and gestured that we were to move towards the door.

'Noooo!' said Mickie James again.

'He's got a gun,' I said. 'I think we better leave.'

We were sitting at a table in a street café in an insalubrious district of Ho Chi Minh City. The sun was beating down and there was a smell of shit in the air.

'What are we going to do?' said Mickie James.

'Move to another table?' I said and Mickie James shook his head and said he meant what were we going to do about the money.

We had found another bank apart from the one where the security guard had been on the point of shooting us and had changed our last remaining yen. We had been thrilled when the teller had slid towards us seven hundred and forty-nine thousand dong.

'We're rich,' Mickie James had said and then I had pointed to a sign. Thirty thousand dong to the pound, it said.

'So that means,' said Mickie James, 'we've got about twenty-five pounds. Do you think there will be any cheap flights from Vietnam?'

It was at that point that I suggested we have a coffee. I knew that most of the important decisions made in the last one hundred years had been made over a cup of coffee. This included all the significant chord changes in 'Let It Be'.

'I could always take my T-shirt off,' said Mickie James, 'and beg for money. People don't like to see a hunchback down on his luck.'

Just then four children appeared at the side of the table. One had only one eye, one had one leg, one had no legs and no arms, and the last one had two normal hands and a third hand growing out the centre of his chest.

'Money! Money!' they all said together and those that had hands held them out.

The waiter came over and shooed them away. He went back to the bar and then a man on a small cart wheeled himself over.

'Money! Money!' he said.

The waiter came back over, put his foot on the cart and scooted it down the street.

'Vietnam, bloody full of beggars,' he said. 'More coffee?'

'Yes please,' I said and Mickie James and I decided to have another think.

It wasn't until we had drunk four coffees and my heart was racing and my eyes were about to pop out of my head that I remembered something.

183

'We've been so stupid,' I said and Mickie James nodded and said he agreed. He said that we should never have left England and that we were going to end up just like the Americans.

'Look how long it took them to get out of Vietnam.'

'No, not that. Octavio gave us a contact at the Ho Chi Minh Rock City. Remember? All we need to do is go there, get a few concerts, and before you know it we'll be the ex-pat group everybody wants to see and we'll have millions of dong at our feet.'

'As long as we've got enough to get us back to England, I don't care about the millions part.'

'A million dong isn't that much in real money,' I said. 'Now, where do you think Rock City is?'

'No idea,' said Mickie James.

Luckily, at that point, walking past the café was a tall man with a long white beard. Over his back he had a banjo. He was obviously a musician so we decided to ask him.

In the end the man with the banjo hadn't spoken a word of English. Mickie James had pointed to the banjo and I had said the words Rock City and the man had taken the banjo off his back and played what sounded like a Vietnamese version of 'When I'm Cleaning Windows'. Then he held out his palm expectantly.

'Do you think we should give him money?' said Mickie James.

'I think he should pay us,' I said.

'Rock City,' said Mickie James in a loud voice and the man started strumming the banjo again.

'On the bright side,' I said, 'if this is the competition, then I reckon we're going to be quids in.'

If I could put to the back of my mind that we had no money, no way of getting back to England, and no real prospects then I had to say that Vietnam was a pretty cool place. Cool apart from being very bloody hot I mean.

There were all these little twisty streets with pavement cafés and men standing next to wooden stands on wheels selling all manner of stuff; Mickey Mouse dolls with huge erections sticking out of them and stylophones with Rolf Harris's face beaming out.

'I didn't know he was big in Vietnam,' said Mickie James.

'He's big everywhere,' I said. 'That could be us one day.'

'Do you think?' said Mickie James and then I put a hand on his arm. Coming down the street was a face I recognised. It was the woman we had seen in the lice clinic earlier in the day. As they say, any known face in an unknown port is worth sticking your anchor into. Taking a long shot I put a smile on my face, put my arm out for her to stop and asked if she knew where the Ho Chi Minh Rock City was.

'Of course,' she said. 'Follow me.'

The woman's name was Binh and she said that she was more than happy to show us the way.

'When you've been looking at penises all day, it's nice to get a bit of fresh air.'

Both Mickie James and I nodded although it was not something that either of us had ever done, not all day. Binh was a good guide and was keen to tell us all about Vietnam. The best part was when we went past this big building that looked like a temple.

'That's a temple,' said Binh, holding up a hand and pointing.

Outside the temple were all these monks, some were

chanting, some were ringing bells, some were banging gongs and drums. Mickie James made us stop and listen and I knew what he was thinking because I was thinking the same thing.

It was a sound we could incorporate into our music. Boy George had done the Hare Krishna thing and that was good but this was different because I knew we would do it in a different way. That's the thing about us, we didn't morph, instead we worked to incorporate new sounds into our style.

'All young men in Vietnam are monks for a time,' said Binh. 'It is said they do a lot of cock-sucking while away from the women. In Vietnam we are easy about this.'

'You speak very good English,' said Mickie James.

'For one year I was a nurse in the Sudan for Oxfam,' said Binh. 'English was the lingua franca.'

The next thing we went past that was worth pointing out was this big cathedral building.

'That's Notre-Dame Cathedral,' she said. 'You know the story, *Hunchback of Notre-Dame*.' Then she looked at Mickie James and she went red. It was the first time I had seen her go red even though I had seen her look at a long line of men's genital areas and talk about cock-sucking quite openly.

'I'm sorry,' she said.

'That's what people think of me, isn't it?' said Mickie James. 'They see me and think Quasimodo. I don't know if I want that any more. I'm not like Octavio. I want to change myself for the better.'

'Who's Octavio?' said Binh.

'I'm not vain,' said Mickie James. 'I just want to look a little bit normal.'

'Is Rock City much further?' I asked.

Binh said it was just around the corner and we set off

again. Mickie James was very quiet. Sometimes I think he is really OK about his hunchback and then at other times it seems to hit him like a large bell on the top of a church or similar building. At last Binh stopped and said that we'd arrived.

There was a sign outside this long two-storey grey building with a veranda round all its sides. 'Rock City', the sign said in large letters. The letters themselves were red and rusty and the 'c' was hanging at an awkward angle.

'Here I love you and leave you,' said Binh. 'But tonight I come and see your show.'

'I don't know if we'll be on tonight,' I said, although in my head I was thinking this was it, our luck was about to change.

Binh smiled. 'I think you will. There's something about you guys. I can sense these things. Now be on with you.'

Mickie James was looking up at the sign and he was kind of nodding. I knew what he meant. This felt right. We had arrived.

Inside, the rock club looked just like any other rock club the world over except this one was somehow typically Vietnamese. There was a stage, a dance area, a bar and some tables and chairs. It was normal but different. For example, the stage had this strange latticework at the front, and none of the tables matched the other ones. On top of this, the whole place smelt of beer and cigarettes.

Behind the bar was a young man with long hair tied back in a ponytail. He was washing glasses but it was more than that. It was like he was dancing with them. As we came in, he looked up.

'We're closed,' he said.

I held up the piece of paper that Octavio had given me. 'We're here to see Quan Hi Truc.'

The barman set down the glass he was polishing and narrowed his eyes. I guessed this was something he had practised; his eyes were pretty narrow already.

'Is he expecting you?'

'Yes,' said Mickie James. I felt Mickie James's hand squeeze my left buttock. 'Most definitely.'

Five minutes later the barman reappeared. Behind him was a small man in a long robe who looked about as old as several mountains. He had a pipe in his mouth which he took out when he saw us.

'Can I help you?' he said in a perfect English accent.

'We're Down by Law,' said Mickie James. Then he said that Octavio, the opera singer, had recommended him to us and I added that we were looking for a gig. We did all this in what I felt was a very professional manner.

The small man gestured us over to one of the empty tables and we sat down.

It turned out that for four years Quan Hi Truc had been assistant assistant manager of such superstar bands as Haircut 100 and the band Howard Jones had been in before he became a top-notch solo artist.

'Eventually the high-speed world of pop stars became too much for me and I retired here to Vietnam and opened this club.' He cast his arms around him.

Mickie James and I were both on a high by this time as it was rare that we got chance to mix with someone who was on first-name terms with so many famous people. When he asked us to do a mini audition we were more than a little nervous.

The barman brought over a keyboard and Mickie James

and I decided to do 'Ain't It'. This wasn't our best song but it is the one with the best opening line, 'I used to be a hooker, now I'm working in this five-and-dime. Life's a bitch, ain't it?' That's the important thing in an audition, to knock them dead in the opening seconds. Top managers like Quan get to hear so many groups, you have to get their attention right off or you're fighting a losing battle almost as soon as you start.

As I stopped singing and Mickie James flicked the off switch on the keyboard we both looked expectantly at Quan.

'There's something early Yazoo-like about you,' he said, 'and yet not. You've got your own sound. I like it.' Quan pulled a black book from out of his pocket and flicked through its pages. 'I'll book you,' he said, 'two weeks tomorrow. I'll put you on third, after Quork. She's from Thailand, models herself on Björk but is more unusual vocally.'

Both Mickie James and I must have looked disappointed because the next thing Quan said was, 'Is there some problem?'

'It's brilliant,' I said, 'but we were hoping to get something a bit sooner. You see, we're brassick.'

'That means we haven't got any money,' said Mickie James.

A telephone started ringing over by the bar. The barman answered it and shouted for Quan.

'Perhaps we should have done "Alien Amore",' I said to Mickie James. 'It doesn't have a good opening line but it's a better song. It might have got us a gig sooner.'

Mickie James nodded and said you never knew with managers. He said they were like buses, you couldn't account for their next movement with any regularity. I nodded my head in agreement. I liked it when Mickie James was metaphorical. It took the edge off things.

Quan appeared back at the side of the table. 'You boys are in luck,' he said. 'That was Hien, lead singer of Headfuck. He was out in the woods earlier this morning and stood on a landmine and blew his foot off. He won't be performing tonight. That puts me one spot down. It's yours if you want it.'

'Fantastic,' I said.

'Shame about Hien's foot though,' said Mickie James.

'This is Vietnam,' said Quan. 'These things happen.'

Quan said we could use Rock City's equipment and that as we were there we might as well do our soundcheck there and then. It turned out that Hung, the barman, was also the resident technical wizard and he ran me and Mickie James through the check.

'It should be a good night,' said Hung. 'You'll be on before Bo Tat. They've got quite a cult following. They're from Cambodia. Quite a few of their songs are about Pol Pot, massacres, that kind of thing. They're good.'

'Your name,' said Mickie James, 'Hung . . .'

Hung pulled a sour face. 'I know what you're going to say.'

'No,' said Mickie James, 'I like it. Hung. I think it's a cool name. If I could have a kid I'd consider calling him Hung. It's much better than Clive.'

After the soundcheck Quan came back over and asked if everything was OK. Mickie James and I said it was and Quan said he would see us that evening about seven. He started to walk away.

'One thing,' I said.

Quan stopped and turned back.

'I don't suppose you know of anywhere to stay. Cheap.'

'We just need a bed,' said Mickie James.

190

'This is Rock City not Bed City,' said Quan. Then he smiled. 'That was a joke. Actually, I might be able to help you. You'd be sharing though and money for the room would come out of your wages.'

'Of course,' I said.

Quan led us through the bar and into the back where there was a narrow wooden staircase. I counted the steps as we went up. There were seventeen.

'I know this person is trying to save money. She'd be glad to share her room for a few nights to cut down costs. She won't mind me saying, she's rather desperate.'

Quan knocked on the door and pushed it open.

The first thing we saw was this big white arse. The next thing we saw was that it was connected to a fat white man. The fat man was upright and bent over in front of him was a very slim brown-skinned woman. The fat man had his hands on her hips and he was pounding away at her.

'Oh yeah, baby,' he said in a loud American accent. 'You like that, don't you, my little Vietnamese whore.'

Quan pulled the door closed. He ran a hand over his forehead. 'As I said, she's pretty desperate. If you'd just like to wait here a few minutes. I'm sure it will all soon be over. Now if you'll excuse me. I must get back to work.'

Mickie James and I didn't have to wait very long. After a couple of minutes the American came out, now dressed in a white shirt and black trousers. He scowled at us, barged past and made his way down the stairs.

'Shall we knock?' said Mickie James.

'She might think we are her next clients,' I said.

'Do you think she does doubles?'

The door opened and the slim lady was standing there. She had a light-coloured gown pulled close around her.

'Quan sent us,' I said.

'We're Down by Law,' said Mickie James.

The woman lifted a hand up to her cheek. 'Well, I don't usually do doubles. The charge would be extra.'

'No,' I said and then I explained about how we were to perform that night and that we needed somewhere to stay. The woman bowed slightly and gestured for us to come in. There was something elegant about her.

Now that we weren't distracted by the big white arse we had a chance to have a proper look around the room.

There was a bed over in one corner, a fan fixed into the ceiling, and wooden doors that opened out onto a balcony. There was a smell of latex and lubricant in the air.

'It's not much,' said the woman. She crossed the floor and pulled back a brown curtain revealing a small alcove in which there was a single bed. 'I don't mind you staying but please can you be quiet? I have a very special event planned here this evening that could raise all the money I need.' She smiled and lifted her hands to her mouth. 'Where are my manners? My name is Suc. Would you like tea?'

Suc made the tea in a clear white teapot and led us out onto the balcony. From here we had a view of the bustling street below. A fat woman in a pink boob tube was shouting loudly at a group of guilty-looking sailors. Three kids were peeing up a wall.

'Can you keep a secret?' said Suc.

She passed Mickie James and I a cup each. The cup was slightly larger than an egg cup and in it we could see leaves spiralling.

'Have you got any milk?' said Mickie James.

'I'm a transsexual,' said Suc. She stood up and opened up her robe.

192

There was the lithe and beautiful body we had seen before. She had perfect pert breasts but nestled between her legs was a dark brown penis.

'I want it cut off,' said Suc. 'That's why I let that American bugger me. Not that that's anything new. Americans have been buggering the Vietnamese for years. How is the tea?'

Mickie James brought the cup up to his lips, blew gently and took a sip.

'It doesn't need milk,' he said. Then he whispered to me, 'What is it with us meeting men who want their balls cut off?'

'Would you like a game of cards?' said Suc.

Down in the street one of the sailors drew out a knife. The woman in the pink boob tube laughed at this and with one single fluid movement she smacked him across the face. The knife went flying through the air.

'Strip poker?' said Suc.

'You're on,' said Mickie James.

Suc was a demon poker player. Even though she was only wearing one item of clothing she never lost a hand. Pretty soon Mickie James and I were completely naked.

'It's because I'm a transsexual,' said Suc. 'For years I had to fight to keep my feelings hidden. I got good at fighting. Poker is like a fight.'

'Is there a toilet around here?' said Mickie James.

'Downstairs,' said Suc. 'Or if you want you can pee off the balcony. That's what I usually do. It's not very ladylike I know, but . . .'

Suc let her last word hang in the air and then Mickie James said he would only do it if I did it as well. He is like this sometimes and as I needed to go we stood side by side on the balcony and peed into the street below.

Afterwards Mickie James said he was tired and so we excused ourselves and went into the little alcove behind the curtain.

We talked a bit about that evening's gig and then we had sex and after that we fell asleep without even washing ourselves off. I was dreaming that a mobile hot-dog stand had pulled up outside Rock City and Mickie James was shaking me and telling me to wake up as he fancied a hot dog and then I did wake up and Mickie James was shaking me.

'We've been asleep for ages,' he said. 'We're due onstage in twenty-five minutes.'

I'd read about a lot of people who got stage fright before they went on. Barbra Streisand was probably the worst although she had nothing to worry about because she had such an awesome voice and everybody loved her anyway; except those people who had it in for Jews full stop. But I never got nervous. It was the opposite with me.

I got this buzz before I was to go on and it was like I was never properly alive unless I was onstage. Apart from when I was with Mickie James because I was alive then too and come to think of it that was most of the time because I couldn't remember the last time when I was apart from Mickie James for a long time.

Downstairs the club was already full and a band was already on the stage. The band were four women and they were all wearing these enormous blue hats.

'They're called the Blue Hat Band,' said Suc. She was leaning against the bar, smoking a cigarette in a long gold holder. She looked quite the picture, there was no doubt about it. 'Translated from Vietnamese, that is. All their songs are about items of clothing. This song is called "Pink Pants". They're a bit jokey but they have this feminist undercurrent. Things aren't so hot for a lot of women in Vietnam.'

Part of me had expected the club to be full of Westerners but I was wrong about that, there weren't any. Everyone was Vietnamese. There was smoke in the air and everyone was sweating. Over by the bar people crowded for drinks.

The only other reference point I had had with the Vietnamese before was from American war films. In those films the Vietnamese were always ruthless soldiers, killing indiscriminately. I had only been in Vietnam a few hours but I was already beginning to doubt that. Everybody had been pretty awesome so far. Better than awesome in fact, look how much trouble we had had getting a gig in London. This was way better than that.

Onstage the four women took off their hats and bowed from the waist and then Hung appeared from the wings; Hung was the compère as well as the sound man, he was multitalented like that. I guess you have to be in these Third World countries.

Hung started talking in Vietnamese. I couldn't understand a thing but I heard our name said and then a large part of the crowd started shouting 'Headfuck'. That was the name of the band that we were replacing.

'Go on,' said Suc, 'you're on.' She squeezed my arm gently and leant in close to my ear. 'And remember later, whatever you hear tonight, don't come out from behind the curtain. It's very important. This is a big night for me.'

'And for us,' I said. 'Tonight we try and win over Vietnam.'

Hung passed the microphone to me and I shouted into it a big hello. This is usually how I start a gig. I'm not one of those singers who likes to keep an artificial emotional distance from the audience. That's part of Down by Law's ethos. We're a people's band.

'Do you think everything's OK?' Mickie James shouted over from his position behind the keyboard.

I knew what he meant. A large part of the audience were still shouting 'Headfuck, Headfuck' over and over. They weren't doing it in a nice way.

We had never had to play to an audience that was hostile to us before. Because of this we started with 'Manos Sucias'. We don't usually do this one until the middle of the set. It's our best song. By doing it first I thought it might get the audience on our side.

As we hit the middle bit, the part with the flamenco routine in, I did my usual thing of spinning and gyrating around the stage. That's another Down by Law thing, even though there are only two of us, we like to own the stage.

Unfortunately this stage was new to me and on top of this I was a little disturbed by all those people who were still shouting 'Headfuck'. Somehow I managed to spin right off the stage and land in a heap on the dance floor. Behind me I heard Mickie James grind to a halt.

First I thought, shit, I've hurt my foot, and then I thought, shit, will Quan still pay us if this whole gig goes down the pan, and then there was someone helping me up. It was Binh, the nurse who we had met earlier in the day.

'Whoops-a-daisy,' she said. 'I told you you'd get a gig, didn't I? A word of advice, do you know any Duran Duran covers? Headfuck are a Duran Duran cover band. You should see Hien, he is the spitting image of Simon Le Bon. I mean if Simon Le Bon was Vietnamese. Actually, I heard he lost his foot today. Simon Le Bon is two-footed, I suppose.'

I managed to climb back up on the stage and I told Mickie

James to start doing 'Rio'. 'Rio' was one of the first songs we had ever done together.

The change was immediate and dramatic. The people that had been shouting 'Headfuck' now stopped and started singing along to 'Rio'. A couple of them even held lighters up in the air until a big bouncer bloke came up and snatched the lighters off them. I knew what that was about, the whole place was made of wood.

After 'Rio' we went straight into 'Girls on Film' and then we even did 'Wild Boys', although I didn't know all the lyrics. It didn't seem to matter though. Everyone seemed pretty happy shouting 'Wild Boys' over and over with me. I guessed that 'Wild Boys' was pretty much a Vietnamese 'I Will Survive', the kind of song that everybody likes.

As we came to the end of 'Wild Boys' I went over to Mickie James and told him to go straight into 'Alien Amore' without even waiting for the applause to start or finish. I figured that if we could keep the audience with us then we could win them over with our own songs. That's the kind of thinking on your feet you have to do when you're a performer. You have to learn how to play the audience.

It seemed to work. We were halfway into the first verse, 'Alien Amore, Do you want to hear a story, About this man who came down from Mars, Drove about in flashy cars', before half the audience had even stopped shouting 'Wild Boys' and then when they realised it wasn't Duran Duran any more they carried on shouting anyway.

From there on in the gig built and built. 'Wacky Iraqi' went down a storm, 'The Uniting of the Potato Two' had them doing this weird kind of one-heeled spinning dance, and 'Ain't It' had them practically shouting down the roof,

'Life's a bitch, ain't it?' There was no doubt about it, it had been our best gig, especially as it had started off so shit.

As we came off the stage Binh was waiting for us. She was holding two pints of lager.

'You guys were great!' she said. 'How come you don't have a record deal?'

'We're on our way,' said Mickie James. 'All this is background work.'

'We have a saying in Vietnam,' said Binh. 'It says that if a foreigner wins a Vietnamese heart then he will have it for life. If a foreigner makes a Vietnamese enemy then he will have an enemy for life.'

For a second I thought of that American buggering Suc and then Bo Tat were coming on the stage and the audience were going mad again.

It was cool watching Bo Tat with Binh. As each song finished, over the cheering and whooping of the Vietnamese around us she told us what it was about. The best song was this one called 'Year Zero' and it was about when Pol Pot had gone into Phnom Penh and killed thousands of his own people. It had this really cool hi-hat drum section in the middle.

'That's supposed to sound like a gun,' said Binh. 'You know the Vietnamese army tried to help the Cambodian people but the Americans bombed us for our trouble.'

'Why?' said Mickie James.

'There isn't a why,' said Binh. 'Would you like another beer?'

'I'll get them,' I said.

Hung was at the bar now the music was over. 'These ones are on the house,' he said. 'And any more you want. I thought you were great.'

I took the drinks back and told Mickie James what Hung had said and he said that Ho Chi Minh City was probably the best place he had ever been and I said I had to agree with him. All in all things had worked out better than expected, better probably even than that.

It was three hours later when we went to bed and we were both pretty pissed although it would be fair to say that we were as high on life as we were drunk on alcohol.

We crept quietly into the room, and sure enough there was the same fat American buggering Suc. We remembered what she said and how important it was that we didn't say anything so we crept behind the curtain to where our bed was waiting and were about as quiet as it is possible to be.

The last thing I remember is Mickie James saying that he was just nipping for a piss and then I fell asleep.

When I woke up in the morning Mickie James wasn't there. I didn't think much of it because my head was banging and I was still on a high from the previous evening. That was all I was thinking about.

I stuck my head through the curtain.

The room looked a mess, there were beer bottles and clothes everywhere. On the bed was the American and lying next to him was Suc. No Mickie James.

I got out of bed and padded quietly across the floor. I gently rocked Suc's shoulders and her eyes flicked open, as if she'd been having a bad dream.

'You haven't seen Mickie James, have you?' I said.

'What?' said Suc. Then she saw the American. 'What the fuck is he still doing here?' she said. Her voice sounded panicky. She sat up on one elbow. 'Oh fuck!' she said.

'Mickie James went for a piss,' I said. 'Just as we came upstairs.'

'And he didn't come back?' Suc looked at the American again. 'Oh fuck, I don't believe it,' she said quietly.

'Believe what?' I said.

'They can't have done.'

'Done what?' I said. The edge in her voice was starting to make me panicky too.

Suc gave the American a final look as if she couldn't believe it and shook her head.

'They've taken the wrong guy,' she said.

'What?' I said. 'Who've taken the wrong guy?'

'It was all supposed to be easy,' said Suc.

'What?' I said. 'What was?'

'They'd come and he'd go.'

'Who'd come?' I said. I was beginning to feel more than a little uneasy now. Something didn't seem right.

'The Vietcong,' said Suc. 'I think the plan has gone horribly wrong. The Vietcong have got your Mickie James.'

Suc had said 'fuck' a lot, over and over and then had woken the American up and practically kicked him out the door. She didn't let him bugger her this morning. Overnight a lot of things had changed, the biggest of them being that apparently Mickie James had been kidnapped by the Vietcong.

Suc made some tea in the teapot and we went out and sat on the balcony. The sun was coming up over the building opposite and I could smell the smell of fish frying.

'Is he going to be OK?' I said. 'What do they want, money?'

Suc put her head in her hands and her long hair fell forward so it was nearly touching the floor of the balcony.

'They must have thought he was the American,' said Suc.

'Mickie James has a hunchback,' I said, and then Suc told me the story from the beginning. It was like a fish swimming upstream.

She was a woman growing up in a man's body. For the past two years she had been having hormone injections. She now had breasts but more than anything she wanted rid of her penis. That's the only reason she slept with men, to raise money to pay for the operation.

The American we had seen was one of her best customers. He was rough but he always paid well and in American dollars. She had never known who he was or what he did until one day she had been approached by a man with no teeth at the fish market.

'He was part of a Vietcong cell,' said Suc. 'He told me the American who was fucking me was a big cheese at the consulate. He worked for American investors who wanted to exploit the Vietnamese market. He said that this man was not only fucking me he was fucking the whole of Vietnam.'

Suc said how the man had taken her to a coffee shop and had told her the plan and what she had to do.

'The man was well guarded. Ever since 9/11 all Americans in his position were. However, because he wanted to keep it quiet that he liked putting his cock up the bums of transsexuals, when he visited me he was without his guard.

'The Vietcong man offered me a lot of money. He said that if I could get the man to stay with me all night on a particular date then they would arrange his capture. They want to make an example of him.'

My head snapped up at these words. From across the street a fishwife unexpectedly mouthed the opening bars of an aria.

'These people are desperate,' said Suc.

'What exactly are they going to do to the American?'

Suc shook her head. 'I don't know.' She paused. 'But something bad. They are the Vietcong, they have a reputation to live up to.'

I stood up and gripped tightly onto the railings of the balcony. Down below a dog chased its tail. It didn't catch it.

'We have to get him back,' I said.

'I'm a transsexual,' said Suc, 'not Rambo.'

'You told me you knew how to fight,' I said. 'Fight is what we are going to do.'

Ever since Mickie James and I had been in a group I had never considered being a solo artist. We had been through a lot together and even the things I had done by myself, like those porn movies, I had done with Mickie James in mind.

When Mickie James was upset about his hunchback it was me he leant on. When he had an idea for a new song it was me he came to. We were Down by Law and in a world of manufactured pop we were more than the sum of our parts.

I explained all this to Suc and I think she got it because she said she would help me.

'After all,' she said, 'I'm to blame. It was me getting fucked by that American. That's what started this whole thing off.'

She got up from her seat, collected the tea things one by one, washed them in the small sink and then went over to a chest and took out a gun. Suc slipped the gun in a handbag, applied some lipstick and put on her high heels.

'I have a plan.'

'Come on then,' I said, jumping up. 'Let's go.'

Suc looked me up and down. 'Hadn't you better put on some clothes?' I was still naked. 'You know what? You have narrow hips and great legs. Have you ever thought of doing drag? You'd be great. As long as we strapped that penis out of the way. And I know a great trick for pushing the balls back up inside you.'

'Do you know how to use that gun?' I said.

'Hopefully, I won't need to. It's a long time since I've killed anyone.' Suc stuck a cigarette in the end of her holder and lit it. 'Joking. Now get a move on, it's time to rumble.'

Downstairs the bar was empty, outside the sun was bright. The street was half full. The same dog I had seen from upstairs spun round and round as it chased its tail. Over by the wall one kid was trying to light another kid's farts with a silver Zippo lighter. It was hot. It was that kind of day.

In other circumstances I would have been pleased to be seen with Suc. There was no doubt she was cool. But as we walked through the narrow streets I didn't give this too much thought because today I was thinking about Mickie James. I was worried about the whole kidnapping thing.

'Have you ever heard about honour among thieves?' said Suc.

I nodded my head because I had read about this in Bob Geldof's autobiography. There was also stuff in there about masturbating while sharing a room with other guys. That had been hot even if it was Bob Geldof on the other end of it.

'Well, there is no such thing as honour among prostitutes,' said Suc.

We stopped outside a two-storey building with all this curling ironwork. It looked like something you might expect to see in a former French colony.

'Let me do the talking,' said Suc. Then she added, 'Most of it will be in Vietnamese.'

She pulled a chain by the door and inside a loud gong sounded. It was all rather fancy and it reminded me of a docudrama I had once seen about Lillian Gish.

After a few moments the door glided open and standing there was a striking Asian lady dressed in an expensive-looking kimono. She looked surprised to see us but Suc stepped inside anyway and I followed her. There were some sharp words and we were led into this room.

A staircase in one corner went up to a balcony that ran around all four sides above us. Directly in front of us was a fountain shooting up water. Behind the fountain a naked woman was gently strumming a harp and here and there on chairs were men. Most of them were Western. Most of them had erections clearly visible in their trousers.

There was a sound above us and then coming down the staircase was a older woman. She had this enormous hair with loads of chopsticks sticking out of it and her face was painted white although it was obvious she wasn't white underneath it.

'She's the madam,' said Suc and for some reason I bowed. It seemed like the thing to do.

Suc and the madam talked for a while. At one point Suc put her hand in her bag and I thought she was going to take out the gun and shoot the madam, but she didn't. She took out some money which she handed over and then we were going up the staircase.

'The Vietcong soldiers sometimes come here,' said Suc. 'There is one soldier in particular. He is keen on An. He may have told her where the base is. That is what we will ask.'

An was an innocent-looking girl. She couldn't have been more than seventeen, eighteen. When we mentioned her sweetheart, Phuc, her eyes lit up. She asked if we were going out to the base, if we could take a letter to him. Suc said that we could but that we were not sure of the way to the base. An picked up a piece of paper, drew us a map. It was as easy as that.

'Aren't they worried that we will give their position away to the Americans?' I said.

'We are not at war any more,' said Suc. 'Besides, everyone here hates the Americans. No one would betray their own to them.'

'If it's so easy, what do we need the gun for?'

'In Vietnam,' said Suc, 'things have a habit of getting a little complicated. It's best to be prepared.'

'I see,' I said, although I didn't, and then I asked the question that I had asked before. 'What do you think they were going to do with the American?' And in asking this I was asking, in fact, about Mickie James.

'I don't know,' said Suc. 'That, I don't know.'

The road got worse and worse until it was little more than a trail of broken-down grass. Eventually the jeep could go no further and the man driving it told us to get out.

We were about fifty miles west of Ho Chi Minh City. The suburbs had given way to rice fields, the rice fields to jungle. I had never been in a jungle before except for that day when I had gone to Kew Gardens and gone in that big glass house and that wasn't really a jungle.

I tried to rack my brains for any famous singers who had gone out to the jungle and I couldn't think of any. The nearest I got was when Geri Halliwell went to see those kids who lived on a rubbish tip in Manila and they made a documentary about it. That had been a good show because the subtext of it was about how pop stars could change the world.

Suc talked to the man driving the jeep and the man spoke

angrily and banged the wheel. Suc tried to look sexy by crossing her legs and the man banged the wheel again and held out his hand. He wanted his money.

'He won't go any further,' said Suc. 'It looks like we're on our own from here.'

Then the heavens opened and it began to rain. It wasn't like rain I had seen before, it was heavy and warm and it felt like silicon. The man in the jeep let out an angry howl.

'Shit,' said Suc. 'It's a monsoon.'

'Is that bad?'

'It'll ruin my hair, quick, this way.'

Suc slapped some money into the hand of the driver and hopped out of the jeep and made towards the trees. I followed, having trouble keeping up even though she was wearing heels. Behind us I heard the sound of the jeep driving away. We were on our own in the jungle.

I looked around at the trees, the place was full of them. And behind that lot of trees, I thought, somewhere was Mickie James.

'According to this map,' said Suc, 'the camp is that way.' She pointed into the trees.

'Should we blacken our faces with earth or something?'

Suc pursed her lips. 'I don't think that is necessary. It's taken me years of electrolysis to get this skin. I'm not messing it up now.'

I had a lot of questions that I wanted to ask Suc but I kept them to myself. I thought it might be better not to know what she thought would really happen to Mickie James. Besides that, it was tough work walking through the jungle. These frond things kept slapping against me and I kept having to push them out of the way. I was also thinking about jungle animals. I didn't know much about Vietnamese jungles but I guessed that somewhere in them were animals that would eat you first, ask questions later.

Overhead I could still hear the rain hitting the rooftop of trees. It was like a distant drumming. For a second I thought it would sound good in the background of a song and then I felt guilty about thinking of music at a time like this when I should only be thinking of Mickie James.

'How much further is it?' I asked.

Suc stopped and did something with her hair. I didn't like to say that it looked a mess. Sometimes it is the little things that we cling on to.

'It should be round about here,' she said and then we both heard the noise. It sounded like a match flaring.

'Get down,' hissed Suc.

I didn't need telling twice. I was down on my belly along-side Suc. Moments later two men in combat fatigues passed within inches of us. One of them laughed and then the other said something in a high staccato voice. They both then laughed and were gone.

'Go very carefully now,' said Suc. 'I think we should crawl. We must be very near.'

The seriousness of the situation was impressed on me by the fact that Suc no longer seemed to care about her clothes. It was hard work and I had to concentrate. Luckily jumping up and down on a stage gives you a fit body and although I'm not a dancer I can dance. This jungle crawling was a bit like a dance. I could see it onstage, a troop of people in combat clothes, doing just this while Mickie James and I performed 'Wacky Iraqi'. I hoped Mickie James and I would be performing 'Wacky Iraqi' again, and soon.

In front of me Suc stopped. I shimmied up so I was level with her and looked where she was looking.

We were on a bluff. Ahead of us and below was a clearing. In the clearing were a number of dirty tents and one medium-sized wooded construction. It must have been teatime because in three separate locations large fires were burning and around the fires were gathered more of the same lithe men in dirty fatigues. Each was holding a metal tin from which they were scooping food into their mouths.

Obviously we had found the camp. I thought of Suc's gun.

'What now?' I whispered.

And it was then that I felt it. The hardness of cold metal pressed against my head. This was followed closely by a click.

I had seen enough movies to know the sound of a gun.

I passed out.

I woke up in darkness. I was on a floor. It was hard. I could hear breathing near me and then as my eyes got used to the dark I could make out shapes. One was Suc and one was Mickie James.

'Mickie James,' I said.

The shape that was him moved, then sat up.

'Mickie James,' I said again and he said that he had wanted to be awake when I woke up and that he was sorry but he had been pretty knackered and I told him not to be silly and we were together again and that was the important thing, except for being held prisoner which was quite important too, and then I asked him what had happened to him.

'I got kidnapped,' he said. 'And then when they found out I wasn't an important American from the consulate they were pretty angry. They threw me in this hut. Anyway,' said Mickie James, 'what are you doing here?'

'I came to rescue you,' I said.

'Brilliant,' said Mickie James and I could tell by his voice that he meant it. Perhaps it hadn't dawned on him yet that this whole rescuing lark had gone a bit off-kilter. I was going to say something along these lines when the door to the hut opened and standing there holding torches in one hand and guns in the other were two cadres. They gestured with their guns for us to get up and then they said something quickly in Vietnamese.

'I think this is the end,' I said to Mickie James.

The Vietnamese man on the left spoke again, this time more sharply.

'They want you to go with them,' said Suc. She was sitting up and rubbing her eyes. 'Apparently the commander wants to see you.'

It was dark outside, but still hot. It had been hot constantly since we had been in Vietnam. The remnants of the fires were alight with men gathered around them. Closer now I could see that there were not only men but women and children too. The children were all on these little carts. They were all similar but different. Mickie James saw me looking.

'I noticed it too,' he said. 'There's an awful lot of cripples here. It's like a collection of them. There's something going on but I don't know what.'

A dog growled, over by one of the fires we heard a child's laughter, above us the stars were pinpricks in the firmament. Our two guards came to a stop in front of a large square marquee tent. There was a man standing guard here. He gave a kind of salute and we were ushered in.

There was a wooden desk in the centre of an open area. Pinned to the sides of the tent were various pictures, jungle scenes, markets, towns, faces. I guessed these were all images of Vietnam. Sitting behind the desk was a small man with a bald head. He was wearing a green robe and had all manner of papers in front of him on the desk. As we entered he looked up.

'You know,' he said, 'you have caused me a great big headache by not being an important knob from the American consulate.'

'I'm sorry,' I said.

'Are you going to kill us?' said Mickie James.

The man made an annoyed gesture and several papers fell from off the desk and onto the floor.

'It is all arranged. CNN will be here. We have told them we have a hostage and also that tomorrow we will hand the hostage back. Only now we don't have a hostage, we have only you.'

I tried to smile helpfully. 'But we are hostages, aren't we?'

The man blew air through his mouth and shrugged. 'You, you are nothing, nobodies. And besides, you tell me you are English. It is the Americans with whom we have our argument.' He stood up. 'You see this?' He pointed to a map pinned on one of the tent's walls. 'Between 1961 and 1971 America dropped nineteen million gallons of Agent Orange on our country and we are still feeling the effects today. You have seen the children outside? Our youth is being destroyed with spina bifida. And neurological diseases, leukaemia, skin diseases. It goes on. And that Bush man calls other people terrorists. I just wanted the world to know. I guess that they would have ignored me but better to have tried and failed than not tried at all.'

The man sighed and sat down.

'You are free to go,' he said. 'I have no conflict with you. I am sorry to have caused this trouble. We, at least, are a peace-loving nation.'

That, it seemed, was the end of the interview. Mickie James and I headed towards the tent-flaps. It was just as I was about to pass through that I had an idea. I stopped and turned.

'You say that you have reporters coming tomorrow? Well, it just so happens that Mickie James and I are in a pop group. What could be a better story than that? British pop group does concert in Vietnamese jungle for casualties of war. It's a hook, I'm sure.'

'And you are famous in your country?' said the man.

'We will be,' said Mickie James.

'What have you got to lose?' I said.

A stage had been made by putting all these beer crates together and a kind of canopy had been hung over it draped on poles. It was stinking hot. Minh, the commander, was the overall supervisor and ran around telling everyone what to do. Every now and then he would shout, 'Get a bloody move on. We've got CNN coming!' He said this in English. I think it was for our benefit.

Only the kids in the carts did nothing. Nothing that is except wheel themselves up to the front of the stage and cheer wildly every time Mickie James or I made an appearance. Suc explained this.

'Growing up with spina bifida in the jungle isn't that great,' she said. 'They're looking forward to hearing some top pop songs.'

It was about thirty minutes before CNN were due to arrive and forty minutes before we were due on the stage that Mickie James spotted a potential problem.

'What about instruments?' he said. 'How are we going to play without instruments?'

211

As I've said before I don't know what I'd do without Mickie James. He has the kind of sharp mind that can cut to the heart of any problem. I scratched my head and suggested that maybe we could do the set a cappella.

'That might work for one song but it gets boring after that. Look at the Flying Pickets. How many hits did they have?'

Mickie James had a point. We'd look a right couple of tits standing on the stage belting out our hits with no accompaniment. If we had some fake snow falling down on us we might have got away with it but it was a fact that we didn't.

I told Mickie James to stay where he was and I went in search of Minh. I found him with four of his soldiers in front of a large packing case. The soldiers appeared to be attacking the case with a number of crowbars. As I arrived they gave a final push and the front fell forward.

I was more than a little surprised to see amps, microphones, speakers, but best of all a brand-spanking-new Korg top-of-the-range keyboard.

'This was delivered a few months ago by Music Sans Frontières,' said Minh. 'They're a Swiss charity who believe the world will be healed by music. They're largely funded by three of the former members of Abba. I hadn't given them much thought until now. Come on, help me unpack. If we haven't got a story by the time CNN arrive then they'll make one up. You know the kind of thing. "Yeti found in Vietnamese jungle." They'll put some fancy graphics on the screen and fake a few footprints.'

That was one of the best things that I'd ever seen: Mickie James's face when I appeared at the head of the soldiers carrying the Korg keyboard under my arm. I don't think he knew what to do. He stood up, sat down, then clapped his hands.

We had literally just set up and I had said 'one two, one two' into the microphone when we heard a loud rumbling from over the top of the trees.

'Helicopter,' said Minh. 'That'll be CNN. Here's the deal. I make a short speech, then I introduce you, you play a number of songs.'

'We've changed the lyrics to one of our songs,' said Mickie James. '"Alien Amore" is now "Agent O-ran-j".'

'Agent O-ran-j,' I sang, 'rained down on the forests of old Vietnam. More lethal than a bazooka aimed at a pram.'

'If we'd had more time,' said Mickie James, 'we could have written a new song.'

'It's brilliant,' said Minh. 'You guys are brilliant.'

Minh's last words were nearly drowned out by the landing of the helicopter. A woman in a miniskirt and too much make-up jumped out followed by two men in red jumpsuits with CNN emblazoned across the chest.

'OK,' screamed the woman, 'where's the freakin' story? We've got to be in Cambodia by lunchtime. One of the freakin' elephants has given birth and it's going to be the top story in *Children of Asia – We're not so different, you know?*'

Minh cleared his throat and stepped up to the microphone. All the soldiers were now gathered around the stage. The children were still at the front practically jumping up and down in their wooden carts.

'Welcome, America,' he said, 'landing like a bomb. But then you would know all about that.'

Over by the helicopter the woman was smiling and speaking into a camera. 'Vietnam. Jungle. Hostage. Terrorist. A potent brew of the Axis of Evil.'

'Excuse me,' said Minh, 'actually there is no hostage. The only thing that will be held hostage is you by the music of Down by Law. They are here today to raise awareness of the horrific effects of Agent Orange.'

Mickie James played some dramatic chords on the keyboard and the children cheered. Then the soldiers cheered. Minh raised his hands in the air and was about to continue when a man all in beige appeared through a gap in the trees. He was riding a donkey. He had a pith helmet on his head and a notepad in his left hand.

'Roger Korman,' he said, 'BBC World Service. I'm not too late, am I?'

'Freakin' Brits,' said the CNN woman. 'Arriving at the last minute on an ass as usual.'

Minh spoke into the microphone once more. It was a perfect, blue-skied summer day.

'Some say the war in Vietnam is over. I say the war is never over until the effects of war are dead and buried. In this time when the bombing of Iraq is something of a cause célèbre in certain Western democracies it is worth noting that here in Vietnam our people still suffer. Among our population we have higher than average incidents of chloracne, non-Hodgkin's lymphoma, soft-tissue sarcomas, peripheral neuropathy, multiple myeloma, cancers, spina bifida, diabetes and chronic lymphocyte leukaemia. And this list grows every year, the direct result of the indiscriminate dropping of Agent Orange. And if you say that Agent Orange is not used today then what about the weapons that are? The children of Iraq are already suffering from extraordinarily high amounts of cancers, linked to the use of uranium depleted weapons. When will you ever learn? When will we ever learn?' Minh took a deep breath. 'And what can we do? Who knows? But today we are going to enjoy ourselves. Today we will hear the first British pop group that have ever performed in the jungles of Vietnam. Today I give you the quite fantabulous Down by Law.'

That was our cue. Mickie James played the opening notes to 'Alien Amore', now 'Agent O-ran-j', and I took the microphone from Minh. Over the heads of the kids and the soldiers I could see the CNN camera pointing straight towards me. I couldn't resist.

'Good morning, Vietnam,' I shouted and then I started to sing.

When Mickie James and I had first formed Down by Law the thing we used to talk about was how we would make loads of money and live in a big house and also own a yacht. Of course the passion for music was there but somehow, like with all dreams, that passion gets turned into a desire for money. But if I had learnt one thing then it was that our dream wasn't about that at all. The money wasn't important. It was each other and this; people and the connection.

The soldiers had shed their shirts and they had their arms around each other and were jumping up and down. Some had picked the kids up out of their carts and were holding them aloft and the other kids left in the carts were rocking from side to side and everyone was smiling and many were laughing. Even above the music I could hear the laughing and I understood what Robbie Williams meant when he said that onstage you are there to entertain and what is so wrong with that at the end of any day?

After 'Agent O-ran-j' we went into a cover of the Frankie Goes to Hollywood song, 'War'. Mickie James joined in with me on the chorus making a loud 'Uggghh' sound before each 'War!' and then by the third chorus all the soldiers joined in as well. They shouted out 'Uggghh' and threw their arms

215

in the air. It would have looked good in a video and then I realised we would have a video because the man from CNN was still filming us.

As 'War' finished I shouted 'Hello, Mum' into the microphone and then we moved onto some of our own songs. I did my dance during 'Manos Sucias', and I got everyone to sing along to 'Ain't It'. That's the thing about music. It is international. Even though a lot of the soldiers and the disabled kids probably didn't speak English I guess they knew what they were singing when they sang, 'Life's a bitch, ain't it?' Some words have meanings that transcend boundaries. As R.E.M. had sung, 'Everybody hurts'. They were right, they do and you would have known that even if the song had been sung in Polish.

For the last song we did 'Rio'. It was a bit corny but we got Minh up on the stage and Suc too. Duran Duran aren't known for their clever lyrics but sometimes the meaning to a song lies behind the words. That's what's clever.

That day, with those kids and those soldiers, and the camera pointing at us, the words 'Her name is Rio and she dances in the sand' seemed suitably poignant and to sum up the situation perfectly; this image of a beautiful woman on a beach somewhere dancing by herself. But it said much more than that in our hearts. It was about a country, more than one country, and the dreams that we all have for everything to be better.

Both Mickie James and I were sad to say goodbye to Minh and everyone at the camp.

'Thanks for kidnapping us,' I said.

'I didn't kidnap you,' said Minh, 'only the hunchback.' And he pointed at Mickie James.

This, I thought, could have gone two ways but fortunately Mickie James laughed. He understood that, as Minh was surrounded by deformity, he wasn't being singled out for being different.

Suc came with us and it was only as we reached the edge of the jungle that we realised that we didn't have anywhere to go. After the high of the concert we had almost forgotten that we were stuck in Vietnam.

'You can stay in my room,' said Suc. 'I'm not going to let that American bugger near me again. I've decided. I need the money but it's a matter of principle.'

Rock City looked much as we had left it, a two-storey wooden building in a bustling part of Ho Chi Minh City. Suc let us in with her key and we followed her up the stairs to her room. As she pushed open the door she stopped, puzzled, and turned back to us.

'There's a man.'

Then the man stepped forward holding out a hand. He wasn't on an ass but I still recognised him.

'Roger Korman,' he said, 'BBC World Service. I hope you guys don't mind me appearing like this. I thought you were great.'

'Thanks,' I said.

Mickie James nodded.

'As soon as I saw you I got onto the chaps back home. "You've got to hear this band," I said and I played them the tape I made.'

'Thanks,' I said.

'We have this show on Radio 1,' said Roger. 'We play new music. And there's no point beating about the bush, we want you on it.'

'Thanks,' I said and then the words sunk in.

'We haven't got tickets home,' said Mickie James.

'Oh don't worry about that,' said Roger. 'It can be arranged. Now, what commitments have you got here? The show airs on Tuesday. That's four days away. Do you think you can make it?'

I looked at Mickie James and he was looking at me and I could see that he was still nodding.

'We'd want it known where we were discovered,' said Mickie James. 'And why we were there. We're writing this song about Vietnam. We're quite a political group.'

'Yeah,' I said although up until that point I'd never realised we were. But we were. 'We're a bit of an electronic Bob Dylan.'

'Whatever you want, ' said Roger. 'You're going to be massive. I've got this feeling.'

'Do you think?' said Mickie James.

'Yeah,' said Roger, 'I do.'

LONDON CALLING

As it happened Dave hadn't managed to let out our rooms at the top of St Pancras Station so we were back in there like a shot.

'Where've you been, then?' he said.

'Tokyo,' I said.

'Vietnam,' said Mickie James.

'Bloody hell,' said Dave. I knew what he meant. The whole thing did sound a bit odd when you put it in that light.

Later that night I was lying in bed and I was thinking about Roger Korman's offer. We had been around the world and finally it was at home that we were going to make it. Finally.

'If you could have anything at all,' I said to Mickie James, sitting up on an elbow, 'what would it be?' I knew the answer was a number-one single but I wanted to hear him say it.

'A straight back,' said Mickie James.

'What?'

'Like an iron rod,' said Mickie James. From outside came the hum of traffic. The room was lit with London's late-night continuous glow. 'I was thinking, being on TV and having all those people looking, they'll be thinking I'm a freak.'

'You were OK in Japan,' I said. 'And in Vietnam. And those other places.'

'That was different,' said Mickie James. 'It seems real at home. When I'm here, I really am me, and I don't like it.'

'Anyway, they won't be looking at you, they'll be listening to the music.'

'Do you think we really will be on TV?'

I jumped out of bed. I wanted to do something dramatic but it was one of those times when you can't think of anything so I ended up standing there naked. Actually, that did feel quite dramatic.

'People like to put people in boxes,' said Mickie James. 'I'll be in a box marked freak. I'm starving.'

'What?'

'Go out and get me a burger, will you?'

I pulled on some clothes and headed down the stairs. They smelt of piss. Mickie James's favourite poet was this French guy called Rimbaud. That was the sort of thing he would have done; pissed in a stairwell. Apparently he gave up writing poetry when still young and went to live in Africa. All of Mickie James's heroes seemed to have given up at some point. I wondered if this is why they were his heroes.

In front of me in the queue in Burger King was this drunk woman. She had wild hair and a coat about six sizes too big for her. The smell of it was about six sizes too big too.

When she got to the front she asked the girl behind the counter for a vodka Martini. The girl smiled in a bored way, like she was presenting a feel-good story on the news and said it was a burger bar.

'I'll have a vodka Martini burger then,' said the woman.

As I was going back up the stairs I thought that that was perhaps what Mickie James meant about putting people in boxes. I saw that woman as a drunk, that was all. Maybe there was more to her than that. Perhaps she had once been a leading pharmacist. Or walked dogs for the stars. Who knew?

In the room I found Mickie James asleep. He had pushed the covers down and his body was bathed in moonlight. In a nice way he reminded me of a crustacean, his crooked spine looking like a fragile shell and I thought how nice it would be if I had some kind of special powers and I could take away all his pain. Then I thought what a good super-hero that would be and why hadn't anyone thought of it before, kind of a Mother Teresa with muscles.

'Mickie James,' I said quietly over and over and then I sat on the floor and ate the two burgers one by one.

Roger Korman looked different not on the back of an ass coming out of the jungle, more respectable somehow, but I was glad that I had seen him on that ass. It gave him kudos.

We were in his office, which was small and on the eighth floor of a tall building, near to the banks of the Thames. On all the walls were these pictures of old-fashioned radios with famous people posing next to them. It was obvious where Roger's heart lay.

'This is the contract,' he said, pushing a couple of pages across the desk towards us. I picked them up and tried to look as if I was reading but my eyes were too excited to focus on the words.

'I didn't know the BBC gave out contracts,' said Mickie James. 'Not for pop stars.'

Roger Korman put his hands together so they formed a triangle with the desk as the base.

'I should explain,' he said. 'I'm not actually with the BBC. It's all subcontracted out these days. I do this show for them, *Music from the Wild Frontier.*'

221

'We're from Birmingham,' said Mickie James.

'You were in Vietnam,' said Roger. He lowered his palms so his hands now almost made a square. 'Is there a problem?'

I looked at Mickie James. This time I could tell it wasn't about his hunchback. When you've been together as long as Mickie James and I had you can tell these things.

'We had a problem before,' I said. 'We were once supposed to support Showaddywaddy.'

'Then we had a contract in Japan,' said Mickie James. 'That fell through.'

'I was in a porn film,' I said.

'Two,' said Mickie James.

'Showaddywaddy were a class act,' said Roger. He picked up a pen, looked like he was going to write something down, then didn't. He put the pen behind his ear.

'I'm looking to move into pop management. I meant what I said in Vietnam. You guys are great. You've got something intangible. That's what everybody wants. Read the contract.'

'We'll sign,' I said.

'Read it first,' said Roger. 'I want you to be sure every-thing is above board and kosher. But don't take too long. There's this concert planned in Hyde Park. It's to raise money for the tsunami orphans. I know some people, can get you on the line-up. Think about it.' He smiled. 'There'll be loads of famous people there. And you deserve to be with them.'

That night Mickie James had the idea of taking the tube out to the end of the line. As we got on the Piccadilly Line at King's Cross Station this turned out to be Heathrow Airport.

'I expected fields and dogs playing with young children,' I said. 'Do you know what I mean?'

222

There was a huge roar overhead and I imagined, just up there, a 747, cutting the night sky.

'I feel like I'm in a film,' said Mickie James. 'Not a Hollywood one, one by Jim Jarmusch. You remember the beginning of *Mystery Train*? The Japanese couple arriving in Memphis. They stay in a cheap hotel and someone gets shot.'

A train pulled into the station behind us and hundreds of people got off, a lot of them with suitcases.

'We've got a record contract,' I shouted. 'This is supposed to be a happy occasion. Who's going to get shot?'

'Since we've come back I feel different. I've been trying to make myself think that my life is OK, but it isn't. I don't know if I can do this.'

A Chinese man in a pink lounge suit stopped by a chocolate machine and banged it twice with a fist. Then he took a large banana out of his pocket.

'I couldn't imagine my life being any better than a film by Jim Jarmusch,' said Mickie James, 'and that's what scares me. They never have happy endings.'

'Are you going to sign that contract?'

'I feel that we're coming to the end of something.'

'We are,' I said. 'And things are going to get better.'

The contract was short but sweet. We would record one song in a studio, make one video. The cost of these would be offset against any future earnings. There was an option in the contract for it to be extended and it also demanded exclusivity. If we broke the contract in any way then we weren't allowed to sign with anyone else for two years.

'That's what happened to Gina G,' said Mickie James. 'It consigned her to pop wilderness.'

223

He smiled when he said this as if it somehow cheered him up. Mickie James might feel down but he never feels out, not completely.

One possible problem we could envisage was that we were already signed with an agent, although Betsy Wong had been more than a little silent for quite some time. However, that worked out OK.

We went to her office and found that either she had closed down or moved on. The office now appeared to be occupied by a telesales team for a discount pet retailers. There were tins everywhere and pictures of cats and dogs all over the walls.

'Hey, you wanna buy ten trays of Whiskas?' said a young man as we poked our heads around the door. He had a headset on like he was about to direct a failed moon landing.

'What about a job then?' he said, as we shook our heads. 'Read the information off this card. I'm sure you'll be naturals.'

'I've got a job,' I said. 'I'm going to be a pop star.'

The man smiled. 'We've got plenty of those in here. See her, over there? That's Rita, she's going to be on *Pop Idol*. She's just waiting for the next series. And that guy, he's going to be a best-selling author, the new Dan Brown.'

'Tally-ho,' I said to Mickie James which meant, 'let's go'. Betsy's absence was our gain. It's funny how things sometimes work out like that.

I wanted to tell someone about our contract but as I couldn't think of anyone I went to the cheese shop to tell Con. He was standing, as ever, behind the counter, a hundred types of cheese in the display cabinet in front of him.

'Just the man I wanted to see,' he said, as soon as that bell tinkled above our heads.

I wondered if somehow news of our contract had leaked out.

'I want you to start work again. That bloody Marmalade has pissed off. One day he's here juggling cheese and the next he's gone. Just like that Harry Potter.'

'I've signed a record deal,' I said. 'Down by Law are on their way up.'

'No one could sell cheese like you,' said Con. 'You were a natural.'

'We could use the money,' said Mickie James. 'Just until it starts rolling in.'

'You can start right now,' said Con, tossing me an apron. 'We've had a delivery of Gorgonzolas. Big buggers.'

I'd read all sorts of pop biographies about the crazy jobs pop stars had had to take before they became famous; working in a chip shop, or as a ladies' horse groomer, made them somehow authentic.

That was what was wrong with so many of these manufactured boy bands. They are plucked straight from stage school and thrust into the limelight. It's like they believe it's their right.

Could Tom Fletcher from McFly have written Soft Cell's 'Bedsitter'? Or was Duncan from Blue capable of writing something like Morrissey and Marr's 'William'? Actually, Duncan from Blue was from public school. What I'd like to have seen was Blue performing 'Sex Dwarf'. That's the problem with a lot of this modern stuff. It's scared to experiment with its kinky edge.

I liked it when I thought like this. Mickie James and I could have been managers if we weren't destined to make it ourselves.

As it was, our life went back to how it was when we'd first arrived in London. I worked in the cheese shop by day

225

and at night we practised in the loft at the top of St Pancras Station. The only difference was that our travels had given us an edge.

'Our lo-fi hi-fi sound now has an international ambience,' said Mickie James, and I agreed although I still wasn't sure exactly what he meant.

We had to decide which song we were going to record. 'Wacky Iraqi' had been our biggest success so far but neither of us wanted to do that one. It can be bad luck to go back on yourself, and besides, things had gone from bad to worse in Iraq and we didn't want to put out a song that in any way might be seen to be exploiting a poor situation. To be truthful, I had gone off the chorus anyway.

Eventually we decided on 'Alien Amore' and that was because Mickie James had a great idea for the video.

'It can be like an ET/Metal Mickey fusion,' he said. 'These two aliens meet and fall in love.'

'Metal Mickey is a robot,' I said.

Mickie James shrugged. 'Robots are aliens, kind of. They come from the same mindset. They both represent man's attempt to believe he is not the only being infused with a rational consciousness. These are issues we can raise in the video. And besides, kids will love it.'

One day I came back from the cheese shop and I found Mickie James in the rehearsal room backed up against one of the vertical iron girders there. He had his hands up behind his head and his face was contorted in pain.

'What are you doing?'

Mickie James opened his eyes and let go of the girder.

'I've been doing this every day for half an hour. It might straighten my back a bit. What do you reckon?'

Sometimes the truth can hurt.

'Come on,' I said. 'Let's get practising. Not long now until studio time. I want to get that first chorus right.'

'I don't know if I want to be in the video,' said Mickie James.

'What?'

'We could be like the Cure. They never appear on their album covers. Or the Smiths.'

'They were in the videos though.'

'Do you think they'll show our video on MTV?'

That night I couldn't sleep. Back when I was a kid one of my brother's friends told me that if you lay on your back while sleeping and stretched out your toes then you would grow taller. On the other hand, if you slept in a foetal position then you wouldn't grow.

For over a year, every night I lay on my back and said, 'Grow, grow.' I wasn't even short.

It's amazing what others and ourselves can convince us of. If we don't believe that we can change ourselves then life appears redundant.

I eventually fell asleep and when I woke up the following morning I found myself alone in bed. For a moment I panicked, feeling that something terrible had happened to Mickie James, but then I spied him on the window ledge reading a letter in the sunlight.

'What's that?' I said.

Mickie James folded the letter and pushed it into his underpants.

'I say we go out and celebrate.'

'Celebrate what?'

Mickie James shrugged. 'That things are starting to happen.'

'Where'd you fancy?'

'Burger King,' said Mickie James and a big grin cut his face in two. I should have been suspicious right there and then.

As it was a special occasion we went to the Burger King on Leicester Square. It was packed. That's what we liked about it, you could find all types in there. Today there appeared to be what were a group of ballerinas on one side and a group of tall black guys in basketball shirts on the other.

The ballerinas kept trying to catch the basketballers' eyes by doing these fancy pirouettes. However, the basketballers were having none of it, mainly due to their coach who was balling them out.

'Those guys were pussies,' he said. 'Can anyone tell me who was the tallest among them?' Then, 'Whose is this chicken burger?'

'If we were rich where would you want to eat?' said Mickie James.

I took a bite of my chicken burger. It was flame-grilled. You can't get them in all the Burger Kings. 'Probably the Ritz,' I said.

'Where is that?' said Mickie James. 'What kind of food do they serve?' He took a bite out of his burger. 'Isn't the Ritz the kind of phrase people say without knowing what it means?'

One of the basketballers stood up quickly. He was incredibly tall and had a handsome face. I thought he'd look good in a video and I thought how cool it would be if I could walk up to someone and say, 'I'm from Down by Law, I'd like you to be in our next video.'

'I think we might look back on this and think this was the best time in our lives,' said Mickie James. 'Right now, when everything is about to happen.'

The doors to the Burger King swooshed open. Two men walked in. They were wearing motorcycle helmets with darkened visors and each of them was holding a gun.

'Nobody move,' they said together, like it was all rehearsed.

The first thing I did was look to the left and the right, thinking perhaps we were part of a TV show or a publicity stunt. Both motorcycle helmets had the Maltesers logo emblazoned across them.

Then one of the ballerinas screamed and I knew we were in trouble. Screaming girls in tutus don't sell chocolates. I was instinctively sure of this.

The two motorcycle guys moved into the restaurant waving their guns in front of them. As they passed our table one of them put an arm out and grabbed Mickie James around the neck, pulled him up out of his seat and put a gun to his forehead. I could see the barrel right there, flush against his skin.

'Everybody keep still or the hunchback gets it!'

My eyes locked with Mickie James's and he inclined his head slightly. I wasn't sure what this meant, move or don't move, be a hero or don't be a hero.

The other robber had gone to the counter. He held out a red Adidas bag and it was filled in turn from each of the staff at the tills. The whole thing took a couple of minutes, perhaps less. Outside I could see the tourists sitting on the grass, and men in suits talking into mobile phones.

'Nobody move,' said the man holding the gun on Mickie James and then they both left, the door swinging shut behind them.

There was a sound of sirens and policemen rushed into the restaurant. One of the ballerinas fainted, so you could see her knickers, and several basketballers rushed over to help.

'"Keep still or the hunchback gets it,"' said Mickie James quietly. 'That's all I am and all I ever will be.'

'We could write a song about this,' I said. I was trying to calm Mickie James down. I could see that he was pretty shaken by the whole situation.

The policeman wanted us to give statements and concentrated pretty hard on getting everything down in his little black book. When Mickie James said the word 'hunchback' he looked up.

'Hunchback?'

'Yes,' said Mickie James, 'that's me. You know, like Quasimodo.'

'I think I've seen the film.' The policeman tapped his pen against his nose as if he had said something important.

'Come on,' I said.

That night neither Mickie James nor I slept.

'Perhaps it would have been better if that man had shot me,' said Mickie James.

'What?'

From outside came the sound of traffic. Always there, even so many storeys up. People going places or returning. I sat up on one elbow.

'Just before, you said that that moment was possibly the best moment we would ever have.'

'That's what I mean,' said Mickie James.

'I don't get you,' I said. Then, 'I know, let's have a practice.'

We went and fired up the amps and keyboards and went through a whole set. I pretended there was a crowd watching us and in the intro to the second song I said, 'We're Down by Law and this is Mickie James on keyboards.'

The song was 'Ain't It' and it has this really tricky keyboard part in it which was made up of loads of black keys in a row. Mickie James nailed it.

I knew we'd never sounded better. You can use the things that happen to you. They can give you an edge. If your life isn't tough then you're never going to have that. It's not fair, but that's life.

One week passed and Mickie James was acting weirdly. He kept disappearing and not saying where he'd been. I'd heard about this, how fame can mess you up so I didn't say too much. Besides, we weren't even famous yet.

We had another meeting with Roger Korman. This time he had one of his assistants with him. She had hair permed on one side and straight on the other and these glasses in the shape of hearts. She was very attractive.

Roger told us the gig in Hyde Park was definitely on. He said he had managed to squeeze us between Amy Winehouse and McFly. This made me smile and I turned to Mickie James but he was looking out the window. To be honest, I was worried about him. In a way I felt those robbers calling him a hunchback had been the final straw in a long life of straws.

'So you've decided on the song we're going to do?'

'"Alien Amore",' I said. 'It's one of our best.'

'I was thinking,' said Mickie James, 'when we're onstage I could appear in a Dalek costume. You know, my arms could stick out the sides, and I could work the keyboards like that.'

The attractive woman played with the spiral perm side of her hair and pursed her lips.

'I don't think that'd be on,' said Roger. 'People want to see you.'

'Why?' said Mickie James.

Roger laughed in a way that sounded forced and sat back. 'Come on,' he said.

'Why?' said Mickie James. There was something in his voice.

'It's the way of the world. I love your music, but you do look different. You have to admit that. Everybody has a selling point. Don't you see?'

'I think I do,' said Mickie James.

Friday at the shop was what Con called a slow cheese day. It was what I called dead. I took the opportunity to tell Con about the robbery in Burger King.

'They wouldn't want to try that in here,' he said. 'Seriously.' He tweaked the end of his moustache.

'What do you mean?'

'Let's just say I was in the Greek army. Some of these cheeses are booby-trapped.'

I wasn't sure if Con was serious, he has one of those kind of faces.

'I'm serious,' he said.

At around two o'clock, Con said I could go. He said he wasn't expecting any kind of cheese rush. He had been in the business long enough to know that.

I expected to find Mickie James taking an afternoon nap or practising, sitting cross-legged with the keyboard on his knees, or doing his exercise, the one where he tries to straighten his back. Instead, in the room I found Ivan Norris-Ayres and nobody else.

It was a long time since I had seen him and I wasn't that happy to remake his acquaintance. I should have smelt a fish straight away. I knew Ivan Norris-Ayres meant trouble.

'Where's Mickie James?' I said.

Ivan Norris-Ayres tipped his pink fedora in a sarcastic

manner. 'What do you think I'm doing here?' He lifted up an arm and made a big show of looking at his watch. 'It's the last day of the shoot today and the little bugger appears to have done a runner.'

I sat down on the bed. This had a lot to do with the surprise I was feeling. I'd heard how shock can do this to you but I hadn't expected it to happen to me. It was the word 'shoot' that did it. I knew from experience what kind of shooting Ivan Norris-Ayres did and it wasn't grouse.

'I've ploughed a lot of money into that little monster.'

I leapt up and grabbed Ivan Norris-Ayres around the neck. I pushed him back until he was up against the wall. This was much closer than I really wanted to be to him.

'You didn't know?' he gargled. 'I did tell you there was a certain market. And Mickie James came to me, not the other way around.'

As I could see his eyes were beginning to pop I released my grip slightly but I still kept a tight hold. I was pretty angry.

'He said he needed the money, and quick. I thought he'd told you. I'm an impresario, not a mind-reader.'

'So where is he?' I let Ivan Norris-Ayres go.

'I'll tell you what,' he said. He ran his hands down the front of his jacket. 'If you let me hunch you up and you complete the sequence, we'll forget about the three thousand your friend owes me.'

'What three thousand?'

'I paid two-thirds up front,' said Ivan Norris-Ayres. 'Don't ask me why, but I did.'

I sat down on the bed. Mickie James had three thousand pounds. He wasn't here and somehow for the first time in a while everything added up. I knew he had gone.

*

Eventually, in desperation, I called his mother.

'Harold?' she said. 'Harold, is that you?'

She sometimes breathes with the help of a machine and I could hear its noise in the background, cutting in and out. The other boys at school used to call her Davros, after that guy in *Doctor Who*, although I don't think she looked anything like him. She had blonde hair for a start.

I said my name and as that drew a blank I then said I was half of Down by Law.

'Who's the other half?' she said with a kind of dull squeak. She has this way of talking. Then she said, 'Did you say, "in trouble with the law"?' The sound of the machine grew faint as she held the phone away from her ear.

'Chris!' she shouted. 'Chris! I think it might be for you.'

I replaced my end of the receiver and stepped out of the phone box. I remembered how Mickie James had said meeting me had been an escape. He wouldn't go back there however desperate he was. I was sure of that.

I kept thinking he would come back. In the night I found myself sitting up in bed at every noise and peering towards the door in the hope it would open. One time it did but that was just the wind and not Mickie James.

Down by Law was the one constant good thing in my life. I could delude myself about so much that wasn't real but what I felt about Mickie James was honest and true. He was just being selfish. We were about to be famous, what we had worked so long and so hard for. It was like we were finally about to see the light at the end of the tunnel and he had closed his eyes.

On the Tuesday I had another meeting with Roger Korman. I thought that if I talked a lot then he wouldn't notice that Mickie James wasn't there but about five minutes into things he hit the nail on the head.

'Where's Mickie James?' he said.

I felt myself going red. I'm not very good at lying except when I'm bigging up the group and then I wasn't lying because in my head we were big.

'He's got a cold,' I said at last. I smiled. 'It's cold at the top.' This was in reference to living at the top of St Pancras Station and also 'top' meaning the top of our profession.

'We've got your costumes,' said the pretty woman with half a perm.

She stood up and took these two red suits out of a box. They had all these silver buttons on and I thought they were great. A bit like something the Beatles would have worn during their *Sgt Pepper* stage but more modern.

'We wanted Mickie James to try it on especially. What with him being a funny shape.'

'He's not a funny shape,' I said. I put my hands flat on the desk. 'He is a shape, but not a funny one.'

Roger intervened.

'We've also set a date for the video shoot. One week today. How does that grab you?'

By the bollocks, I wanted to say, but I managed to bite my tongue.

I tried to think of other megastars who had split up before they'd even started but I couldn't think of any. That's a thing about being a megastar, you had to make it first.

I hung out in Burger Kings, I pounded the streets, I waited, and there was neither sight nor sound of Mickie James. As far as I could see, it was almost like he had never existed. Except he had because I had loved him.

I wasn't sleeping. It was like everything had finally come to a head, and it was a bad one.

I kept thinking about this film that Mickie James had made me watch. It was about this director who was making a film based on the story of Don Quixote.

On the first day of shooting they had a big flood and after this everything had only got worse, including the main actor having a problem with his arse so he couldn't sit on a horse. For most of the film he was supposed to be on a horse.

The film never got made. This was like that. Our career was the film, Mickie James was the horse and I felt like that sore arse.

One day I opened my eyes and looked at my watch. It was five a.m. and the sun was coming up over London like one of those economy light bulbs. As I needed the toilet I opened the window and went out onto the roof. The part of the sky above the station was full of clouds and it was drizzling slightly, and cold. I felt my balls shrinking, which was OK. There were worse things in the world. Much worse.

Next to the toilet was this magazine. It had been there for ages, it belonged to Mickie James. I wasn't really one for reading on the toilet. I preferred to think of music. It was during one particular session that I had come up with the whole middle eight for 'Ain't It'. This morning, though, the muse had left me. In fact, if I was being sentimental about it, Mickie James was my muse and he had left me.

I picked up the magazine and began to leaf through it. It was a typical Mickie James kind of magazine. There was an article on the social impact of the Beckhams on Spanish society, then there was this article on top academics talking about their favourite children's programmes and how they could now reinterpret them in a Marxist way.

It wasn't really my kind of thing, and before I had finished on the toilet I had finished with the magazine. I looked to the left and the right and finding we didn't have any toilet paper, I thought Mickie James wouldn't mind if I used a page from the magazine.

I turned to the back, where all the advertisements were, thinking to use one of these pages, and it was there that I saw it. In the bottom left-hand corner an advert had been circled again and again in blue pen. I read it once and then read it again. I remembered Mickie James talking about this very thing one day a long time ago.

I felt like some alien creature had just leapt up out of the toilet water below me and was eating its way through my arse. I knew where Mickie James had gone. It was only a question of finding him and bringing him home.

I hoped I would have enough time.

Downstairs in the concourse of St Pancras Station I made some phone calls. What became obvious more or less straight away was that I needed money. My mum always said that if you love someone you should let them go. But then my dad always hit her so when he left I guessed she was pretty glad to see the back of him. I would do anything to get Mickie James back and with anything on the cards I bit the bullet and gave Ivan Norris-Ayres a call.

'I'll do it,' I said, 'but it has to be today. This afternoon.'

It was almost like he had been waiting for me because straight away he reeled off a place and said I should be there at twelve.

The tube was full of the usual suspects, Chinese and French tourists peering at their maps and knocking people over with overstuffed knapsacks, men trying to pick up other men, little kids picking their noses and wiping it on their mothers' arms. I got off at London Bridge and found Ivan Norris-Ayres waiting for me outside Smith's.

'I've got a friend,' he said, 'he rents out rooms by the hour. This should take about three hours.' Then he said, 'Follow me, stallion,' which pissed me off a bit but I kept my mouth closed.

Maurice and Colin nodded as I came in. They recognised me from our previous adventures. The lighting was already set up, as was the scene. There were a number of seats in a row, like bus seats, and on one side of these was the actual side of a bus. You could see where the edges had been cut with a blowtorch.

'The plot is,' said Ivan Norris-Ayres, describing a circle in the air with his hands, 'that this bus driver has been kidnapped by a gang of al-Qaeda terrorists. They think by having a bus they will be able to penetrate the heart of London's transport network. This scene takes place actually on the bus. They have the bus driver tied up over the seats and they take it in turns to have their wicked way with him.' He coughed into his hand. 'They are very wicked.'

'Mickie James played the bus driver,' said Colin.

'If you could put this on,' said Maurice.

'This' was a fake hunchback.

First I had to take off all my clothes. The fake hunchback was made of latex or something and it was heavy. As soon as they put it on I almost bent double with the weight of it.

I wondered if this is what Mickie James felt like. After five minutes my neck hurt. I kind of had to twist it to see straight.

Maurice led me over to the seat and Colin tied me up.

There were ropes that went around both of my hands and around both of my feet.

'Action,' said Ivan Norris-Ayres, speaking into a loudhailer, and a door on the other side of the room opened and these four guys walked in.

The guys were obviously white but their faces had been stained to make them look brown. I'd seen how they did this on a *Blue Peter* special once. That wasn't about a porn film though.

Each of the men was wearing a sheet that was tented in the middle. I didn't need any *Blue Peter* special to explain to me what that meant.

'If we could start with two in the mouth and two towards the rear,' said Ivan Norris-Ayres into his loudhailer, 'and then we'll take it further from there. I think this is going to be my magnum opus.'

'I think you're right,' said Maurice.

'Keep clenching those buttocks,' said Colin. 'Nice and easy.'

I closed my eyes as I saw the cocks lunging towards me.

'This is for you, Mickie James,' I thought. 'This is for you.'

I gazed up at the departure screen, waiting for the correct line to start flashing. In one hand I had my ticket and over my shoulder was a bag. I hadn't packed much, some spare underpants and a T-shirt. I wasn't looking forward to sitting down on the plane. I felt a bit like that Lawrence of Arabia and he'd done it for fun.

'This could make you and the hunchback famous,' Ivan Norris-Ayres had said. 'Al-Qaeda are pretty hot news at the moment. This is one porn film that will be on the tips of everyone's lips.'

I had asked for my money, in cash, and gone straight to the airport. I remembered that time me and Mickie James had come out to the airport together. That hadn't seemed that long ago. That was life, sometimes it drifts by you and at other times it's like a roller coaster you can't get off.

On the plane I was sitting next to this large Texan guy. He had a face as flat as a pancake and as we were taking off he gripped my hand tightly and said he didn't want to die.

'Do you think God meant us to fly?' he said.

Out of the window I could see the ground disappearing. The engines roared. Overhead, one of the lockers sprung open and a packet of dried gravy granules fell down into the aisle, scattering everywhere.

'Have you heard of this man?' I said. I unfolded the page I had ripped out of the magazine and showed it to the Texan. He looked it over carefully, shaking his head, and passed it back to me.

'I don't think that's godly either,' he said.

'But you came on the flight?' I said. 'Flying isn't godly and neither is this.'

'Sometimes you gotta do what you gotta do.'

I pressed the call button and the stewardess appeared. I ordered five drinks. I knew from experience that they were free and I wanted to get drunk. It was the only way I figured that I would get some sleep.

I was dreaming. Mickie James was onstage. There was a crowd in front of him and he was gyrating, spinning round and round his microphone stand. There was something different about him, something important and I couldn't get what it was. It was making me anxious, like the whole world was out of kilter because of this and if only I could work out what it was then everything would be OK. But I couldn't. That was the thing, I couldn't. I woke up.

My body was covered in a cold sweat. Next to me the Texan was snoring, his mouth wide open like a tunnel. As soon as I opened my eyes I knew what had been different about Mickie James in the dream. His head was erect.

The voice of the captain came over the tannoy. He said that shortly we would be making our descent to Las Vegas airport. He said that he hoped we would enjoy our stay in America and that those of us who were staying in Las Vegas would make a killing. This last bit was a joke. It was a reference to gambling and not actual killing.

I looked out of the window. All I could see was miles and miles of flat brown land. It was a desert, and then on the edge of the horizon I saw it, a city rising up from the land. It looked impossible, like it didn't belong there, a place of dreams.

The bus from the airport was enormous with these wide seats, and it had fierce air conditioning like a fridge. If it had been different circumstances then I might have enjoyed it.

Night was falling and from the window of the bus all I could see were these massive hotels. Each one was covered in thousands upon thousands of light bulbs, flashing on and off. One was shaped like a fountain, or it might have *been* a fountain. It was difficult to see with all those lights.

I thought of all the people who had made their fortunes here; David Bowie, Tom Jones, Celine Dion. And yet there was something corny about it. It was the ultimate in inauthentic, in surface glamour rather than reality. I remembered that Mickie James had said that once and he was right.

As I got off the bus the heat hit me for the first time. It took my breath away and burnt me at the same time.

I wandered the streets looking for a small unassuming hotel, but there didn't seem to be anything of that type. So eventually I just chose one with slightly less light bulbs than the rest. It still had hundreds though.

The name tag of the woman behind the counter said her name was Tammy. She looked like a Tammy too, although the only Tammy I knew was Tammy Wynette and I didn't know what she looked like.

I asked for the cheapest room and she pulled a face. It was almost imperceptible but I could see it anyway. I declined the offer of a bellboy and said I could make my way up to the room by myself. I was on the twenty-eighth floor.

I shared the lift with these two fat Englishwomen. They were from Scarborough.

'We've come to make our fortune,' one said. 'This is the city of dreams.'

'I'm fifty pounds down so far,' said the other. 'But I'll pull that back. I'm going to leave here a millionaire.'

The other one did this little dance with her feet. 'Me too!' she said.

I was glad when the door pinged open and they stepped out and I was free to carry on the journey by myself.

The room was small and white. Above the bed was a picture of a lake in a frame and on the bed was a leaflet for the casino downstairs. It said they accepted forty-eight kinds of credit cards, had over two hundred fruit machines and more than one hundred and sixty croupiers. It was all numbers.

I sat straight down on the bed, picked up the receiver of the phone and asked for an outside line. I looked at the advertisement from the magazine and punched in the numbers. I could feel my heart beating in my hands.

The phone rang twice and was then answered by the chirpy voice of an answering machine. I was told that the office was currently closed. It would open again at nine o'clock the following morning and if I wanted to leave a message then I could. I didn't and hung up.

I wondered if I should have read the signs. I lay back on the bed and put my feet on the covers without taking my shoes off. I remembered back to when I had first met Mickie James. One time he had got upset and jumped in front of a train. The train hadn't been moving but still the whole experience had been pretty scary. That was a long time ago and his problems had started a long time before that.

I thought this whole group thing was helping him but maybe it never had. Perhaps by forcing him onto the stage I had made him worse. I had never wanted that. I had only wanted him to face up to himself and like what he saw there. I thought somehow the audience would be like a magic mirror.

I went over to the window. It was night and Las Vegas looked alive. Massive cars ploughed the streets. People zipped in and out of revolving doors on grand hotels and somewhere in the background was that noise of coins going into slots or balls dancing across the wooden surface of a roulette wheel. It was like so many tiny teeth chattering.

I hadn't had a shower since the porn shoot. I took off all my clothes and went and stood in front of the full-length mirror in the bathroom. I could see where the semen had dried on my body like snail tracks. I wet my fingers with my tongue and rubbed them over the stains. Then I put my fingers back in my mouth.

'You're disgusting,' I said to myself.

I squatted down and licked the middle three fingers of my left hand then inserted them up my bum. The pain shot through me, the skin torn and sore. I wiggled my fingers around and pulled them out quickly. I put the fingers in my mouth and sucked.

'This is all your fault,' I said.

In the reflection I could see my tears. They didn't stop. I didn't sleep.

In the morning I used the last of my money to take a cab out to the address on the advert. The clinic was on the edge of the city, a low two-storey stucco-covered building. On one side loomed tall buildings, on the other side desert, stretching as far as the eye could see.

Inside was plush. There was a waiting area on one side complete with low comfortable-looking leather couches and a range of neatly organised magazines. On the other side was a reception desk. Sitting behind it was a woman with perfect features.

'I'm here to see Mickie James.'

'I'm sorry,' she said. 'Do you have an appointment?'

I could see myself in the large mirror hanging behind the reception. My eyes were ringed with dark smudges, my hair was on end and I must have smelt. I could smell myself.

I strode up to the counter and banged my hand down on it.

'I just want to see him! Do you understand that?'

The woman's face didn't flicker. She picked up a receiver, said a few words into it and told me to wait.

I walked over to the leather couches and sat down. I ignored all the magazines but instead pulled out the advert.

This was the place it was advertising. According to the information they did facelifts, nose jobs, boob enhancement. But it was the final bit of information that was the nail in the coffin. 'Hunchback corrective surgery', it said.

At last a door opened and a man appeared. He was small and wiry and had grey curly hair. He was wearing a white coat.

'Come, come,' he said. 'This way.'

I followed him into an office and took a seat. Everywhere on the walls were certificates in wooden frames. On the desk was a small plaque. It said 'Dr Weissmuller' in bold black letters.

'You are a relative, yes?' said the doctor.

'I'm his partner.'

The doctor smiled. 'Ah yes, he talked about you. Your name is –'

'Can I see him?' I said. Then quickly, 'He's here?'

Dr Weissmuller made his hands into a triangle and rested his chin on them. 'He was most keen to go through with the operation at the earliest opportunity. I have never seen such a pronounced case. In textbooks, yes, but in the flesh, no.'

'Can I see him?' I said again.

'It was because of this that we were able to arrange the extra funding so quickly. Medical journals will pay for this kind of thing. Rather like your *Hello!* magazine. You know, photographs and interviews. But in this case for the furtherance of medical knowledge.

'The operation was a long one. Twenty-eight hours, but we were able to manipulate fifteen vertebrae.'

'So you have straightened his back? Is that what you're telling me?'

Dr Weissmuller took his hands from the desk and removed his glasses.

'I'm sorry,' he said. 'Not exactly.'

'What?' I said.

'I think you should see for yourself.'

The bed was in a room by itself. Out of the window was a view of the desert, it seemed to stretch off forever like a picture on a biscuit tin. By the side of the bed a machine beeped and a line made a journey across the screen, left to right, on and on.

Mickie James's eyes were open, the rest of his body was one big bandage.

'So you found me then,' he said.

'We were supposed to be onstage with McFly.'

'Look,' said Mickie James. Very carefully he lifted back the covers on the bed and then very carefully he put his feet on the floor. I made to help him but he gestured me away. Slowly he shuffled across the floor to the wall. There were some markings here.

Mickie James put his hand flat on his head and then stepped away from the wall leaving his hand there.

'I'm two inches taller,' he said. 'That means I've got two inches less of a hunchback.'

'Are hunchbacks measured in inches?' I said. I was angry.

Outside a car pulled up, its tyres sending up clouds of dust.

'They told me they can do more operations. This documentary-maker said he'll pay for it. He said this kind of real-life show is popular here in America. He said he could probably sell it to all the different syndicates, that I'd be famous.'

Mickie James took his hand from the wall. He looked like he wanted to put it in a pocket, then, finding he had none, he dropped it by his side.

'I said no,' he said. 'It was as they were putting me under that I realised I wasn't running towards the operation, I was running away from being famous. I don't want to appear on the stage with McFly.'

'You don't want to be in Down by Law?'

'I was thinking about what made me happy. This last year has been brilliant, except the parts that were crap and looking back they were brilliant too. We've entertained orphans, the Vietcong, the Iraqi people, we've made friends with a magician and a giant. If we were really famous we wouldn't be able to do any of that. They'd keep all that away from us. That's what happens when you're famous, you have to fit in.'

'David Bowie has always done his own thing.'

'What about "Let's Dance"? That was pure commercial stuff. What we should do is carry on trying to be famous, having these adventures, and if there is ever any chance we really will be famous we should run away quick. I mean, what could being famous give us?'

'A decent toilet?'

'I'm being serious.'

'So am I.'

'Look,' said Mickie James. 'Tell me how *Batman* ends, or *The Bridge on the River Kwai*.'

'They have happy endings.'

'But what happens after that? That's the thing about life, it's the doing of it that is the experience, not the ending.'

I went over to the bed and sat on the edge. I remembered all those pop biographies I had read and one thing they had in common was how after they had made it pop stars generally had a crap time. It was the getting there that had been fun.

'I've still got a bit of money,' said Mickie James. 'From this magazine article they did on me. We could use it to buy some studio time. We could record some songs and then the next time we did a gig you could say at the end, "If you want to buy our CD then it's available at the front".'

I nodded my head, that would be cool. I could see where Mickie James was going with this. We'd sell our CD and then maybe some kid would buy it and he'd love it and he'd give it to his friend and then this friend to another friend.

There'd be this big buzz about us and then some agent would hear about us and would beg to sign us and before you know it we'd have that number one we'd always dreamt about. Or rather, we wouldn't, because the dreams were the thing, not the reality.

'So,' said Mickie James, 'what do you reckon?'

'You might be on to something,' I said and I went out into the corridor. I'd seen a payphone here. I wanted to call Roger Korman and tell him we didn't want him to represent us after all.

As I picked up the receiver and looked for some small change I thought about everything. It was all suddenly very clear.

I'd wait here in Las Vegas until Mickie James recovered. Then we'd find some cheap hotel together, hopefully one full of penniless gambling addicts selling their bodies for a few bucks. We'd stay in a room on the top floor, or in the basement, a room with dirty sheets and no en suite so we'd have to pee in the sink.

One night we'd hit the town and sneak into the Celine

Dion show and get drunk and say how crap she was, but we'd know all the lyrics and we'd sing along at the tops of our voices until we got thrown out.

Then that same night we'd decide to crack America. Where Robbie Williams had failed, we would succeed. We'd toss a coin, heads for the East Coast, tails for the West. And we'd set off, thumbs out, hitching our way, thinking up fantastic songs, huge pop ballads inspired by the landscape. We would be together.

I told Roger Korman all this but I'm not sure if he got it. That's the problem with other people, they're not me or Mickie James. We have this way of thinking. That's what sets us aside from other people. We're Down by Law and always will be. On and on. Forever and ever.

There was a song in this. I wondered if Mickie James would be up to the writing of it. With a smile on my face I headed back into his bedroom. He didn't have his Korg keyboard with him but that didn't matter, we would improvise. We would go with the flow and see where it took us. All in all we hadn't done too bad so far and things were looking up. There was no doubt about that. Down by Law were about to conquer America. After all, America was what dreams were about, wasn't it?

Thanks to Peter Burton, who first published a Down by Law story, and to Tony Cook and everyone at ABCtales.com who encouraged me to carry on writing about Me and Mickie James. Thanks to Gary for giving me the time and space to write this, except for the time you took the door off! Thanks to Felicity, my agent, for the title and being so enthusiastic about the book. And finally to Will, for believing I could do it.